GAME RUNNER

B.R. COLLINS

BLOOMSBURY

LONDON BERLIN NEW YORK SYDNEY

Bloomsbury Publishing, London, Berlin, New York and Sydney

First published in Great Britain in July 2011 by Bloomsbury Publishing Plc
36 Soho Square, London, W1D 3QY

A CIP catalogue record of this book is available from the British Library

ISBN 978 1 4088 0648 7

Mixed Sources
Product group from well-managed
forests and other controlled sources
www.fsc.org Cert no. SGS-COC-2061
© 1996 Forest Stewardship Council
FSC

Typeset by Hewer Text UK Ltd, Edinburgh
Printed in Great Britain by Clays Ltd, St Ives Plc, Bungay, Suffolk

1 3 5 7 9 10 8 6 4 2

www.bloomsbury.com

PART I

NOTHING IS IMPOSSIBLE

He knows he'll get killed here, and he does.

He swings round the corner, a micro-em from the edge of the wall, trying desperately for the extra millisecond that might make all the difference. In front of him there's only the dark and a pale tunnel of light that lurches as he runs. Somewhere there has to be a door, if he can just get to it. But he's only human. His lungs are full of fire, his throat burns with acid, his heart is going so quickly it's a roar in his ears. The floor slips backwards under his feet. Faster, faster, faster . . .

And behind him the shadows have woken, spun themselves into shape and gathered speed, thirsty with keen, deep malice against the little people who carry lights and speak aloud, breaking the old rules. The dark has turned against him like a tide: mindless, malevolent. It's his own fault, he knows that, and it slows him down. If only he hadn't — the light, the stupid *light* . . . but it's too late now. The feeble cone of silver bounces in front of him, not showing anything but long blank walls and floor. He feels liquid spatter on his hands and doesn't know whether it's his own sweat or spit spluttering out of him. He'd call out, but there's no help here.

There's a glint. A fractional corner of something, sliding in and out of the torchlight like a metal tongue. He can't stop, can't run straight any more, can't think, but somehow there's just enough energy left in his body to throw him forward. A door, there has to be a door . . . He grabs for his belt, undoing it as he runs, feeling the weight drop away, but it's too little, too late. Just ten more seconds, five, two . . .

Suddenly the back of his neck is burning, an electrical itch pressing on his atlas vertebra like a thumb. The in-range signal: the shadows are close now, close enough to get him. It's too late — or almost, almost too late. He could turn and fight, but he'd lose, and in any case *now* — he chokes with bitter laughter and fury — now he's dropped his weapon-belt . . .

He sees the blade just in time. It flicks out at him, waist-height, smooth and automatic as an insult, and he's lucky — no, he's *good* — and his body takes over and smashes him to the ground, his chin hitting the floor with an impact that hurts more than he's expecting. He hears the air sing above his head and the whine and click as the trap resets. But there's a flash in the corner of his vision — one, two, three flashes. The impact's damaged something, and for a split second he thinks it's his eyes. What has he done? His torch, oh no, his torch . . . The whole world pauses. Then the torch goes out.

He knows it's all over, then. He lets his forehead rest on the clammy floor, lets his lungs fill with a long, slow breath of defeat. Because without the light . . . how could he run this quest in the dark? *Whine, click*, goes the blade-trap again. And he only has a second left, maybe two, before the shadows swallow him. Maybe in the dark they'll take longer to find him — but it's seconds, not minutes. He knows that. So really there's no point jumping to his feet, especially with the trap *zing*ing above his head, making it even harder . . .

But he's desperate. So he struggles to his hands and knees, his triceps aching, the pressure on the back of his neck almost painful now. Somewhere there's a door. There's always a door. The first rule: nothing is impossible.

Zing. Zing. Zing . . .

One second more, while he closes his eyes against the dark, learning the rhythm of the trap. And then — gods, if he could only see himself . . . because even now, even hopeless and gasping for breath, he can't help admiring the way he leaps up — sharp as a flame — and dives forward to the floor, dropping and rolling. He knows he's judged it perfectly because he's still alive. Brilliant. It's such a shame that he's going to die anyway.

He runs.

There's something ahead. He blinks frantically, forcing the sweat out of his eyes. A doorway outlined in gold; somewhere there's sunlight, gods, *sunlight*, which means he's nearly out, he's nearly done it —

Zing. He drops, rolls, automatic now, ignoring the fire in the muscles of his back. *Zing*. And again. *Zing*. And again —

Only this time he sees it, in the faint daylight that clings to the metal like grease. A long scythe, whipping round, rhythmic, slow, at the level of his ankles. Easy to avoid, if only he wasn't already throwing himself forward; easy enough to avoid, if he hadn't smashed his torch, if he'd only seen it in time . . .

It's too late to stop himself. He hits the ground. Everything slows down, so he has time to watch the scythe swinging round on its arc, deliberate, leisurely, leaving a silver trail in the air. The corners of the world go red.

His eyes are stinging from the sweat. He doesn't even bother to watch the last micro-ems of the scythe. He lets his head drop back and looks up at the ceiling, waiting to die. The adrenalin's fading, now. He can't even be bothered to swear.

Blackness. Total blackness, like blindness. And the temperature drops so sharply it hurts. The sweat on his skin burns with cold. He holds his breath and counts, feeling a drop slide down his ribcage like a fingertip. Ten seconds, twenty . . .

And then light so harsh he has to cover his eyes. He screws his face up, filtering the glare through the gaps between his fingers. This is the bit he hates. The world in front of him wavers as if he's underwater. Slowly, stickily, he peels his hands away from his face. He's back where he started, looking at the entrance to the quest. Nice of them, he thinks, to put the soul-tree just outside. That way I can start all over again, straight away . . . Ha. The doors are massive, forbidding, even now, seen through the pale haze that ripples across them. He has to tilt his head back to see the arch at the top. But he doesn't care how impressive they are, any more. His corpse is there, slumped on the steps, and he sits down next to it, turning his head to stare through the ghost-shimmer, narrowing his eyes, stupidly, as if that could help him see.

Oh, brilliant, he thinks. Three hours, and now he's dead and it's all wasted. And it was a solo, so no loyalty, no owed favours — *nothing*. Not even a debt or a vendetta. He hasn't gained anything but a reason to be grateful that he's got an infinite account. If he hadn't . . . but he does. Daed has his uses, after all.

He squints through the mist at his corpse. It looks like him, except for the hair and the eyes and the muscles. He wishes, suddenly, that he could just reach out and pat its shoulder — comfortingly, paternally — but of course he can't. If he touches his corpse, he'll resurrect, and he doesn't feel up to that right now. He stands up, glides up the steps and pushes at the door, because this might be the day he'll find a bug — maybe it'd let him run the quest again as a ghost . . . Gods know he deserves one, statistically, after this much time in the Maze, but all he gets is a line of text at eye-level: **You are a ghost. To open this door, resurrect and try again.** He pushes again, until his shoulders burn with the effort. More text hangs in the air: **To resurrect, touch your corpse.**

He skims down one step, then two, towards his sprawled body, then pauses. He could go back into the quest, but there's no way he'll get further than he just did, not the way he's feeling now. His legs are shaking all over the place; it's just as well he's a ghost, or he wouldn't make it down the steps. No; enough's enough.

He ought to cool down, but he can't face it. Normally he'd spend a dutiful ten minutes flying, skimming over water, whatever — it's the only thing being a ghost is good for, after all — but he's too sore, still aching and fed up. Another five seconds in that corridor, and he might have made it . . . He says, 'Log off, please.' The screen in front of him goes to flat mode, and he blinks, fighting the nausea as his eyes adjust. He's been playing too long. The gateway music swells and loops, once, twice . . . He says, 'Shut up,' through the pounding drums, and grins mirthlessly at the gateway ikons when the tank goes quiet. He eases the gamecap off his head, then the undercap. He feels the wet silk catch on the stubble on his scalp, and makes a mental note that he needs to shave his head before his next session. He drapes the cap on the hook behind him and leans against the wall. The tank is filled with dim electric light, making his skin look green. He licks the salt off his lips, taking deep, conscious breaths. He hasn't been this tired for ages. His wrists tremble as he undoes the straps on his waist and ankles. The screen says, **Goodbye**, and snaps to black.

2

It was a relief to get out of the tank into the liquid grey of real daylight. He paused for a moment, taking in the wide-screen windows, the huge panorama of the real world, the way he did every time; and thought — the way he did every time — how depressing it looked, compared to the Maze. Even when you were dead, there was sunlight in the Maze . . . He pressed his hand on the outside panel of the tank to sign out and grabbed his towel and water-bottle from the locker. He caught sight of himself reflected in the window and winced. There was a real bruise on his jaw. He watched the water pour down over his face and imagined himself standing where his reflection was, in mid-air twenty storeys above the streets of Undone, unprotected in the acid rain . . .

'Good session, Rick?'

Paz's voice made him jump about an em in the air. He wished she wouldn't *do* that. He scrubbed frantically at his sweaty forehead and then turned, dropping his hand, trying to look cool. 'Yes, thanks.'

'Looks like it.' Paz looked him up and down, smiling.

Another rush of sweat broke out on his forehead, like his body wringing him out from inside. He looked down and scuffed the toe of his runner on the floor. He could still feel her watching him, amused, faintly disgusted, noting the dark continents of wetness on his T-shirt, the way it clung to his breastbone and under his arms. He knew exactly what she was seeing: a sinewy, sweaty kid. What did she care if he could run the Maze better than anyone else in the complex? He was Daed's son. That was all that mattered.

'Any bugs? Glitches? Anything we should know about?'

Ah, he thought. Research. *That's* why she's talking to me. He forced himself to meet her eyes. 'Don't think so.'

'Well, tell your — tell Daed, if you find anything.'

'I always do.'

'Good.' Another little smile, like a reward. Then she walked away, and finally he had the space to look at her without her looking back. He hated the way he *had* to look, but he couldn't help it. He stared at her back, taking in her shape, her histro clothes, the long seams of her stockings, her high heels. She was so . . . but *beautiful* wasn't the right word. He didn't *like* her, he just . . . She wasn't like Perdita, say — the kind of person you could talk to, who you *enjoyed* talking to. Sometimes he tried to imagine Paz with Perdita's personality, but it didn't work. Perdita couldn't be anything but ugly, and Paz couldn't be anything but . . . whatever the word was. Overwhelming. Irresistible. He took a mental screenshot and stored it away for later.

He got the rest of his stuff out of his locker and closed the door. He tipped forward and gazed at the window, leaning on his bruised jaw, cupping his hand over the locker's click-wheel so he didn't reset it by mistake. A design fault . . . He stared past the petrol-lustre of the chemiglass and the swirling grey on the other side. When he blinked and focused, his reflection had been watching him for a long time; it looked faintly surprised that he'd finally noticed. Behind it the sky had started to flicker. Storms tonight. That would be good — he got bored in the long hours between 2100 and 0500, when he was locked out of the Maze — but there was always the danger of a power surge. Once the tanks had gone down for twenty-three hours and he'd thought he'd go mad. The Maze itself couldn't go down, of course, but that made it even worse, knowing other people were running it, taking all the gilt and the best loot . . . Crater — the company who owned the Maze — lost billions of new dollars, too, because the survey team couldn't get in either. That put Paz in a bad mood. And when Paz was in a bad mood it spread through the whole complex like a demic. Even Perdita had been terse and uncommunicative — and Daed . . . Rick grimaced: he could still remember what Daed was like, that week.

He shook his head suddenly, and the grimace turned into a grin. Gods, what kind of world did he live in? It was crazy. He couldn't remember what it was like, before he and Daed came to Crater, he was too young; but he'd heard the stories, seen the occasional report on his computer. Out there, in the streets of Undone, where he'd been born, there were kids running wild, abandoned or orphaned so young they couldn't speak Inglish; there were gangs who'd mug you for your hood, leaving you bare-headed in the corrosive rain; there were people starving. That could have been him. It *would* have been him, if Daed hadn't . . . Not that he knew exactly what Daed *had* done, to end up with Crater. Except been a genius, he thought. That probably helped.

He imagined them walking in — a younger Daed, with Rick just a hooded bundle in his arms — through a great golden gate, with Paz there to greet them with open arms, kissing Daed on both cheeks, calling for warm milk for little Rick. Ha ha. No, it would have been more like hours of automated security clearance, Daed sitting calmly on the floor, ignoring Rick's screams, and Paz nowhere to be found — Paz in an office somewhere, making deals with the Inglish government. He could imagine her, driving a hard bargain: OK, we'll keep our complex in Undone in spite of the pollution and security risks, and in return you run all your decisions past me . . .

You had to hand it to Daed, though. Getting a job with the last corporation left in Ingland? However he did it, it couldn't have been easy. And without him, Rick would have been one of those Undone kids. Here, now, he ran the Maze for fun. But for them . . . The Maze kept them alive. It was an opportunity to scavenge gilt that they could sell on the black — and there was always the chance that they'd find something *really* valuable. A special sword, a potion, something unique: and then they could sell it and make their fortune, get enough real money to start a new life . . . There were people who'd sell themselves for an hour in a tank. Even if it was illegal, even if it was *dangerous*, because their tanks were botched and shoddily built and might malfunction at any moment. Rick thought: And here I am, worrying about whether Daed's in a decent temper.

Paz had said to him once — back in the first few years of the Maze, when she was so pleased with Daed she was almost talkative — that there were two kinds of people in the world. The people who would sell their gilt for good new dollars: and the others, the proper Mazers, who would pay real money for a purse of gilt at the right time. *They're our kind of people. Our demographic,* she'd said. *You're one of them.* At the time he'd thought it was a compliment.

A cat-o'-nine-tails of lightning arched out across the sky, and he shivered, abruptly aware of the sweat on his skin. It was always like this — after he got out of the Maze he was useless, slack and dreamy, good for nothing. If he could get a heads-up display on himself right now, his power bar would be down to 1. He grabbed his stuff and made for the shower.

'Rick. *Rick.*'

For a moment he didn't know where he was. He turned over, opening his eyes, sleepily registering the new aches in his shoulder blades. The pillow was wet and he was clutching the sheet in both his fists. He must have been dreaming. But it was still night; he could see the flickers of lightning through the half-darkened chemiglass. He caught himself sliding one hand down towards his belt before he realised this wasn't the Maze and he wasn't armed.

'For gods' sake, Rick. Wake up.'

Daed. Of course: who else? There were other people who could override the lock on his door — Paz, for example, or anyone in Marketing, or even Perdita, although she wouldn't come in without knocking — but he couldn't imagine why they'd bother. Rick sat up, wincing. He really shouldn't have left the tank without cooling down. He said, 'Time, please,' and watched the digits flash up on the top corner of the window. *0315.*

'Don't turn the light on.'

'What are you *doing* in my rooms at — never mind.' He drew his knees up to his chest, covered himself with the sheet, and waited.

There was a metallic scratching sound and Daed's face was suddenly hovering a few ems away, gold-red and flickering. He was holding a flame between his fingers, raising it to his lips. Then there was only a little red glow and the bitter, archaic smell of a cigarette. Rick looked away. He liked seeing fire — he was like a kid, he still got excited — but there was something shameful about seeing Daed smoke. It was so Last World; like he was only doing it to make everyone feel uncomfortable. 'Did you disable the fire alarm?'

'Naturally.' He turned and coughed the smoke to the side. Rick narrowed his eyes. Daed's cough was as much a part of him as his mind: but tonight it sounded thicker, frothier, a full-fat kind of cough. Rick waited, but the cough died to silence and Daed didn't say anything else.

Rick yawned. 'Are you going to tell me what you want, or can I go back to sleep?'

'I need you to do something for me.'

'*Now?*'

'As soon as I've told you what it is, yes.'

Rick rolled his eyes. 'I'm going to put the light on.'

'No, don't —'

'Lights, please.' He added, 'Level one,' as a concession, but even so Daed groaned and covered his eyes with his forearm. He didn't sound tired, but then he never did. Rick leant back against the wall, his hands clasped round his knees, and watched him. Gods, *0315* in the morning, and Daed wanted him to run some kind of errand . . . He didn't know much about fathers, but he was pretty sure they weren't meant to deprive you of sleep and breathe poisonous chemicals at you. Then again, there was always the possibility that Daed wasn't his father. He could be his uncle or his older brother or even . . . Rick remembered half overhearing someone make a joke about Daed and calling him *she* — but he was pretty sure that was the joke. You couldn't be completely sure, from looking at him, but . . . Rick shut his eyes, trying not to let himself think too much about it. Daed was a mystery, even — no, especially — to Rick. Even if Daed was his father, he didn't know who his mother was. Or if he'd had one. When he was small — smaller, anyway — he'd tried to pretend Perdita was his mother, but it didn't really work. She wasn't a mother kind of person, really. And Daed told him once that he'd been hatched.

He opened his eyes, looked at Daed, and thought: Daed, my father. My father, Daed. It was the easiest way to stay sane.

'Next time,' Daed said, lowering his arm, so the fumes from his cigarette wafted upwards, 'I'll disable your lights as well. Why you need to *see* anything is completely beyond me.' He grimaced. He was good-looking, of course — there was a rumour that he'd designed his face himself — but there was something a bit weird about his eyes, like a deliberate mistake. It got to Rick every time.

'I just . . . forget it.' Rick shrugged. 'Lights off, please.'

'Better,' Daed said, in the dark. 'Now listen. I want you to go into the Maze —'

'Now?'

'Yes, now — and fight someone.'

'Why — wait — sorry but lights on, please,' Rick said, and leant forward, because he had to see Daed's expression. 'In the Maze? Now? Fight who? Why?'

Daed was still blinking, but he didn't cover his face this time. 'There's someone causing me problems, and I want you to sort him out.'

'Can't a gamemaster do it?' Rick watched Daed's fingers holding his cigarette like a pen; they were shaking. 'If he's doing something illegal —'

'I don't think he is.'

'So . . .' Rick paused. He remembered, for no reason, the way he'd had to stop in front of the doors to the quest, this afternoon: the way it took him five seconds to take in their sheer size. 'So, Daed, how is he causing you problems? If it's something technical —'

'Nothing technical.'

'So . . .' He stopped. Daed's doing this on purpose, he thought. Shutting me up, so he'll be able to tell me in his own way and his own time. He waited.

'He's in the Roots,' Daed said. 'He's doing the Roots of the Maze. He's looking good. He's probably using some kind of cheat, but I can't track it. I don't want him to complete them.'

Rick could taste air conditioning. He realised his mouth was open. He said, 'He's going to complete the Roots of the Maze?'

'No,' Daed said. 'He isn't. Because you're going to stop him.'

'You want me to go into the Roots of the Maze?'

'Yes.'

'But I've never — it's not —' He didn't know what to say first: But, Daed, it's the hardest quest there is. People say it's not possible. If you die in the Roots, you don't resurrect, you have to start again, from scratch, you forfeit all your gilt, your *everything* . . . He licked his lips and settled for something simple. He said, 'But it's an instance. How can I —'

'No, it isn't.'

'All the solos are instances,' Rick said. 'That's the point. There's a new version for every player. You're always on your own. You can't interact with other players, not real ones, because every time someone runs the quest, the server creates a new version, that's what an instance *is* —'

'I know what "instance" means, Rick.'

'But the solos — all the solos are —' He was burbling.

'The Roots aren't. The Roots are real. Universal, I mean.'

'Then . . . oh.' He took a deep breath and formed the words carefully, like someone testing for quicksand. 'You want me to run the Roots of the Maze. And take out the other player.'

'You're so quick to catch on, Rick. I wonder if we're related.'

'That's *illegal*,' Rick said, tripping over the words. 'You know that. Commissioning one player to assassinate another —'

17

'No, it isn't. It would only be illegal if I paid you.'

'Oh well, that's a relief,' Rick said, piling on the sarcasm, not letting himself feel the unease underneath. What the hell was going on? Why didn't Daed just get one of the gamemasters — or even the techies, if it was a bit shady — to sort it out? He thought: What's this got to do with *me*?

'All right? Get up.' Daed walked to the window and stood there, smoking, watching his reflection. 'And you need to shave your head.'

Rick rubbed his hand over his scalp, feeling the hair prickle against his palm. 'Yes, I know. Daed . . .'

'Now. Do it now.'

Slowly he swung his legs over the side of the bed, trying to think. 'This is important, right?'

Daed didn't bother to reply, but that was an answer in itself.

Rick said, 'What're this guy's stats? His reputation?'

'His reputation's just maxed out. Two days ago. He announced to his guilds that he was going to run the Roots.'

'So . . .' Rick said to himself: It's OK, *everyone*'s reputation score maxes out when they say they're taking on the Roots, and then it flatlines when they die . . . But the nerves in his fingertips started to tingle. 'And his fight stats?'

'There aren't enough data to make a reliable prediction about how you'll measure up.'

Oh, great. Rick said, 'You mean he always wins.'

'So do you, don't you? The surves say you do.'

'Yeah, but —'

'Come on, Rick. I just don't want Paz to — I don't want

Crater to make a big deal of it. Just sort him out. It shouldn't be too hard. It'll be a walkover.'

That bit was a lie, obviously. Rick dropped his gaze and flexed his wrists, testing the ache in his forearms. 'You said he had a cheat.'

'Maybe. I'm not sure.' Daed breathed out smoke, hissing through his teeth. Suddenly he spun on his heel, as if something had snapped. '*Now*. For gods' sake! You're wasting time. This is important.'

How is it important, Daed? *Why* is it important? What the hell are you playing at? But Rick didn't say anything at all. He slid out of bed, wishing he wasn't naked, or that he hadn't turned the lights back on. He could feel Daed looking at him as he went into the bathroom and started to put shaving gel on his scalp. He reached out with one bare foot and opened the cupboard behind him with his big toe, picked out a clean pair of pants, dragged them back to where he stood: he didn't want Daed to watch him, but at the same time he hoped he was impressed. Not everyone could get dressed and shave his head at the same time; it was this kind of coordination that made him the gamerunner he was. Oh, hell. He felt a trickle of blood roll down his ear. He said casually, 'So what do I get?'

'Marks out of ten? Only a seven, I'm afraid. You're a bit scrawny.'

He gritted his teeth. 'If I win this fight.'

Daed's voice changed, hardening. '*When* you win this fight.'

'All right. So what do I get?'

'We'll talk about that afterwards.' Which meant: nothing.

'Daed, come on . . .' A pause. Rick wiped the margin of gel off his forehead. 'You've *commissioned* me. What about taking off the bars on my account? As I'm doing this for *you*?' His face looked back from the mirror, guileless.

'Don't push it, Rick.'

'Shouldn't we agree the terms before I go into the Maze?'

'Yes,' Daed's voice said. There was a pause. Something made Rick look round, and Daed was there, in the doorway.

Daed smiled at him in the mirror. He moved nearer, until he was right behind him, and leant forward so that Rick could smell the smoke on his hair. 'My dear boy, you're quite right . . .' His voice was very, very gentle; but not loving. 'We *should* agree our terms. Yes, let's agree our terms, right now.' His breath smelt of fire and chemicals. 'Listen. These are our terms. They're very simple. You do exactly, *exactly* what I tell you. And in return I will continue to protect you from everything you need protecting from.'

Rick wanted to turn away, to reach for a shirt or trousers or . . . but he couldn't move. He stared into Daed's reflected eyes and wished he knew what was so wrong with them.

Daed held the stare. He said, 'Do you accept those terms?'

'Yes,' Rick said. A wave of fatigue rolled up his legs. He felt faintly sick.

'Good,' Daed said, and moved away. He opened a drawer, took out a T-shirt and trousers and dropped them casually into Rick's arms. 'Get dressed.'

'Yes,' Rick said.

Daed gave him an odd, lopsided smile, like he'd made a

very lame joke. 'Light of my life,' he said. 'Come on, then. Let's go to my office. You can look at the blueprints before you log in. Oh, and what did you do to your face?' He went through the doorway without waiting for an answer.

Rick followed, still struggling into his clothes. As he logged out of his room it occurred to him, for the first time, that this was a fight he might not be able to win.

3

The Roots of the Maze.

Rick stared at Daed's flatscreen and opened his mouth, but there was nothing to say.

The Maze had other dungeons, but the Roots were different. They ran for miles — light-seconds — twisting, hungry, pitch-black, a labyrinth so elaborate and pitiless Rick could almost believe they'd grown on their own. They were the nest, the nebula of every monster in the Maze: the deepest, most hostile corner of a hostile world. It made Rick's ears sing — buzzing with danger, ringing sickeningly like tinnitus after a bomb blast — just to look at the blueprints. He closed his eyes, but he could still see the design on the inside of his eyelids: endless networks of traps — clever, interconnected, trip-one-and-you-trip-another-one-five-minutes-away traps — and hungry scraps of dark, with teeth, swarms of them, too many to fight, multiplying as you ran . . . and it was a maze, of course, the only bit of the Maze that really *was* a maze, so even if you survived you might never make it to the end.

Finally Rick's breath and his mouth matched up and made a noise. He said, 'You are *joking*.'

A flicker of a smile went over Daed's face; then faded, as

if he'd realised this wasn't the moment for professional pride. He tapped one polished fingernail against the screen. 'It's designed to take anything between an hour and a year. Not that anyone would last that long.'

'A *year*?' Rick frowned. 'You mean it's designed to be impossible?'

'Nothing is impossible.' Daed met his eyes. There was a tiny flicker of complicity: it was one of Crater's slogans, the First Rule of the Maze, and they both knew it wasn't true, or not quite. 'It's designed to be . . . hard.'

'No one's ever done it.'

'No.' Daed leant back, ran a hand through his hair. 'That's why I think this guy is cheating. Somehow. But I can't trace the code. From this end it looks legit.' He swallowed; Rick could see it hit him hard to have to admit that. 'In any case . . . I'll disable as many traps as I can — not all of them, it'd take too long, and someone might notice — and I'll give you a map, so you can see where to go. Not to complete the quest, understand? You track this guy —' he flipped to another frame — 'Herkules404 — and kill him. Gods, why can't these morons think up original names?' He flipped back to the blueprint. 'Repeat that back to me. You *do not complete the quest*.'

'I don't complete the quest,' Rick said, automatically. 'Why?'

'You find him, kill him, and then you kill yourself.'

Rick opened his mouth to argue. What was going on? Why did Daed even *care* what he did, after he'd killed Herkules-whatever-it-was? But something else occurred to him,

23

suddenly, and he said, 'Wait. If I kill myself in the Roots, I don't resurrect. So —'

'It's all right, I've found you another avatar. Apart from anything else, I don't want anyone to trace you back to me.' Daed's fingers skimmed the keyboard, calling up a file. 'Look. Tonight you're — oh great — Athene. Athene Glaukos. Well, at least she made a *bit* of effort,' he added.

'She doesn't look anything like me,' Rick said, before he could stop himself.

'Why would you want to look like you?' Daed said, shrugging. 'She's fine. Same height and weight as you, so you won't have to adjust. That's all that matters. Oh, and she's careless with her card details; practically anyone could have hacked her account. I've given her all the equipment you're used to.'

'And . . .' Rick swallowed, realised he didn't have anything to say. He just wanted to put off the moment when he had to go into the Roots. What if he couldn't do it? He said, 'Daed, what if I can't do it?'

'It's simple,' Daed said, without looking at him. 'Find our little friend and take him out. You're good. Stop worrying.' A pause. 'And *do not*, whatever you do, *do not complete* —'

'Yes, you said,' Rick said. 'Don't complete the quest. How *do* you complete the Roots, anyway?'

Daed turned, his attention suddenly focused on Rick. 'Don't even *think* about it.' He narrowed his eyes. 'I'm sending you in because it's important, *vitally* important, that *no one completes this quest*. I will be . . . there will be trouble, if someone does. OK? Have you got that?'

'Yes, I just . . .' *Why?* he wanted to say. Why is it so important?

Daed nodded, slowly. 'Rick . . . I'll explain another time, all right?' A pause. 'You trust me, don't you?'

'Yeah, 'course I d—'

'No, not *of course*. Do you trust me?'

He couldn't quite hold Daed's gaze. He heard his voice again, silently. *These are our terms. They're very simple. You do exactly, exactly what I tell you. And in return I will continue to protect you from everything you need protecting from.*

I'd trust you, Rick wanted to say, if you trusted me. I'd trust you if I wasn't just a game you played. I'd trust you, if, if . . . No, I don't trust you. Tell me what the hell's going on.

He said, 'Yes, Daed, I trust you.'

'Good,' Daed said, and if he wasn't convinced it didn't show. He turned back to his screen. 'Weapons, armour, map . . . Is there anything else you need?'

Speed. Strength. Stamina. But those all had to be real.

'No, I'm OK.'

'You're ready, then?'

'Yeah.' The back of his neck tingled, then burnt, as if the **enemy in range** signal was already activated.

'Good,' Daed said again. 'Better get going, then. Don't waste any more time.' He didn't even look round.

Rick stood for a second, looking at the back of Daed's head, noticing the way his hair glinted in the light from the flatscreen: hair just long enough to announce that he'd never worn a gamecap in his life, just long enough to proclaim his disdain for the people who actually *played* the game he'd created. Rick's skull felt cold, clammy, like the palms of his hands. He thought: What if this is just something Daed thought up when he was bored? What if this is another crappy game?

'Get a move on, Rick.'

Gods, what had he been expecting, a goodbye kiss? Rick said, 'Yes, Daed,' and went. He shut the door quietly behind him.

4

For the first time ever, he warms up before he signs in.

He shuts the door of the tank and stands in the swirling blue light of the gateway screen, feeling sick. The tank's soundproofed, naturally, but all the same he thinks he hears the patter of the rain on the window outside, slowly eating into it, etching patterns into the chemiglass. He wonders how long the panes will last before they have to be replaced. Last time it was two months; the time before that, three. Or maybe Maintenance will forget, and one day as he comes out of the tank the window will shatter in the wind, exploding inwards in a storm of fragile shards and acid, and he'll be left standing there, drenched in corrosive rainwater. A death sentence. An elegant way for Paz to get rid of him, if she wanted to; or Daed . . .

Stop it. He takes a deep breath, and another, trying to concentrate. He stretches his legs, shoulders, rolls his neck and back, going through the different kinds of traps in his head. Ones you duck, ones you jump, ones you crawl under . . . Come on. If he leaves it too long, it might be too late. He puts on the undercap, the ankle- and wrist-bands, the belt, then finally the cap itself. He runs his fingers over the silver mesh, trying to summon some enthusiasm, but it doesn't work; there's just dread. Then he logs in.

Daed works quickly, you've got to give him that: at the touch of Rick's hand the pointed feminine face of the new avatar looks back at him from the screen, already his default, as if she's always belonged to him. He tries to catch her blinking, but the synchro's spot on; he winks at her, just to see her mirror him. It feels weird. There's something odd about her body language; for a second he thinks the mimic program is malfunctioning. Then he realises it's just that she's moving like him, like a boy. Her gaze is too direct, too aggressive.

For a second he considers switching back to his own avatar. But his body is still lying, dead, on the steps outside that instance; from where it is, it might take him a couple of hours to get to the Roots, even if he knew where the entrances were. He needs Daed's programming to get him to the right place. He's going to have to put up with her, and the stupid way she moves. He tilts his head to one side, brushes imaginary hair away from his face, wiggles his hips. She mirrors him, awkwardly, and then shakes her head and cracks up. They laugh at each other. All right, he thinks, we share a sense of humour. That's something.

It feels a tiny bit better, knowing she's on his side.

OK. He takes a deep breath and says, 'Load the Maze, please.'

Latest location was Knossos Palace, North Side. Return to latest location?

'Yes.' His mouth is already dry.

The tank swirls round him as it loads 3D mode. He [?] his eyes shut and waits until the light on his eyelids [?] before he opens them again. He's expecting huge doo[?] the instance he did yesterday, but he's staring at a w[?] washed wall with a crack in it, the kind you'd never both[?] to look at twice. Of course: the Roots have lots of entrances, and he knows from Daed's blueprints that the only way to last five minutes is to find one of the secret ones. So, he thinks, this is the one Daed's chosen for me. He says, 'Optimise equipment. Load map of the Roots of the Maze.' A second later he sees where he is: at the entrance to one of the straighter tendrils of the Roots, with a clear run for three hundred ems before he hits the first traps. And Herkules404 isn't too far away, moving quickly but oddly, pausing for a few moments (probably waiting for a trap, Rick thinks) and then doubling back, zigzagging, slowly closing on one of the widest tunnels. Rick waves the map away — it hovers, improbably, an em above his head, where he can still see it — and takes a deep breath: he can smell grass and sunlight. Nice touch, Daed.

He steps towards the crack in the wall, turns his body to get through.

Suddenly the world freezes. For a second he's disorientated, dizzy, as he steps sideways and the world doesn't adjust to his movement. What the —?

You are about to enter the Roots of the Maze. If you die while attempting this quest, your account will be closed. Are you sure you wish to proceed?

He hisses with relief, because for a moment he thought

ed. He says, 'Yes,' and the world comes

sudden, absolute, sliding across his vision
e slips sideways through the crack in the
sunlight into darkness. The smells change,
...p and iron. He hasn't done anything yet, but his
eartbeat is already faster.

He doesn't bother with a light at first. He navigates by the glowing lines of the map above him, the little blue spark that shows his position. He jogs, easily, letting the exercise soften the stiffness in his legs, swinging his arms to loosen his shoulders. It's weird, running into the dark, knowing he's in a tank that's only three by three. He keeps his eyes on the map, until the blue spark gets close to the red crosses that mark the traps. Then he stops. 'Light, please,' he says, and hears his voice echo off non-existent walls. Gods, Daed must have spent years on these effects . . .

The walls are of stone, but the floor is earth, and there are loops and webs of tree-roots hanging from the ceiling, like pillars. They could take you out, if you were running fast enough; Rick threads his way through them, swiftly, without pausing to wonder what would have happened if he hadn't kindled his light in time. He runs carefully round the curve in the passage, then slows to a walk, assessing the traps ahead. Only blades; easy. He takes another few steps. The rhythm of the blades speeds up. After another step they're whizzing impossibly fast — too quick to get past . . . He takes a step back. They slow down. He walks back to where the passage curves: the blades are almost languid. OK, Daed, you smart-arse, he thinks. It's clever, but it's not unbeatable. It's just a question of getting the timing right. Look, you do it like *this* —

He runs, front-flips for speed, lands and rolls forward, on to his feet, still running. He sees the next trap ahead and keeps going, flips, runs, on and on, three blades, four, his heart pounding and his head full of nothing but yes, I can do this, *easy* —

Until he glances up, stumbles, staggers and stops dead, reeling and flailing for balance, his feet right on the edge of disaster. Automatically, gasping, he jumps for the bar in front of him, grabs, swings himself over the pit, drops, rolls. He says, 'Ow, hey, ow, *ow*,' laughing, because finally the fear's gone, completely. Daed may have made the Maze, but only *I* — Rick thinks — only I can run it. Ha. This is my place; this is where I'm meant to be.

He runs up the vertical stone in front of him, grabs at the ledge at the top, scrambles up and feels — hey, Daed, the effects are *good* — actually feels it crumbling under his feet. He half drags himself, half vaults through the opening, twists and spots the ground as he drops. It's just as well: he has enough time — a split second, a flash — to throw himself backwards, one hand reaching for his weapon-belt, gasping with shock and concentration. At the bottom of the wall there's a nest: huge, nightmarish, a mesh of shadows that shudders and slides as his torch moves. If he'd landed in it, he'd be dead by now. He almost stands and stares; then his instinct takes over and he's running away, glancing up at the map above his head. Thanks, Daed, you could have marked *that* on the map . . . although now he can see that it *is* on the map; he just hadn't looked properly. Come on, concentrate . . . Something's coming after him: he hears the whisper and rattle of pursuit. The back of his neck prickles and flares. The map flashes information at him: **beware! wyrmlings' nest!** He mouths, 'No, really, I *want* to be digested alive,' and keeps running, ignoring the stats sliding over the ceiling. **3 wyrmlings in range, strength 1,200, speed 0.75 m/s** . . . He can see fire-traps ahead; if he can get through them he should be safe, for a while. Wyrms don't like fire. **4 wyrmlings in range. 5 wyrmlings in range. 6 —**

Yes, thanks, I get the idea, Rick thinks. He takes one last long in-breath and holds it, puts on a final spurt of speed, his lungs stinging as if they're already full of smoke. Come on, come on . . . He runs towards the dancing lines of fire, taking a final second to absorb the pattern, then throws himself left. Something grazes his ankle and the whole world goes gold-red, flaming into his face as if he's running into the heart of an explosion. *Damn*. What the —?

He breathes out, emptying his body of air in one harsh huff. There's no time to turn so he keeps going, finds himself on the other side, in sudden darkness, and his health bar is blinking at him pathetically like a dying animal. **Your health is critical. Find a doctor as soon as you can. Your health is . . .**

He gasps, sucking at the air as if he's been underwater. If he'd inhaled the flames, he'd be dead. He leans forward, dizzy and trembling. He says, 'Time, please,' and he's only been in the Roots for three minutes. Oh, gods, gods . . . He says, 'Sorry, Daed, I'm sorry, I can't . . .' and then shuts up, because there's no answer but the echo, and the sibilance of the fire-traps. When he looks back the wyrms are dancing like cobras, their tongues tasting the smell of his sweat, only kept at bay by the flames.

Gods . . . He can't do this. It's too hard. He could kill himself — kill Athene — now. But the target — Herkules404 — is only a few turnings away. He has to try.

You do exactly, exactly what I tell you . . .

All right, he thinks. Nothing is impossible.

He looks up at the map. There's nothing ahead of him but a time-trap and a steep gradient: speed and stamina, that's all he needs. Nothing he hasn't got. A brief respite, before he goes left, right, and left again, to intercept Herkules404 in the central tunnel . . . OK. He takes a long breath, says, 'Hide stats,' because he can't bear the sorrowful flicker of his health bar, and jogs up to the invisible line which triggers the next trap. Then he's sprinting, concentrating on his speed — because it's simple, speed is the only thing that matters here, and it's possible, it has to be, it *is*, it's possible . . .

The floor rumbles and collapses behind him, the vibrations spreading through the soles of his runners. But it's OK: he's fast enough, just. He scrambles up the last section of wall, grabbing for purchase with his hands, catches something with his ankle, suddenly loses his grip, slides back . . . not far, but he loses a second, loses an em, damn, damn —

The space in front of him flashes into a waterfall of gold

and crimson, pouring heat into the air, a shield of fire that would have incinerated him, if he hadn't slipped. He thinks: Oh . . . A tripwire. How histro. Hey, that nearly —

He glances up at the map, but there's no time to look at it properly; the ground rumbles and this time he's careful where he puts his feet, which means he only just has time to —

He gets to the top and jumps down into a wider corridor, as he hears the roar of the passage behind him self-destructing. His knees almost buckle underneath him as he lands. If there are more traps here he's dead, no question . . . but it's quiet, still. There are torches burning on the walls; he turns his own light off, to save the battery. He can't get enough air into his lungs. He looks up at the map and it looks like he's safe, thank gods. He needs the recovery time, before he gets close to Herkules404.

And Herkules404 is only a couple of turnings away. Oh, hell, Rick thinks, I'm too tired. It must be about four in the morning. He leans forward, wrapping his arms round himself to stretch the muscles between his shoulder blades. He gives himself ten seconds of long, rasping breaths, and then looks up again at the map.

Here the Roots are straight, intersecting one another at right angles, like something man-made. If he climbs up to the hole in the wall opposite, and gets through, he'll be in a square hall — booby-trapped, of course, and with a circling swarm of hostile red dots, but with Herkules404 only a hundred ems or so away, now. He might even be in eyeshot. Rick runs a hand over his weapon-belt, watching the ikons

34

flash up. Sword or spear or double daggers? But it's best to wait and see; no point choosing now.

He scrabbles at the wall for handholds, kicks his feet into it for extra purchase, gets two ems off the ground and then can't reach any further. Great. He lets go, in spite of himself, and scrapes his face on the wall as he drops back to the ground. The friction burn glows and stings with sweat. Oh, come *on* . . . this isn't high-tech, it's not even complicated. All he has to do is get to the top of the archway, where the bricks have crumbled. He says, aloud, 'Everything is possible.' He's trying to make himself believe it, but his voice comes out like Daed's, dripping with irony. He clenches his jaw, scanning the wall for more handholds. This *is* possible. If he were half an em taller, it would be easy. So come *on*.

He tries five more times. By then he's crying with frustration, swearing, pummelling the wall with his fists. He looks up at the map and Herkules404 is getting away. He's going to lose this, and Daed will kill him.

On the sixth attempt he makes it. He's so surprised he almost lets go. He fumbles gracelessly for a foothold, gasping, and drags himself through the gap in the bricks. The wall's thicker than he expected and he has to squirm forward and drop into the hall head first, flipping before he hits the ground. He's in a massive, high-ceilinged hall, with crumbling pillars round the outside like a cloister; but there's no time to look. He runs straight through the storm of sucker bats, relying on the split-second delay before they register him as an enemy. Run, run, run . . . too many to fight, and even if he could he doesn't have time. Herkules404, you loser, where are you? Come out, come out, wherever you are . . . He threads his way between pillars, in and out, the bats singing and whining round his head. Their screams echo in the vaults of the ceiling, but they haven't touched him yet, not yet. He runs. Faster, *run*, for gods' sake, Rick, your HP's critical, one bite in the wrong place and you're gone. And once one of them tastes blood . . . The back of his neck blazes with sudden electricity. Oh, *damn*. There's nothing he can do, except go on running; but it's hard to get enough speed, when he knows he's going to die anyway. The bats surround him with shadow, whirling round him in a sickening vortex. How the hell did Herkules404 get past these? It's impossible. It's —

Nothing is impossible.

It's not Daed's voice; it's not even his own. He could swear it's Athene's. And she spins, quick as a spark, her daggers in her hands, and he almost believes she's moving him, that for a second he's her avatar, not the other way round. He's standing his ground, blades weaving so fast that they're a shield, looping and flashing through the air around his head and torso, spraying the nearest walls with liquid dark. The bats squeak and glow reddish-orange, enraged. Great, he thinks. Impressive. But I can't keep this up.

Nothing is impossible.

He thinks: Daed thought I could do this. But I can't. I can't . . .

There's no time to think. His wrists are starting to hurt; his shoulders have been hurting for a long time. The daggers shine, never still, never hurried. The bat blood hits the floor with a noise like someone spitting. Rick thinks: What am I doing? This is a *game*. If I lose, it's not the end of the world. Death by sucker bat — it could be worse . . .

It's the thought of Athene, dying here, that makes him breathe, relaxes his wrists and neck, shifts his weight so that his spine is straight and his balance is even. There. Thanks, Athene, he thinks. That helps a bit. Now I can go on for, oh, another thirty seconds, probably . . .

Daed thought I could do this, no problem.

Yeah, well. Daed said he'd disabled the traps, and *that* wasn't exactly —

Some of the traps. He said he'd disable *some* of the — wait. What if —?

He knows how Daed's mind works. There should be a trap just before the great doors, the route Herkules404 took. You don't get doors like that without *something* to make it harder. But there's nothing marked on the map. So —

Please. *Please.* Let this work. It's not much of a plan, but *please* —

He inches his way towards the doors, spinning so fast he can hardly keep his sense of direction. But he can't lose his concentration now; not when there might — just might — be a chance, after all. The bats dance and scream, glinting like petrol and wet ink. Gouts of black blood spray around him. If this were real, he'd be covered with the stuff; as it is he can smell it. It's a nasty, heavy scent, like tar. He keeps moving, breathless, pushing himself harder and harder. Gods, it's like trying to keep raindrops off his face by dodging between them. He glances sideways — where are the doors? He should be there by now — and immediately there's a flash of red in the corners of his vision, punishing him. *Damn*. A bat-bite; one won't kill him, but another one might. **Your HP is 3. You are dying. Find a doctor as soon as possible. You are dying. Find a —**

Yes, yes, OK . . . 'Hide the stats!'

They've tasted blood. Now he can't see individual bats, only a shimmering fog of dark. And he *still* doesn't know where he is. How the hell did Herkules404 get through . . . ?

He spins, his whole chest hurting now, the joints of his shoulders and wrists burning as if there's sandpaper between the bones. No more, he thinks. No more. Five more seconds, and I'm going to let them kill me. He doesn't know where he's going: he takes a step back, then forward, giddy and off-balance. Sorry, Athene, you're going to —

He steps back, and his ankle gives way, unexpectedly, throwing him down and sideways as deftly as a judo opponent. He's on one knee, suddenly helpless; he watches in a kind of appalled slow-mo as one dagger skitters away across the floor. His kneecap suddenly flares into a blaze of pain. Something makes a noise like a portcullis dropping. Oh, for gods' sake — there is a trap after all, he misread the map again . . . He squeezes his eyes shut, waiting for the silence and cold that'll tell him he's dead.

His heartbeat rattles in his ears. The bats are still screaming.

Slowly he opens his eyes again.

It's worked.

He's kneeling in the space where the trap should be,

watching the storm of bats circle confusedly around him. They won't touch him; they think the trap's still there. Daed's disabled it, but some of the code is still functioning: the sound effect, the clear space around him. He gets to his feet and stands, panting, in the pocket of safety. He's giggling with exhaustion. Oh, thank you, thank you, Daed.

He doesn't want to move, ever again, but he's going to have to. He tilts his head back, wearily, and looks at the map. Herkules404 is at the opposite end of the next tunnel.

Too hard, he thinks. There's no way I can fight someone in this state. But then Herkules404 had to do this, too; he might not be feeling any better. And Daed wants me to do it — wonderful, brilliant Daed, who disabled that trap for me . . .

He crouches, retrieves his dagger, and walks towards the doors, scuffing the floor with his runners. The bats swirl and hover, noticing him again, but they're not quick enough to come in for the kill before he gets to the door. He pushes it open — he's got just enough strength to do it — and slides through the gap. There's no need to close it after him: the bats won't desert their territory. He stands in the shadows, looking down the corridor. And there he is, running the traps at the far end of the passage.

Herkules404.

5

Rick stands and watches him, making the most of the time before he notices he's not alone. So, Herkules404, what're you like? Short — even smaller than Rick — and stocky, silver-blond hair, flashy armour, faint glow of golden light . . . more gilt than sense, then. Sure, it looks good, but try a stealth assassination when you're *luminous*, for gods' sake.

And . . .

Rick squints, peering through the torch-light, wondering whether it's safe to put his own light on. If only he could see more clearly — because there's something . . . he can't quite put his finger on it. Herkules' speed is OK, just about — but the way he's running the traps, it looks too . . . sloppy. No flips, just sprinting, a couple of leaps, a pointless cartwheel in the middle, as if he's showing off. No precision, Rick thinks; no economy. He should be *dead*, running like that. Rick steadies his breathing, hissing through his teeth. That blade-trap — easy, of course, but . . . he could have sworn Herkules just ran *through* it. But he doesn't falter. On to the next — and gods, he *is* just running through the blades. The speed's right, but he's not even bothering to time it properly: the blade spins right through his legs, and he should be dead, he should be *dead*.

'Enable PvP,' Rick says. If he can see Herkules' health bar, that should tell him —

Player versus player mode enabled. All speech will be relayed into the arena. There's a pause. **No live players in range.**

Oh, my gods, Rick thinks.

Herkules404 is *dead*. He's a ghost.

So what the hell is he doing here?

He starts to run, pauses before he gets to the nearest trap, and calls, 'Hey! Herkules!'

Herkules looks round. His mouth moves and there's a tiny silence before he says, 'What do you want?'

Foreign, then, Rick thinks: that's the translation program causing the delay. He says, 'What're you doing? You're dead. You can't complete a quest when you're dead.'

'None of your business.' He's standing on top of a pressure switch: a claw is swiping at him, passing harmlessly through his chest and resetting itself, over and over.

'You're spying out the Roots, aren't you?' Rick feels a rush of relief: he won't have to fight this guy, after all. He's not going to complete the Roots: he's just come in for a recce. 'You think you'll come back when you're alive, and you'll know where to go. Look, mate, it's not worth it, honestly. No one can complete the Roots. You're wasting your time.'

'Go away.'

Rick's pretty sure that wasn't an accurate translation. He says, 'I'm just giving you some friendly advice.'

'I'm not doing anything wrong. So muck off and stop bothering me, you skinny little girl.'

Rick clenches his fists. Of course, he's Athene. He's a girl . . . He says, 'If you're working for a tankshop, it's illegal.' But he knows it's a long shot: Herkules *might* be spying out the Roots for a tankshop, but then again, he might not. And he's spent money on his avatar: with that look, he's probably some rich eastern kid, not a tankshopper.

'You think I'm doing something illegal? So call a GM. Report me.'

Rick shrugs. 'I'm just trying to help.'

'What do you want, a big kiss?' Herkules leers at him. 'What guilds do you belong to, anyway?'

Oh, hell. He doesn't know. His own are the Assassins, the Heroes, the Alpha Omega, the Silver Shield — but Athene's? He says, 'The Alpha Omega,' and tries to look like he believes it.

'The Alpha —? Oh, yeah, right. Sure you do. If I were alive, I'd *love* to take you on. You'd be on your knees . . .' Herkules pouts at him and flutters his eyelashes.

Gods, who does this cretin think he is? Rick says, 'Up yours,' and wonders how it'll translate.

'Sorry, sweetheart. Not now. I've got things to do. Now run away and play with your dolls.'

'Oh, whatever,' Rick says. It's not much of an exit line, but he's knackered. He leans against the wall and slides down until he's sitting with his knees up. That's it for you and me, Athene, he thinks. We didn't even need to be here. What a waste of time. I am going to *kill* Daed.

He watches Herkules, idly, as he runs the barrage of claws and blades and darts. Why is he running? He doesn't have to run, if he's a ghost . . . He must be running for the surves' benefit, Rick thinks, so that they don't notice there's a ghost in the Roots. He's trying not to draw attention to himself. Because . . .

I'm not doing anything wrong . . . So what *is* he doing?

Rick's too tired to get a complete grasp on his own thoughts; but his body is suddenly buzzing again. A hunch, that's all: like a pinprick in the wall of his stomach, hardly noticeable at first, until he feels the unease slowly starting to leak out. He levers himself to his feet, pressing his hand against the wall for balance.

It's mad, of course. Now he knows that Herkules is dead, he's not sure if it's even possible to follow him. But he should try, at least; he knows he should. Rick thinks: Wait. Daed didn't know he was a ghost, did he? Daed thought he was alive, and I could kill him. So he's not showing up as a ghost, on the survey computers. It's not just that they haven't noticed, it's that the server thinks he's alive . . . So there's definitely something dodgy, he must be cheating, somehow. And you have to be alive to run a quest, to complete it . . . He must be doing something, he must have a plan, he *must* be cheating. I have to go after him. I need to do something . . .

Like . . . Like *what*? I can't fight him . . .

For some reason it's the thought of Daed — not how he normally is, but how he was tonight, shielding his eyes from the light — that makes up Rick's mind for him, finally. He'll do everything he can, for Daed.

He sets off after Herkules. He's lucky he's used to spending hours in the Maze: he can flick his concentration on and off, like a switch. He imagines the traps as part of him: their rhythm is his rhythm, the volume they take up is an extension of his own body. It's a trick, but it works: he can judge the spaces perfectly, the split-second opportunities for him to move. *He* doesn't need to be a ghost. He feels the confidence running through him like water, but he stays careful, not too tense, not too relaxed, because the smallest mistake and he'll be dead. He tumbles, rolls, skids, goes round a treacherous corner — thank gods, a line of disabled traps, so he can run for a few seconds without thinking — and Herkules is there, jogging up a long slope, towards a blank wall.

Rick glances at his map. Yep, it *is* a blank wall. Nothing special about it: just a dead end. So why doesn't Herkules turn round and come back?

Herkules slows to a walk, then stops, rolls his shoulders. He reaches down between his shoulder blades with one hand, pushing his elbow back with the other. He stands easily, facing the wall, rocking from foot to foot. Suddenly the pretence of tension has gone out of his movements: he looks like someone stretching after a fight, taking his time before he loots his enemy's corpse. *No need to rush*, his body says. Whatever he was trying to do, he's done it.

And there *is* a corpse. Rick sees it before he understands what it means. A corpse; a short, slumped shape, half sitting, half lying against that blank, impassive wall. A vaguely person-shaped, glittering mound of jewelled armour and blond hair, glowing faintly golden.

Rick didn't think he could run any faster: but it's as if Athene adds her strength to his, and together they're

44

sprinting, kicking up against the wall to get the height to vault a spindle-trap, dropping, rolling, the air whistling as the next trap activates in a cascade of razor-sharp scales like a dragon's back. Rick's mind is blank: he's a camera, a machine, nothing but eyes and muscles, dancing his way through the last ems of danger. He has to get to Herkules; now he understands what's happening, no, he *will* understand, as soon as he's got time to think . . .

He opens his mouth to shout, but he hasn't got any breath; and when he surfaces from the next roll something stops him trying again. It's like Athene whispering in his ear: *No, Rick. Not yet. Wait.*

He staggers to his feet, dragging the air into his lungs, scans the space in front of him and sags with relief. A line of plate-traps glints dully, deactivated. Thank you, Daed. He moves forward — soggy and trembling, you couldn't call it a run — until he's only a few ems away from Herkules and his corpse. He's not particularly quiet, but Herkules is staring up into thin air, and doesn't seem to hear him. Rick thinks, with an irrational pang of shock: *He*'s got a map, too. Where the hell is he getting these cheats from? When this is over, someone has to tell Crater . . .

Herkules rubs his eyes, wipes sweat off his forehead, and nods. His lips move, but there's no sound. Then he takes a step towards his corpse, checks the map one last time, and kneels to touch his body.

There's a blue swirl of light around the two identical figures; the corpse dissolves into stars and smoke. When it clears, Herkules is grinning.

PvP mode is enabled. There is one live player within range. Do you want to engage him?

'Yes, please,' Rick says, just loud enough for Herkules to hear.

Herkules turns round, slowly.

Rick meets his eyes and feels laughter bubbling up inside him. He says, 'Surprise!'

'What on earth are you doing? Go away and leave me alone.'

'What the hell are *you* doing? How did your corpse get here? If you die here, your account gets wiped. There's no way you could leave your body here. You must have cheated.' He smiles, showing his teeth.

'Look . . .' Herkules says. 'So I might have found a bug. So what? It's none of your business. Anyway, now you know about it too.'

'And the map?'

'What map? I don't have a . . .' He stops. His eyes flicker — he must be reading something that Rick can't see — and his hand creeps towards his belt. Rick keeps his eyes on Herkules' index finger, ready to dodge as soon as a weapon materialises. 'You want to fight me, do you?'

'Yep.'

'That's stupid. Look,' Herkules says again. Either the mimic program isn't working properly or he hasn't got the hang of sounding reasonable. 'There's no reason to fight me. We can both complete the quest — and you'll get more reputation from that than from killing me. And anyway I'd win. Give it up, sweetheart.'

'Nope. Sorry. No go.'

'What?'

Rick shrugs. His muscles are so tired it feels like his shoulder blades have got stuck together behind his back. 'I've got to fight you,' he says, trying to sound like he's taking it seriously.

'Oh,' Herkules says, and turns away, fiddling with something at his waist.

And spins back, catching Rick off-guard.

He's fast. Gods, he's fast. Rick hears his own voice saying, *You mean he always wins.*

Stop it. Stop *thinking*.

Rick ducks, rolls, inelegantly, smacking his shoulder on the ground, but he's out of the way, just. He grabs for Herkules' ankle, but the other foot swings up and stamps down into his face, and he has to block with both forearms. He rolls forward and on to his feet, and spins to face Herkules, his back against the wall, breathing so hard he thinks his lungs might spring a leak. He rests his hand on his weapon-belt. Double daggers? Sword and dagger? Does he want speed, or range?

Herkules says, 'Well then, sweeth—'

And swings his sword in the middle of the word: a nice trick, but this time Rick's ready. His hands have already chosen his weapon — daggers; if he doesn't have speed he doesn't have a chance — and the blades meet and cross in front of him, catching Herkules' sword at eye level and swinging it away. The metal catches the light and shines like lightning. He lets the momentum carry him off the vertical and kicks with his free foot, but Herkules pulls his sword away and jumps back, on guard.

'Nice try, little girl.'

It's stupid, how much that annoys him. He takes a long breath, diluting the anger. He thinks: I'll kill him. Then he'll be sorry.

He relaxes his arms, standing ready. The dagger hilts tremble under his fingers, as if they've got a mind of their own. He wishes that they did; he needs all the help he can get. He edges forward, sideways, keeping his weight balanced, ready to go in any direction. Makes an experimental feint —

But Herkules is there before he is.

He smashes his sword blade down on the guard of Rick's dagger. The hilt leaps, biting into the bones of his hand. Rick's fingers open. He can't stop them. The dagger drops to the ground. He looks down at it, his guts sinking. The vibration runs up to his shoulder like an electric current, stinging. He thinks: Another centi-em and he'd have disabled my hand. And then: How the hell did he do that? I'd only just *moved* . . .

Not that it matters, right now.

Herkules punches with his other hand, smiles at Rick's desperate block, dodges his counter-punch smoothly, and swings the blade of his sword up and round, until it's under Rick's chin. It's all so easy; like he was reading every move as it came, like he was hardly bothering to try.

Oh, gods, Rick thinks, he's going to kill me. And then Daed will kill me, too.

'So you're one of the Alpha Omega, are you?' Herkules says.

'Yeah,' Rick says. He wants to close his eyes, but it seems cowardly, somehow.

Herkules laughs. 'Sure you are. I'll look you up. What's your name? You might as well tell me. When I kill you your account will be wiped anyway.'

'Athene,' Rick mutters.

'Such a pretty name for such a pretty girl.'

But he doesn't answer. He stares into the expensive high-cheekboned face and wonders why Herkules doesn't just kill him. In the Assassins they call it Bondvillain Syndrome: the need to gloat, the subconscious need to give your victim a few more minutes of life. A weakness: you can lose a fight that way.

Or win it, Rick thinks; if you're the victim.

'Thanks,' he says. 'You're not too bad-looking yourself.' There's something in his left hand: the other dagger. His arm is hanging limply at his side, and he wouldn't have time to do anything before the sword blade went into his throat. But it's interesting. It sets something off in Rick's mind: a mental itch, the beginning of a plan.

Herkules frowns. He's clearly not used to people being polite, before he kills them. 'Er . . .' he says. 'Right.'

That's good, Rick thinks. I've surprised him. He doesn't know what I'm thinking. There might still be a chance . . .

What would Daed do?

Herkules says, 'How come you got this far?'

'In the Roots? Oh. Well. I'm good.'

'No one's that good. Who's your Cheat?'

Rick takes a second to understand: the translation program

again. He opens his mouth to say 'No one', then hesitates. The sword blade hovers in front of his larynx, and the **enemy in range** signal is so strong it hurts. He says, slowly, 'Daedalus.'

'*Daedalus?* Don't wind me up, you little —'

'I'm not winding you up. How do you think I got here?'

'Daedalus isn't *real*, you silly girl. Daedalus is a myth.' Herkules laughs. 'Look around. You think one person could create this? It takes *hundreds* of designers, years of work, player feedback, and a hell of a lot of of AI code to create this. *Daedalus* is just a convenient idea. Not a person.' He tilts his wrist, ready to strike, and grins. 'So don't muck me around.'

'It's true.' Rick's pushing it; any moment now he'll get that sword through his throat. 'I'm from Crater. Daedalus —' He swallows. What would Daed do? *Think* . . . 'Daedalus is a friend of mine, one of the designers. He sells cheats on the black. I had to give him a couple of grand for this. But it's risk-free. Whoever your Cheat is, Daedalus is better.'

'So how come you're the one with a sword pointing at you?'

Rick tries to smile. 'Good point. But if you kill me I'll just come back tomorrow. After I've reported you to a GM.'

The bluer-than-blue eyes narrow. 'How can cheats be risk-free?'

'Crater turn a blind eye. Because it's him. Daedalus. He can do what he wants, as long as he goes on working for them. A few cheats running here and there — who cares? As long as he's still on their side.' Rick's talking too fast; but it's OK, the translation program will cover it.

'I don't believe you.'

It takes every ounce of self-control Rick has to shrug; but he manages it. 'Fine. Kill me.' He tilts his head back, as if he's bored, surrendering himself for the coup-de-grâce. 'Herkules404, isn't it? Exploiting a bug . . . or commissioning a Cheat . . . the GMs won't like it . . .'

A pause. Rick stays still.

'Does Daedalus . . . this Cheat, whatever . . . sell to anyone who can pay?'

The sword blade hasn't dropped; but there's a tiny, tiny bit more space between Rick's neck and the edge of the metal.

'Yeah, if you can contact him. But he's hard to get hold of. Has to be.'

'So how would . . . how do you contact him?'

Rick stops himself from laughing. Just. 'I told you. He's my mate. I meet him face to face, tell him what I want, where I want to go . . . how hard I want it to be, even. Sometimes it's good to have a challenge. To know that even if I'm technically cheating, no one else could do what I'm doing. *You* understand.'

Herkules' eyes flicker, searching Rick's face. He stares back, steady, because that's the only thing the mimic program will render exactly.

'He's expensive, though? Daedalus?'

'Not too —' He stops, smelling the danger, and smiles. 'Well . . . yeah. Sure. What do you expect?'

Herkules frowns. 'Suppose I . . . if this is true — and I'm not saying I believe you — how would, for example, how would *I* contact him?'

'If you let me go, I'll give you his real name.'

The tip of the sword dips, wavers, slides absently away to the side, above Rick's shoulder.

One strike, he thinks. Just the one. One chance.

The tension in Herkules' sword-hand relaxes. 'Yeah. Right. And how do I know this isn't a —'

Rick steps sideways and punches with his left hand, dagger blade straight into Herkules' windpipe. There's no resistance — the tank doesn't sculpt PvP combat — so only his eyes tell him that he's done it. He jumps back, because it would be stupid to get killed now, but there's no need.

Herkules goes straight down; his ghost stays where he was, the transparent face full of disbelief. He says, '. . . a trick?'

There's a five-second pause. Then the corpse starts to evaporate — as if this was an instance, and it was going to reappear outside . . . The way it would have done before, Rick thinks, if Herkules hadn't been cheating.

The ghost turns to watch it go, helpless, his expression turning to fury. His transparent fists clench. The translation program says, 'Muck you, little female dog, muck you, *muck* —'

Rick watches too. All that expensive armour, he thinks; all that expensive body-moulding, all that virtual beauty . . .

Then the ghost disappears; not dissolving like the corpse, but gone cleanly, like a candle flame. Spat out of the dungeon, to the nearest soul-tree . . . no. Wait.

Rick puts his dagger blindly back into his belt, suddenly trembling. That, he thinks, that was someone dying for *real*. Or nearly. The ghost hasn't gone to a soul-tree; it's been wiped. No resurrection for him.

He says, 'A trick? Honestly, the idea! Nice girl like me . . .'

He's done it. He's won.

6

Rick drops to the floor and lies flat, staring up at the ceiling. Even that's modelled perfectly. He starts to laugh.

You have defeated Herkules404 in PvP combat. This account has now been closed, so the corpse is unavailable for looting. All items have been transferred automatically into your inventory.

Oh. He'd forgotten about all that stuff. He says, 'Open inventory,' and watches the scroll unfurl against Daed's beautiful ceiling. Armour — well, fat lot of good *that* was — winged sandals, which he already has and are overrated anyway, a sword, which should raise a decent sum at auction . . . hundreds of gilt, a library of maps . . . Gods, who cares, anyway? He can't keep this stuff: now he's got rid of Herkules, he's got to kill himself. Well, Athene. And she'll be wiped, just like Herkules, blinking out of existence, because when you die in the Roots . . .

He wonders vaguely where Herkules got his cheat. It was a good one. Clever. He thinks: Hats off.

He gets slowly to his feet. The euphoria has gone. He thinks: At least now I can go back to bed. And Daed will be pleased with me. That's something, isn't it?

He looks listlessly at the line of disabled traps stretching back the way he came. Beyond them there's a spindle-trap, still active, that he remembers vaulting over, a lifetime ago. That'll do.

But he can't bring himself to do it. Not yet. He tries to recall the rush of triumph he felt a moment ago, but it's faded, drying to nothing, like sweat. He's never worked this hard, not for anything. He raises his eyes to his inventory — Athene's inventory — and wonders what she'd do if he didn't kill her, if she logged in tomorrow and found all this stuff in her account. Would she ever find out what he'd done? She might work it out: that armour might be custom-made . . . a map of the Roots . . . But she won't be able to log in, tomorrow, if he kills her. She'll have to open a new account.

He says, 'Open map of the Roots.' It unfolds into place, over the map that Daed gave him, and he waves it sideways so that he can compare them. Yep — a pretty good copy, less detailed, but —

What the hell is that?

Herkules' map doesn't show a dead end. It shows a hidden portal.

Rick turns slowly. He looks at the blank wall.

A hidden portal. Oh, gods.

He really, really hates portals. You need more guts, more nerve for a portal than for a boss fight or a brawl or — well, almost anything else. You have to run at them. *Fast*. If you're wrong or not fast enough, it's just a wall. And the tank will sculpt a wall: if you hit one at speed, it hurts just as much as it would in real life. Fifty per cent of Crater's personal injury litigation is something to do with portals, and it's not surprising. There are people who can do everything else, but they never get the hang of portals.

That's why Herkules met his corpse here, Rick thinks. Because it's the end of the quest. Just beyond that wall . . . Daed didn't trust me. He made the map lie, just in case. He thought if I got this far . . . He thought that if I got this far, I wouldn't be able to resist finishing the quest.

And he was probably right. After all, Daed's *always* right; that's one of the things Rick hates about him. Yes, it would have been hard to turn away from that portal, knowing Daed trusted him, steeling himself to walk into that spindle-trap. If the portal had been on the map, it would have been a temptation: possibly too big a temptation. OK, Rick thinks. I don't blame you, Daed. *I* wouldn't have trusted me, either.

And it makes it easier, in the end. So you expect me to be untrustworthy? Rick thinks. OK. Suits me. Serves you right if I *am* untrustworthy.

And I've earned this quest. I've got here. No one else could have done it. That portal is *mine*.

He licks his lips, tasting sweat and the acid tang of exhaustion. Then, slowly, he moves to the blank wall and runs his hands down it. It's only the tank, sculpting the shape of old bricks and crumbling mortar, he knows that; but right now he could swear it's real. He's come to the end of the Maze. It's the end of the known world. He thinks: I'm the first person, the only person, ever . . .

He feels the excitement rising, a sly edge of it breaking the surface like a dorsal fin. The wake of it ripples through his head, nudging him off-balance. He's scared; but not of failing.

He takes five steps back, and an extra one — not for luck, but something else. A mark of respect, maybe, a gesture of appeasement . . . He thinks: Sorry, Daed. If you'd trusted me . . .

Then he shields his head with his arms, takes a deep breath, and runs at the wall as fast as he can.

Four steps, five, six, and —

He keeps running, stumbling, hunched against the impact, but it doesn't come, still doesn't come, *still* doesn't —

And when he opens his eyes he's bathed in golden light and there's nothing, only infinite space and light, empty and beautiful.

He hears a laugh — a soft, delighted sound, not of amusement but sheer pleasure, like someone who's died and discovered it's not too bad after all — and realises it's his own voice. The acoustic relays it back to him with a clean, deep note, like music. Gods, he thinks, this is heaven, Daed's designed *heaven*.

He laughs again. The glowing mist around him swirls and dances.

Congratulations, the screen says to him.

'Thanks,' he says. 'Thank you very much, ladies and gentlemen. I can't express how much this means to me. I'd like to thank everyone at Crater and especially Daed, my mysterious possibly-not-father-at-all, who has always been there for me, if only to criticise and order me around. Thanks, Daed, this one's for you —'

You have successfully completed the Roots of the Maze, the screen says, ignoring him. The mist begins to clear, slowly, like Rick's sobering up. Behind it there's a garden: grass, trees, fountains, the kind of garden that would be riddled with traps, if it were just another part of the Maze. **Thank you for playing. Game over.**

The words disappear. Rick takes a step forward into the garden, hands on his weapon-belt, through force of habit. In the Maze, there'd be enemies, at least. You'd never find a garden that was . . . just a garden. But here there's nothing. Just the sound of the fountain. He keeps walking, savouring the scent of . . . what? Jasmine? Something old, anyway, something extinct. The grass makes a soft, agreeable noise under his feet. Yes, heaven. Peace. Game over . . .

He stops, then, and looks back over his shoulder. The portal has gone; there's only more garden where the door would have been. No way out. And no traps, no enemies, nothing.

Gods, what is he supposed to do here? *Sleep?*

He steps forward again, a strange impatient ache in his throat. He can still see **Game over**, as though it's branded on his retina. He rubs his eyes, pressing the heels of his hands into his face, suddenly sick of the faint gold haze. He feels moisture on his wrists and the brief sting of sweat on his eyelashes. When he looks up again he's sure that something will have changed: he waits for a threatening note in the music, an ominous shadow behind the vines . . . Come on, he thinks. Please. Am I *dead* or what?

But . . . yes. Something *has* changed.

Faintly — very, very faintly, so faintly he isn't sure that he's really seeing it — the air is shimmering, forming itself into words. He blinks and frowns.

The words are just a ripple in the haze, insubstantial, like writing in water. They're hard to see; but he can read them, just.

Welcome to the endgame.

He reads them again and feels the grin spreading across his face, like there's someone putting their thumbs at the corners of his mouth and pushing. He hasn't won. Thank gods . . . It's not over.

Welcome to the endgame.

He closes his eyes. Suddenly he's tired. He could lie down on the floor of the tank and die, right now. He opens his mouth to log out.

There's a noise he recognises. A brief, mechanical, *swishbuzz* sound, something so familiar he can't quite, can't *quite* —

He opens his eyes and Daed's there, right next to him, blurry, too close. The nausea rises as he struggles to focus. Daed's shouting. Rick says, 'Wait, Daed, I can't see, I need time to adjust,' slurring his words. 'Just a second, Daed, what's going —'

Then there's pain exploding into his face, and he feels himself fall, straight down into blackness, like a magic trick.

PART 2

WELCOME TO THE ENDGAME

7

He woke up. He hurt. He looked at the ceiling and didn't know where he was, or who, but he knew he was in pain. Bits of his body demanded his attention. Slowly words came back to him, unscrolling like windows on an old flatscreen computer. Shoulders. Abdomen. Ribs. *Head*.

And then, finally, his own name.

Oh, yes, he thought. Rick. Me.

It should have been a relief that he'd remembered who he was, but the pain cancelled it out. He took a deep breath, and another, testing. He had to close his eyes for a moment, because there was a sudden surge of nausea, swirling up into his vision like a cloud of ink. After a while it faded. He tried to imagine that his body was made of gas: thoroughly insubstantial, weightless. He sat up.

The room was dark, full of bluish shadows, and he was alone. It could have been any time of day, any time of the year. But at least it was his own room, and he was in his own bed. Presumably he wasn't dead, or dying, then. He said, 'Time, please.' The digits flashed up on the blacked-out window: *0543*.

He looked at them until they said *0548*. Then he dragged

his fingers over his forehead, trying to drive away the ache. He said, 'Date, please,' and then looked at the numbers and realised he had no idea what they meant. It wasn't like he ever needed to know the date. He wasn't absolutely sure he knew what year it was meant to be.

The last thing I remember, he thought. Was . . .

Welcome to the endgame, just clear enough to read.

And —

He ran his hand over his jaw, gingerly. What else? The sound of the — yes — that's it, it was the noise of the tank door, opening. The blur as his eyes adjusted, and Daed's face, shouting at him. And then the pain and the darkness.

Rick's hand paused. He moved it upwards, wiped his mouth with his fingers, pressing harder than he needed to. It hurt. His lip was swollen, and there was a sharp stab of pain as his finger dug into his gums. He explored with his tongue and tasted metal.

Gods, he thought.

Daed *hit* me.

Daed hit me so hard he knocked me out. He overrode the security on the tank and opened the door manually and came in and *hit* —

The nausea came back in a rush. This time breathing didn't help. Rick jerked forward — Maze-trained reflexes, he thought, at least they're good for something — and vomited on to the carpet. It was like being thrown against a wall. He retched and spat. The wet patch on the carpet split into two identical twins of itself. He let his head drop on to the pillow and watched them dance.

I'm *ill*, he thought. Where the hell is everyone?

He tilted his head back, so he was facing the nearest hidcam, and said, 'I think I need a med. Please will you send me a med.'

Nothing changed. He thought: They have to send someone, right? They've seen me puke. They know I'm ill. They have to help me. I'm important.

The digits on the window said *0556, 0557, 0558* . . .

He rolled on to his side, away from the smell of vomit. His mouth tasted of acid and the sore place on his gum was stinging. He thought: What if no one comes, ever?

He closed his eyes and thought of Daed's garden, full of shimmering golden mist, with the words hanging there in front of him like a mirage.

Welcome to the endgame.

What happened? he thought. What's going on?

What did I do?

When he woke up he was starving, and his skull felt too big for his head, but he was feeling better. He could sit up without being sick, anyway. He folded himself over, rested his head on his knees, and felt his lungs expanding into the small of his back. Yes, better. Although his ribs . . . 'Lights, please,' he said, then pulled up his T-shirt and wished he hadn't, because seeing the bruise made it worse. He didn't know how he got it, either, and didn't want to think about it, because if you looked at it from the right angle it looked like a footprint. Gods, Daed wouldn't . . . would he?

Rick told himself it wasn't as bad as it looked, covered

it up again and got out of bed. The feeling of carpet under his bare feet was a good one. He was alive. That was something.

'Time, please.'

1803.

OK. No wonder he was so hungry. He walked carefully to the door, and opened the delivery box. He'd been out twelve hours, so there should have been two meals waiting for him . . . but there was nothing. He ran his hand over the bottom of the box, disbelieving.

He slapped his palm against the comms panel so hard it didn't sign him in immediately and he had to try again, more gently. Then he said, 'Housekeeping, please.'

A pause. **Hello, Rick. How can I help you?**

'I want some food, please.'

Glad you're feeling better.

'Breakfast,' he said. 'Green tea, Spanish omelette, bananas, buttered toast, bacon —'

Housekeeping said, **I will be delighted to send you a protein-and-vitamin shake. Would you like painkillers with that?**

Great, Rick thought. They don't send a med, but they stop me eating decent food now I'm feeling better. 'Look, I'm fine, I just want —'

Would you like painkillers?

'No, I'd like —'

Your breakfast will be with you in a few minutes, Rick. Enjoy, and get well soon! The comm cut off. The panel went back to silver.

'Caviar,' Rick said to his reflection. 'Champagne. Lobster. Honeyed dormice. Nightingales' tongues.'

Silence. He thought: This is a punishment. No one gives a toss what I eat, really. It's Daed. He must have told them not to give me what I want.

Rick closed his eyes and slid slowly down the wall, until he was sitting on the carpet with his knees up. The floor undulated, tilting from side to side like a ship. He didn't know if it was really moving or not; although he could hear the wind and the smack of rain against the windows, so it might have been.

He thought: Daed told me not to complete the Roots of the Maze. He told me over and over again. He was very clear about it. And . . .

. . . and I completed the Roots of the Maze.

He heard Daed's voice, as though the words were burnt into his brain. *You do exactly,* exactly *what I tell you. And in return I will continue to protect you from everything you need protecting from.*

Rick opened his eyes, because he was getting dizzy. He took a deep breath and gasped at the twinge of pain in his ribs. If Daed did stop protecting me, he thought, and then deliberately bit down on his sore lip to distract himself. If —

Imagine.

But it can't be *that* big a deal. Whatever I've done, it can't be *that* serious.

Can it?

He waited until there was the click of Housekeeping signing in, and let his head roll sideways to watch the door slide open. The man with the tray — it wasn't anyone Rick knew — raised his eyebrows, but didn't say anything. He crouched down and put the tray within Rick's reach, and left again, silently.

The milkshake was brown and tasted foul. Rick managed to swallow three big gulps and then had to stumble to the bathroom to wash his mouth out. But he could think a bit more clearly now. He put some trousers on — if he'd had more guts he'd have done something about his bruises, but even the thought of it made him wince — and logged out of his room.

His body took him to the tanks, out of habit, although he only realised when he staggered on the stairs and asked himself through clenched teeth where he was going. He couldn't play in this state, he knew that. But the instinct was too strong; and anyway where else was there to go?

The tanks were all free. He went to his favourite one, at the end, and pressed his hand against the panel to log in. It wasn't working. He tried the one next to it, and the one next to that. They all said the same thing.

Sorry, there seems to be a problem with your account. Please contact Crater Customer Services.

'For gods' sake, just let me *in*.'

Sorry, there seems to be a problem —

He smacked his hand against the panel, wiping his prints over the screen to register them. 'Come on . . .' Behind him the rain splattered and spat against the glass, and he felt the skin on his back prickle. He said, 'I've got an infinite account! Let me in!'

Sorry, there —

OK. He took a long breath. There was the smell of disinfectant, and, underneath, the clinging odour of sweat. It made him feel queasy.

He was locked out of the Maze. Someone had closed his account. Daed, presumably.

He stared at the panel. He said, aloud, 'Hey, Rick, you didn't want to run the Maze in this state, anyway, did you? What's the big deal? It's just a glitch.' His voice sounded reedy, like a bad-quality recording. 'Bound to be. An error. Isn't it.'

No one answered.

They'd *closed his account*.

He shut his eyes. He felt sick and unreal. For no reason he thought of the skull Daed had on a shelf in his office: empty eyes and unchanging grimace, balanced on a pile of dusty old flatgames. Rick knew it must have been a person, once, but it had never seemed real. It was only now, standing in front of the locked tanks, that he thought he might be starting to understand.

Daed. The thought went straight to his heart, sending a shot of heat through his veins. He didn't know if it was anger or something else; but in any case it helped him to move.

OK. It was too far to the lifts; he went up the emergency steps. Now that he had somewhere to go it was easier to ignore the pain. He found himself almost on all fours, helping himself up the stairs with his hands, but the floor felt reassuringly solid. He heard his own breathing and he was shocked — a little bit — at how much he sounded like an old man.

He said to himself, Daed. Daed will be in his office. He can't do this to me. He's my —

Whatever he is. He can't — he won't —

It's going to be OK, Rick thought. I trust Daed. It's going to be OK.

And this time he believed it.

8

The door to Daed's office was closed and Rick didn't even stop to take a breath before he slapped the comms panel so hard he felt the shock resonate all the way up to his shoulder and between his teeth. He said, 'Let me in. Let me in. I need to talk to you.'

A ripple of petrol-lustre blue went over the screen: the panel was working, but no one was answering. He said, 'Daed. Please. Please, come on, I need to talk to you. *Now.*'

Nothing.

'Please. Come on, Daed, I know you're there, please, stop being such a —' He caught himself. 'Please. I'm sorry, OK, I'm sorry! But they've — you've — someone's closed my account, and I just need to talk to you, for gods' sake, please, *please.*' He took a deep breath, waited. 'Daed. Daed, come on.' He was running out of self-control: he could feel it evaporating off his skin. Any second now he'd start crying. 'Daed, please don't do this to me. I —' And there it went, his voice: cracking like glass in the rain. He swallowed. 'I'm sorry, OK? I don't know what to do. Daed, please don't —'

The door slid open. A voice he didn't recognise said, 'All right, Rick, you can come in if you promise to *shut up*.'

He stumbled through. The light was silvery-blue, and the corners of everything glinted at him like eyes. He felt overwhelmingly sick. For a minute all he could do was grab hold of something and resist the urge to throw up again.

When the world was back to steady he opened his eyes. The voice said, 'Sit down.' Rick didn't like obeying people he didn't know, but he couldn't deny that it was good advice. He let his knees go and there was a chair there, waiting for him. He was impressed, in spite of himself: whoever the voice was, they were as good as Daed.

He said, 'Thanks.'

'I thought I told you to shut up?'

Rick started to say, 'I was being poli—' and then his larynx cut out, because the voice *was* Daed. He blinked, because the face was almost as unrecognisable as the voice. It was only the two of them together that told him that it was Daed, standing there.

He was *grey*.

Rick knew he was staring, but he couldn't stop. How could someone change so much in a day, in two days? He could already see the death's-head behind Daed's face, just waiting for the rest to rot away. Only the eyes were the same: and now he knew exactly what was wrong with them. They were too old. They always had been. But before the face didn't match, and now it did.

He opened his mouth to say something, but the mechanism of lungs and voicebox and mouth wasn't working.

'Don't bother,' Daed said. 'I would be surprised if you had anything to say. Anything worth saying, that is.'

He was right. Finally Rick heard himself say, 'You *hit* me.'

There was a pause, but not a long one. Daed said, 'Yes. And?'

Rick looked at him.

'Yes,' Daed said again. 'I did. You deserved it. I think we can agree on that. Am I right?' He asked as if he didn't know the answer; so it was surprise as much as anything that made Rick respond.

'Yes, Daed.' In spite of himself he meant it.

'Good,' Daed said, but he didn't sound pleased. He didn't sound *anything*, come to that. 'Was that all?'

Rick stared into his face, wondering — not for the first time — who Daed was, how old he was, where he'd come from. He swallowed. He didn't want to think like that; he was happier when he tried not to think at all, when he told himself Daed was just Daed, always snide, always right. He wanted to burst into tears. He wanted to tell Daed what it was like to wake up ill and alone in his bed, to ask for meds and food and get turned down, to be locked out of the Maze. Somehow he thought that — after all — Daed might understand. But he didn't *want* Daed to understand. He said, 'No. Do you have any food?'

Daed made a strange sound, like a laugh. He turned away and sat down at his desk. He was running his fingers over his flatscreen, creating a mesh of lines, a glowing hypnotic pattern. After five seconds he said, without looking up, 'On the shelf. If you're that hungry.'

Rick looked over his shoulder and there was a tall plastic cup, full of something viscous and brown: a P&V shake, like the one they'd given Rick. There was a drinking straw stuck in it, like an insult. Rick's stomach heaved. He said, 'I'm not drinking that. I want green tea and proper food.' Silence. Finally he said, 'Please.'

Daed didn't react. His fingers traced shapes on the flatscreen, weaving filaments of light together. He dragged everything sideways, started again with an empty frame.

Rick said, 'Why did you order *that*?'

'Basic rations,' Daed said. His hands were building another pattern, fluently. 'That's what everyone eats, Rick. In the real world we'd be lucky to get that.'

'Yeah, but it's disgusting —'

'I didn't order it,' Daed said, and the mesh on his flatscreen grew and grew. 'I've had my food credits withdrawn. As have you, I imagine.'

'You . . . ?'

Daed didn't say anything else. His pattern spread and flowered, and Rick realised that it was exactly the same as the last one. Daed dragged it sideways and started again.

Rick said, '*You*'ve had your food credits withdrawn.'

'I have access to basic rations,' Daed said, as if it didn't interest him much. 'We won't starve. Yet.'

'But —' Rick stopped, waited for Daed to interrupt him. But Daed didn't look up; he just went on constructing the same pattern over and over on his flatscreen. Rick stared at the glimmering blue lines, willing Daed to come up with something new. But he didn't.

Rick licked his lips and tasted dryness. He said, concentrating on the consonants, 'Why have they taken away *your* food credits?'

'You know what Paz is like when she's annoyed about something,' Daed said, as if this happened every day, as if it was no big deal. It was only his fingers, flickering uselessly over the screen, that gave him away.

Rick took a deep breath; there was a grey, blank panic threatening to take him over. He looked up at the lights in the ceiling, but even the silver-blue neon didn't help. It was like he was seeing everything through a fog. He didn't want to move, or speak. He wished he could just . . . disperse.

'Daed,' he said, and let the silence stretch until Daed looked up. His eyes were blank and ancient.

'Daed,' Rick said again, hanging on to the word like a handhold. 'What's going on? What did I do?'

For a second the Daed he recognised was there, looking back at him with a glint of disdain. Then the old man resurfaced. He said, softly, 'You did exactly, precisely the worst thing you could have done.'

'I'm sorry —'

Daed raised one shoulder, shrugging the words away. 'Irrelevant,' he said, without rancour. 'I should have known. You're a kid. Kids like to win.'

'I only —'

'*Only?*' Daed said, and his voice made the word silver-sharp, so Rick could almost see it catch the light. 'No. *Only?* No.'

'Then . . .' Rick swallowed. The grey fog of fear had got

75

into his bones, aching. 'I just . . . it didn't seem important. I did what you told me to do, and —'

Daed stood up. He walked around his desk to where Rick was sitting, and crouched in front of him, so that his face was on a level with Rick's. Rick stayed absolutely, perfectly still. And if he'd thought he was afraid before he was wrong, because *now* —

Daed said, 'You did *what I told you to do*? Oh, no. No, you didn't.'

If Rick could have spoken, he would. But there was nothing to say.

'Oh, no,' Daed said again, very softly. 'No, no, no. I think you must have misunderstood. I told you what you had to do, and you chose the exact opposite. You know that, don't you?' He looked into Rick's eyes. 'Don't you?'

'Yes,' Rick said. In the Maze there were serpents that could turn you into stone with a glance. Now he thought he knew what that would feel like.

'Good boy,' Daed said. 'At least you can admit it.'

He leant forward and took Rick's head in his hands. His touch was light and firm and even if Rick had tried to get away he couldn't. Daed held him like that for a second — two, five, ten. Rick stared back, until he couldn't bear it any longer.

Then Daed kissed his forehead, embraced him, and let him go. He stood up, took a deep breath as if he'd put down a heavy weight, and went back to his desk. Rick could still feel the warmth of Daed's mouth, as if he'd left the print of his lips on Rick's skin.

Rick said, 'Tell me what I did.'

Daed glanced over his shoulder and away again. He wiped his hand across his eyes. He said, 'It'll be OK. I can deal with it.'

'But —'

'It's OK, Rick. I promise. It'll be all right. Go and put something on your face. You look appalling.'

He hated it, this new voice, this softness. It scared him. He didn't want Daed to reassure him; he wanted Daed to tell him what a stupid little git he was. He said, 'Please, Daed —'

But he didn't know what he was going to say, and he never found out, because Daed's comms panel lit up and Paz's voice said, 'I'm coming in.'

Daed looked at him, then. 'Go away, Rick.'

'I . . .' He wanted to stay. He didn't want to be on his own.

'Get out.'

Paz opened the door — no need to wait for Daed to let her in, naturally — and paused in the doorway as if she was posing for a screenshot. She said, 'Rick. What a surprise. Run away and play.'

'I can't,' Rick said. 'Someone's closed my account.'

'Oh dear,' she said, and smiled at him. It was the same smile that you saw on the tygers in the Maze, just before they ate you. He thought: Daed must have done that on purpose.

Paz turned her head, dismissing him. She said to Daed, 'I suppose you already know what I've got to say. Don't you?'

'I suppose you'd better say it anyway,' Daed said.

'Then get rid of your dependant, please. I don't want to give him nightmares.'

She turned away and stood looking out at the towers of Undone, waiting for him to leave. Rick looked from her to Daed and back again. He never wanted to leave them alone together; normally it was jealousy, but now he felt . . . protective. But Daed caught his eye and jerked his head at the door.

'OK, I'm going,' Rick said. 'Can I take your P&V shake, please?'

Daed frowned, but he nodded.

Paz turned and leant against the glass, her hands spread on either side of her. She watched Rick as he went to Daed's shelf and picked up the cup of brown sludge. He heard her lick her lips; then she said, 'I hear they're very good for you. Of course I've never tried one, myself . . .'

'I *love* them,' Rick said, before he could stop himself. He went to the door, tapped precisely on the panel and stepped through the moment the gap was wide enough. He heard Daed clear his throat as he walked round the corner, out of sight.

But it wasn't the shake he wanted: it was the straw.

He dragged it out, sucked the shake off the end, and he was on his stomach and waiting for the door to close before he even had time to grimace at the taste. Then the door slid shut, and he slipped the straw into the gap and upwards. It stuck just below the electrolatch. The door paused, confused, leaving a micro-em of space.

Rick smiled, and checked the comms panel. Nothing.

Safety mechanisms, he thought. All that technology and you can keep a door open with a drinking straw. Honestly.

But the flash of triumph didn't last. How could it, when he could hear Paz's voice, faint but clear? She said, 'We don't like people who break their promises, Daed.'

'I don't recall ever *promising* you —'

'Oh, but you did. Don't you remember? The perfect product. A game that would never be obsolete.'

'It isn't obsolete!' The response came too quickly, too fiercely. 'All right, I promised you that — but it's still true. It *is* the perfect product. There's no reason why —'

'A game no one could win, you said. Always another quest to run, always something *more*. Our unique selling point, I think you said. As well as the RPG elements — *real*, classic gameplay — that would never be completed. Tell the world they can win it, and keep the end just out of reach.' Rick heard a faint rasp, and realised that it was Paz's stockings, as she moved. 'I hope some of this is ringing a bell?'

'There was a cheat. The avatar who got through the Roots was cheating. You can't hold me responsible for —'

'If he cheats and gets away with it, I certainly can.'

A pause. Rick wished he knew what they were doing; but there was only silence. The gun-grey metal in front of his face blurred and came back into focus.

Paz said something else, too low to catch, as if she was standing right next to Daed. Rick imagined her touching him — his face, or his arm — and shivered. There was an answering murmur, and Paz laughed.

'Let me recap,' she said, her voice quiet but so precise

Rick could have been reading the words. 'You promised us infinity. You promised us a game which would never be won. You said that no matter how long our customers spent in the Maze, no matter how hard they worked, there would always be something they couldn't do. You promised us a game without an endgame.'

Daed said, 'No one could win against the Roots without cheating.'

There was a noise like something cracking. A split second later Daed laughed, or gasped, Rick didn't know which. Something heavy fell off a table.

'I *don't care* if they were cheating,' Paz said. Rick heard her sigh. 'Oh, Daed . . . The Roots were your masterpiece, weren't they? Constructed to show us how good you were. We gained hundreds of new accounts, because the best players couldn't resist, and the Roots couldn't be beaten. Perfect. But now — I'm sorry, Daed, did I hurt you? — *now* we can see that your masterpiece is flawed. Or, put simply . . .' She paused. 'Would you mind? My shoes were rather expensive, and Housekeeping have such problems with blood . . . I do apologise, I forgot I was wearing a ring. No, as I was saying, Daed, the problem now is that your work has turned out to be worthless.'

'Hardly *worthless*.' Daed's voice was indistinct, as if there was something in his mouth.

'Well . . . certainly not adequate. We'll have to consider very carefully whether to renew your contract.'

Silence. Rick closed his eyes. He thought: This is only a new bit of the Maze. If I say *log out*, I can stop it all. Please . . .

Daed said, 'There is no way you won't renew my contract, and you know it.'

Rick tensed, waiting. Then, unexpectedly, he heard them both laughing: not like friends, but like opponents, taking pleasure in the game.

'Perhaps you're right,' Paz said. 'But on the other hand you have nowhere else to go. So this is the deal. I'm putting you on probation.'

'Gods,' Daed said. 'What kind of bull—'

'You're lucky, in a way. I've just had news of the release date for the new gametank. The iTank.' For a moment he can hear her smile. 'Good title, don't you think? So classic, so seductively simple, so — *sleek* . . . We would naturally release a new version of the Maze at the same time, for the new platform. So you have a month to come up with a new expansion.'

'A month.'

'Oh, I'm being kind to you, Daed. A new *expansion*, I said. So twenty-first century, don't you think? So *flatgame*? But I've learnt my lesson, you see. You're human. I don't expect anything spectacular. Just enough to keep the best players at bay for a year or so . . .'

'You're not asking for infinity, you mean?'

'Naturally not. It wouldn't be fair. I see that now. You're only human; just a person, like any other Creative . . .' A tap, like a polished fingernail on a smooth surface. 'But . . . the thing about people, Daed, is that they're . . . dispensable. I like people, as long as they're useful. It's just a pity that sometimes . . . they stop being useful. And then — well,

Crater is a business. Were you — for example — to stop being useful, I couldn't guarantee your contract.'

No answer. Rick heard a tiny rustle and a click and didn't know what it was until he smelt the smoke.

Paz said, 'Incidentally, cigarettes kill you, you know.'

'Yes,' Daed said, and it was because there were only two people in the room that Rick knew it was his voice. 'Yes. Funny you should mention that. As it happens, I do know.'

'I hope I've made myself clear.'

'So . . . I understand.' Daed coughed, for too long, and Paz made a sudden sound of disgust. Finally he cleared his throat. 'You'll pay me for as long as I keep ahead of the gamerunners. But after that —'

'After that I shall stop paying you.'

'OK . . .' Daed said, and his voice still had rough edges, as if the cough was just biding its time. 'Suppose I call your bluff? There are new games being commissioned all the time, you know. Crater may be the biggest company now, but . . . You need me as much as I need you.'

Paz laughed. 'You want to leave? Feel free. The quickest way is by the window.'

Daed didn't answer. Rick imagined them there, looking at each other in silence. Even from here he could hear the rain splashing against the glass; he thought he could hear the hiss as it corroded.

'Splendid,' Paz said, at last. 'I'm so glad we've got that sorted out. Creative meeting tomorrow, zero-six-hundred hours, followed by Marketing and a working lunch. I've told Housekeeping to give you caffeine, amphetamines, whatever you need.'

'Morphine.'

'If you're good.'

'And Rick —'

Rick moved, instinctively, and grimaced. But it was OK, he hadn't made any noise.

'Yes?' Paz said. 'He's looking rather battered, I must say. Be careful, you don't want Wellbeing to get involved. That could be complicated for both of you.'

'I want decent food privileges for him. And his account reopened.'

'How touching,' Paz said. There was a pause. 'All right. For as long as your work is satisfactory.'

'Thank you.' There was a clean, bell-like note, as Daed reactivated his flatscreen. 'Now I'd like to work, if you'd excuse me.'

'Certainly.' Paz's footsteps moved towards the door, and Rick got ready to run. 'Oh,' she said. 'One more thing . . . Could you forward me the account details of the avatar who finished the Roots? The surves could do it, of course, but this sort of thing can be awkward if it falls into the wrong hands.'

'She's — yes,' Daed said. 'No problem. I doubt it was actually her, though. Her card details —'

'Oh, please, Daed. Who would steal an avatar to run the Roots? I'll get someone to pick her up, make sure the word doesn't get out. And to get the name of her Cheat, as well.'

Pick her up . . . Rick looked at the grey door in front of his face, and for a second he couldn't remember what other colours looked like.

'I —' Daed coughed again; but this time it didn't sound

quite real. 'Paz . . . I don't think it's worth it. It's perfectly possible that her account was hacked — if she's not the one who actually ran the Roots —'

'Since when did you make policy decisions? If it wasn't her, too bad. These things happen.' A fractional silence. 'As I said . . . people are dispensable.'

There was a noise like a footstep, and Daed's chair skidding on the floor. He said, 'Paz . . . look, I think that's a step too far, when there's no guarantee that it was her.'

A silence. Rick strained his ears, but — right now, the moment when he most wanted to know what they were doing — there was nothing.

Paz said, 'Hmmm,' and from the tone of her voice Rick knew she was smiling. 'Daed, there are a few things I'd like you to understand. Sit down.'

A footstep, and a tiny creak.

'Good. Listen to me. I'm not exactly sure what happened in the Roots, the day before yesterday. The surves tell me that there was something . . . not quite right. Something . . . unusual. Now, I'm sure you will agree that it's out of the question for us to let word of this get out. Imagine the chatrooms, for example. Whoever it was running the Maze, they must never have the opportunity to discuss their victory. You're with me so far. Yes?'

No answer; but from the way Paz went on, Rick thought Daed must have nodded.

'I'm glad you're being reasonable. Incidentally, I believe it's perfectly possible to trace the specific tank in which a particular player was running. So, if we did have any reason to suppose that there was anything . . . irregular . . . in what happened . . . well, it would be easy to discover the identities of the people involved, and . . . take appropriate action. Do I make myself clear?'

Another silence; Rick supposed there must have been another nod.

'As I am personally convinced that there is no reason to look further into the affair, I'm going to authorise Customer Services to pick her up and neutralise the situation.' Her voice was as smooth as her stockings. 'But if you have anything you want to tell me — any details, I mean, which might be useful — then now is the time.'

Rick closed his eyes. For an instant he saw Athene looking back at him. He thought: She's not real. That face isn't real. She probably doesn't look anything like that. I don't even *know* her.

Please, Daed . . .

Daed said, 'On second thoughts, Paz, I dare say it's unlikely that anyone hacked her account.'

'That's what I thought.' Her heels clacked on the floor; there was a small, soft sound, that Rick couldn't place. Paz said, 'You're a sensible man, Daed,' and laughed. 'Or . . . whatever you are.'

Rick thought: She kissed him.

Suddenly he felt so sick he could die of it. He didn't even care how much noise he was making as he struggled to his feet. He had to get back to his room before he threw up, that was all. He stumbled away, concentrating on staying upright. He kicked something, heard the plastic cup hit the wall and felt a splash of something damp and thick on his face. Behind him, Paz said something else, laughed. He could smell the P&V shake, and Daed's cigarette smoke. He swallowed and tried to breathe. The corridor turned a right-angle and he hit the wall and rebounded, kept running. He couldn't hear their voices any more.

But he didn't make it to his room before he vomited.

9

He floated face down, watching the shark in the water below, the slow flick of its tail from side to side. It rolled a little, showing its teeth. He dived, swam above it, then stayed where he was, holding his breath. He reached down and half knocked, half slapped the glass, fighting the inertia of the water. He didn't know whether the shark was real or not. If it was a projection, it was good: he'd never seen it repeat an action. Now it saw him and surfaced a little, until it was close enough for him to see the water flowing over its gills. He hovered, waited, feeling the familiar frisson of almost-fear. Then he ran out of air, and surfaced.

He rolled over and looked up at the glassed-out sky, moving as little as he could, kicking gently to stay afloat. It was only just after noon, but the clouds were massed so thickly it could have been evening. For once, though, it wasn't raining: if the ceiling broke, he wouldn't die. Or not so soon, anyway. There'd be radiation, of course, Old World chemicals, the last exhalation of the Alternative Energy Source century still hanging in the air. He imagined the poisons slipping invisibly into his lungs, the seeds of cancer growing, putting down roots. He shut his eyes.

Daed designed this pool, he thought. A glass box, between a great white shark and the outside world. Nice one.

A metaphor.

Gods, what was *wrong* with him? He held his nose and somersaulted, blinded by bubbles and cool blue light. Then he found his feet and waded to the edge of the pool, dragged himself out. He saw the massive fish-shaped shadow move away, blurring as it dived deeper. Either it was a *really* good program, or . . . He paused, wiped the chlorine out of his eyes. Or there was an aquarium, directly below the pool. It was mad; no one would do that. But . . .

He'd never wondered about it, before.

He reached for his towel and wrapped it round his shoulders so that it covered him like a cloak. He went through the archway and sat heavily on his bed, not caring if he dripped everywhere. He'd got so much time to *think*. He should have been in the Maze, right now — if not actually running it, then talking to his guilds, getting supplies, politicking . . . His reputation would die, slowly, if he stayed away too long. He had a couple of vendettas, and he still had to finish the solo he was running, the day he —

The thought made him wince.

But if he didn't run the Maze . . . what was he meant to *do*?

There is another world, Rick, he thought. The real one. The one where, if you die, you *really* die. Ring any bells?

The one where, if someone gets killed because of you, they *really* —

The real world.

But he didn't know how the real world worked. He didn't know what to do. He'd spent all his life in the Maze.

Well then, he thought. Time to find out.

The cameras followed him as he logged out of his room and walked down the corridor, his hands deep in his pockets, his rainhood under his jacket, where the lenses couldn't see it. He could feel the rigidity of the breathing panel pressed against his chest. There was already sweat building up on his breastbone. What was he doing? The hood was there for emergencies, anything that might mean he had to leave the complex, like bomb threats and fire drills and electrical failures. You had to practise once a year, getting it on and off, but apart from that he wasn't allowed to touch it. He thought of the sign next to the hook where the hood normally hung: *PENALTY FOR IMPROPER USE.*

Some people had to wear them every day. If you lived in Undone, and didn't work for Crater, or the government, or . . . well, OK. Just Crater or the government. He imagined what it was like, being used to the hood and the rain and the outside world . . . There were thousands of people like that. Millions. And not just the ones who were alive now, but their parents, and their parents' parents, all the way back to the Alternative Energy Source pollution, and the nuclear disasters. It was . . . *normal.*

Just not for me, Rick thought. I've never been outside, not since I can remember. I'm protected. I'm privileged.

I'm a freak.

Thanks, Daed.

He gave a V-sign to the nearest camera and went down the stairs.

He went down and down and down, until he lost count of the storeys. Maybe the stairs were actually an optical illusion, not going anywhere. But just as he was starting to think about trying to find a lift, he got to the bottom. There was just a door, wire-reinforced chemiglass, glinting like a net. When he put his hand on the comms panel it said to him, **Ground floor. Please select your destination.**

The menu came up, but only some of the options were illuminated. Rick tried to select **outside access**, but the screen didn't respond. The words were faint and greyish, like **meeting room**, **creative department** — everything, in fact, except **canteen** and **toilets**.

Rick selected **toilets**.

The comms panel said, **Enjoy your visit, Rick!** and the door slid open.

He walked down the corridor. He didn't know where he was going, but he knew from the Maze that it was better to go quickly in the wrong direction than too slowly in the right one. Anyway, there was only one way to go: ahead.

Then he came out into the atrium, and he stopped dead, in spite of himself.

It was like something out of the Maze: but real.

It was huge. He hunched his shoulders, taking a deep breath. That's what it's designed for, he thought, to make me feel tiny. There was a staircase opposite him — a hundred ems away, or more — but he could see that the steps were the height of a man, too big to climb. It curved up spectacularly, a double helix, twisting on itself like a strand of DNA, all the way to the roof, until Rick felt a sort of vertigo just looking at it. There was no reason for it to be there, except that it said: You are not important. You — are — too — *small*.

Then he saw it was a fountain. It shone and trickled with water: clean, uncontaminated water, more clean water than most people would ever see in their lives, probably. More water than anyone had a right to.

You — are — *poor*.

But it was silent. Rick wondered for a second if it was a fake, a projection, because surely the water would make a noise, hissing gently over the stone, dripping . . . Then he swallowed soundlessly, and realised there were wave absorbers, deadening everything. It was like he'd gone deaf.

You — are — *trivial*.

This is the heart of the complex, he thought. This is Crater.

The worst thing was, he was pretty sure Daed had designed it.

He wanted to turn around and run away, back to his room. He shouldn't be here. But he couldn't move. He thought of the shadow-rats in the Maze, how if you turned a light on them they froze and stared blankly and let you kill them.

Get out, he thought. Now.

But in the Maze he wouldn't turn back, would he? And this — the real world . . . It's just the endgame, he thought.

Welcome to the endgame . . .

He ran forward. His feet didn't make any noise on the stone. But his body worked the way it was supposed to. He could hear his heartbeat, just. Not even Crater — not even Daed — could take that away. He ran until he had to swerve sideways, round the staircase, and he could see past it.

There were doors in the walls of the atrium, each with a neat histro plaque on the door. *Meeting Room*, the nearest one said. The door was twice the height of a man, smooth and platinum-slick. There was no comms panel.

He skidded past it — felt the friction under his runner, and wished he could hear the sole squeak — and on. *Marketing Department. Creative Department. Security Office*. None of them had comms panels. He thought: Maybe no one ever goes in or out. Maybe you have to be *born* in there.

Opposite him — the other end of the atrium from the door he came in by — there was an archway. It had to be three storeys high. And through it he could see a glass wall with airlock doors, and through *that* a vast hall with more glass walls, glinting with comms panels and —

People.

He wasn't sure he'd ever seen so many people, all at once; not in real life, anyway. There had to be six or seven of them. They were pulling off their hoods, changing from face-less shadows into Crater employees, pressing their hands against the panels to check in, saying things over their shoul-ders . . . They'd come in from the outside. They stripped down to their in-clothes, dropped their out-clothes into a basket, and queued for the airlocks.

He stood where he was, trying to learn the procedure. All that trouble, just to stay alive. He crossed his arms over his chest, squeezing his hood into his ribs. It didn't look the same as theirs. And they had suits, as well. What if, when he went outside —?

And they had guns . . .

They started to trickle out of the airlocks. The first one out waited for the others. Rick smelt something harsh and chemical, burning the back of his throat, and knew it must be rain.

He waited until they had gone — they shot him an odd look as they went past, and stopped talking — and then walked slowly to the door of the nearest airlock. The comms panel swirled blue. He looked through the glass. Beyond the airlock there was the entrance hall, with more panels; and then more glass, and then . . .

He put his hand against the comms panel.

I'm sorry, you're not authorised to access this area. Please contact your administrator.

He said, 'I want to leave the complex.'

I'm sorry, you're not —

'I want to go outside.'

I'm sorry, you're not —

'I'm Daed's son, I can do what I want! Now let me *out*.'

I'm sorry, you're not —

He took a long breath in. Then he put his hand carefully back on the panel, and said, 'Request personal response.'

A long pause.

I'm sorry, there's no one available to help you right now. Please try again later or contact your admini—

No. He turned away; not because he was giving up, but because he thought he'd explode if he didn't. He focused on the great staircase, trying to calm down. But it didn't help. It said to him, indifferently: You — are — *trivial*.

He had to get out. Why couldn't he get out? What was this place, a *prison*?

He thought, too late: Shut *up*.

The giant steps ran and trickled with water, telling him how rich Crater was, how much they could afford to waste. The impossible silence pressed like fingers into into Rick's ears, right into his brain.

You — are — *nothing*.

He spun, shielded his head with his arms as if he was running a portal, and threw himself at the glass.

It clanged and resonated, silently. Rick heard himself cry out, very faintly, as if he was a long way away. But the pain was loud, and right here. He staggered backwards and swore, hearing the air suck the words away before they were fully formed. Black specks buzzed in the corners of his vision like swarms of flies. He knew they weren't real because he could hear them.

Please be careful. Your nearest first aid point is —

He turned himself sideways and ran at the wall, again. It hurt, again; but at least in different places. The glass vibrated and sang without a sound.

Please be —

He hissed and drew back, shaking. It was glass, for gods' sake. He had to be stronger than *glass*. Even if it was reinforced, special, bullet-proof —

He didn't let himself finish the thought. Because if he couldn't break the glass, he couldn't get out, and if he couldn't get out —

One more try. This time he knew the wall would crack, at least. He drew his hand back and made himself believe that his arm was stronger than the glass wall. Stronger than Crater. Then he punched.

He dropped to his knees, cradling his hand, rocking back and forth. He heard the faint distant sound of his breath, sobbing in and out. With an effort he straightened his fingers and fought the new wave of pain. He blinked until his eyes focused again. He looked up. There was a red smear on the glass.

Please, the comms panel said to him. There were more words than that, but he didn't get to read them. Something was pulling him to his feet and fastening his wrists firmly behind his back before he had time to resist. A voice – a human voice – said, 'OK, that's enough.'

A human. Not a robot, or a recorded voice; because humans were useful, and cheap. Rick stayed on his feet, breathing. Suddenly he could hear again; whoever was there must have some kind of portable device, an audio-enabler or something. He struggled against the warm, rubbery things on his wrists. It didn't help. He turned round, slowly.

There was a small, under-designed man in a Security uniform. He said, 'What can I help you with today, sir?'

'You can take off these handcuffs and let me out of the door,' Rick said.

'I'm afraid I can't do that, sir. If you give me the name of your account admini—'

Rick smashed his forehead into the Security man's nose.

In the Maze an enemy wouldn't have missed a beat; but the

Security man swore and bled and reeled. It surprised Rick, and he faltered, looking at the blood. It was real . . . And Rick wasn't used to feeling the impact, either; his skull hurt. It slowed down his reflexes. He only just had time to dodge the man's retaliatory punch, drop to a crouch and sweep his leg round. It was hard to balance, with his hands behind his back. But the kick worked; the Security man yelped and fell to the ground. His hands flailed at the air for a split second and then his head smacked on to the stone floor.

Rick flipped to his feet, poised on the balls of his feet, waiting for him to get up. You *could* kick enemies when they were down, but it wasn't great for your reputation. If his guild saw him —

But he wasn't in the Maze.

And the man didn't get up.

Rick stared at him, and then prodded him, not gently, with his foot. The fight couldn't be over that quickly. No one's health bar was *that* small . . .

The man made a noise like a broken air-con unit. He didn't move.

Rick looked down at him. He didn't know what to do. In the Maze he'd loot the body. Was that what he should do now? Somehow it didn't seem . . . right.

But he needed to get these cuffs off. So he crouched, twisting to go through the man's uniform with his joined hands. In the end he had to lie down to get the right angle, navigating the contents of the pockets by touch. He felt the porto-panel, finally, and scrabbled it out with his fingers. Then he pressed the man's limp hand against it — which was harder than it should have been — and held his wrists in the force-field to unlock the handcuffs. They loosened and retracted. He put them in his own pocket and rolled his shoulders.

The Security man made another noise, and his ribcage spasmed.

Rick thought: He must be important. He's got a gun.

He must be important. And important people can go outside . . .

All I need is his prints, to log in, and the comms panel will let me through . . .

But Rick didn't move immediately. The thought of doing that made him feel odd. He thought: All I need to do is drag him over to the comms panel, and lift him up so I can put his hand on the screen. It's not hard.

I don't even know if he's *alive*.

There were footsteps, coming towards him from behind his left shoulder. They got faster and faster until they stopped.

At his back someone — someone he knew — drew her breath in, sharply. He didn't want to look at her; but he glanced down and sideways, and he saw her shoes. They were dirty and flat-soled — histro, but not chic like Paz's — and they'd paused mid-step. She said, 'Rick, what have you done?'

He felt a sudden hot lump in his throat, because of the way she said his name. He clenched his jaw and thought: Thank you, *thank you*, because of all the people in the complex — Daed, Paz, people he didn't know — the gods sent him Perdita. It could have been so much worse.

She said again, 'Rick . . .'

He looked at her, in spite of himself.

Her face was pale and strained. Her eyes flicked from one security camera to the next and the next, until she was staring past the staircase; and she was afraid.

He started to say, 'I just wanted to get out —'

'Come with me.'

She took hold of him, grabbing his arm sharply and pulling him away. It hurt. Rick looked down, half expecting to see his feet on the edge of an abyss. But there was only the Security man.

'Rick,' she said, 'come with me. Don't argue, don't procrastinate, don't ask. Come with me. *Now*.'

He took one last look at the glass wall. The smear of blood had dried to a kind of rust colour. Beyond that wall was the outside world. If he gave up now —

But . . . the expression he'd seen on Perdita's face.

He turned away and followed her.

10

The moment her workshop door had closed behind him, Perdita said, 'Advance warning on, please,' and the watchdog ikon flashed up on the comms panel. Rick stood where he was and watched it, not wanting to look at her. The ikon had three heads, for some reason. Three sets of teeth snarled and dripped saliva. Yeah, right, he thought. The watchdog could tell you if someone was coming, that was all; it couldn't actually keep anyone out.

She said, 'Do you want to tell me what you were doing?'

'Not really.'

'OK.' She went over to one of the workbenches, and he heard her fiddling with some bit of ancient techno. He heard the sound of running water, and she said, 'Tea?'

He stared at the watchdog's six hostile eyes. Please, don't be nice to me, he thought. Anything but that.

'He didn't look in good shape, that Security guy,' she said. 'That . . . was you, I take it?'

'I didn't mean to hurt him,' Rick said, and couldn't help turning to look at her. 'He just . . . I mean, I thought he'd . . . in the Maze —'

She looked at him. She nodded.

'I was trying to get out,' Rick said. 'The comms panel wouldn't let me out — and the atrium was making me feel weird, and then he came up and put handcuffs on me —'

'The Nucleus,' she says. 'The atrium, that's what it's called. Yes, I know. It's creepy. Meant to be.'

'But I wanted to get *out* —'

She laughed. 'No kidding.'

Something in her voice stopped him saying anything else. He watched her as she poured steaming water out of a plastic jug into two bowls. She prodded the contents with a spoon and then passed one of the bowls to him, carefully. He smelt something acid, like lemon.

Perdita took a sip from her own bowl and sat down. She looked around for an empty space on the workbench, but there wasn't any room, even for a bowl. In the end she kept it in her hands, holding it like it was a ceremony. She seemed to have forgotten that Rick was there. He was glad. He looked around, comforted by how little her workshop had changed since he'd last seen it. It was so like Daed's office; and so different. There were pictures nailed up on the walls, overlapping one another, and bulging boxes piled against the window. There were shelves and shelves of bits of things, junked prototypes, wires and antique toys, even a couple of books. The benches were covered with components and old mechanisms and coloured wire. The room was full of things that wanted to be touched. Rick thought: She does with her hands what Daed does with his mind. I think I like it better.

She still hadn't said anything else, so he took a sip of his tea, finally, and the taste surprised him. It wasn't bad. The warmth ran down his throat and past his heart.

Perdita frowned at the sleeve of her overall, folding the fabric into lines. Rick watched her hand, short-nailed and sinewy, and then looked at her face. She was ugly. She must have chosen to be ugly. She was a Creative, after all, she must have got a decent wage. But she'd still got a flat-ish nose and plump cheeks, she'd still got nothing-coloured eyes. Rick wondered why anyone would *choose* to be ugly. But somehow he was glad Perdita had. He liked the way she looked.

She caught his eye, while he was staring. She said, 'You could be in really big trouble, Rick.'

He felt his eyes narrow. He said, 'Why, are you going to tell Paz?'

She shook her head. 'It's all on hidcam, Rick. Whatever you did to that poor . . .' She hesitated. 'I don't have to tell Paz anything. Not that I would.'

He stared at her, hostile, until she looked away. Then he stood up and said, 'I'd better go. Thanks.'

And then he started to cry.

At first he thought he was ill. He knew what crying was, but he'd never done it before — not that he could remember, not like this. It was like vomiting, he couldn't control it. In the Maze the non-player characters sometimes had water trickling from their eyes when they asked for help; but not like this. They always wiped it away and carried on speaking. No one ever covered their face with their hands. No one ever lost the power of speech. He didn't know it could happen like this.

But he wasn't in the Maze.

In the Maze the Security man would have got up after Rick hit him.

Perdita said, 'Sit down. Breathe.'

He did. (He might as well do what he was told. He'd made a real mess of *not* doing what he was told.) And it helped.

Perdita waited. Finally she said, more gently this time, 'Rick . . . you know there are cameras. There's no way Paz won't hear about what you did. With any luck she'll be decent about it. But the way things are now . . . with Daed in troub—'

She stopped.

He looked through his fingers, at the bench. He said, through snot, 'In trouble. You know about that, do you?'

'Everyone does,' she said, because she was the same as Daed, like that, she didn't believe in white lies.

'He's working on the expansion, isn't he? That's going OK, isn't it?'

'Yes,' she said. But her tone wasn't agreeing.

'What's wrong?' Rick said.

'Nothing. With the expansion. But . . .' She looked at him, and he saw her consider whether to go on, and decide that she might as well, now. Maybe *that's* the point of her face, Rick thought. It lets you see what she's thinking. It's not a mask, like Daed's. 'It's just that expansions are so . . .'

She searched for the word. But she didn't need to; Rick could remember what Paz had said. He said, 'So *flatgame*?'

'Yes.' She shrugged. 'Honestly. Daed, designing an expansion? It's like Aeschylus, writing an episode of *Undoners*.'

He didn't know who Aeschylus was — a genius, presumably, like Daed — but he got the gist. He said, 'But . . . his contract's OK, right, he's still . . . important —?'

'Yes,' she said, slowly. 'It's just that now . . . well, it's not the best time for you to attract attention. When that game-runner won in the Roots, everything went . . . Things changed. Daed's having a difficult time.'

He looked at the bench, and prayed. Please let that not have been pity in her voice. Please — oh, gods, if she *pities* Daed —

He wanted to ask another question. Anything. What relation are you to Daed, anyway? Did he ever say anything about my mother? Do you think he really cares about m—

Too late. The comms panel growled. Perdita glanced past him and said, 'Oh, hell.'

He followed her gaze.

The comms panel said, **Daedalus will be here in 15 seconds. He has full entry rights. Daedalus will be here in 14 seconds. He has —**

Perdita said, 'Oh well. Looks like he'll be finding out that you're here, then.'

'He can't.' Rick saw the grey veil of panic drop over the world. 'Please — Perdy, he can't see me here, I don't want him to know —'

'He'll find out anyway,' she said. 'You weren't exactly subtle.'

'He doesn't have to find out like this — please, he'll kill me —' Rick knew Daed *wouldn't* kill him; but somehow that was worse. 'Can't I — Perdy, if I hide, just don't tell him I'm here, and later on I can explain to him, properly.'

Daedalus will be here in 5 seconds. He has —

She looked at him, and he knew she was only giving in because she was so much older than him, and she felt sorry for him and Daed both, and she was nice, the kind of person who'd be ugly just because that was how she was born. She grabbed him and pushed him backwards. He didn't mean to resist, but he didn't know where he was going, so he tripped. His head hit something and hurt. He saw Perdita shutting a door in front of him. Then everything was pitch-black.

Oh, gods. He didn't like small spaces. Especially not in the dark.

He shouldn't have asked to hide, then, should he?

He reached out slowly and touched something on either side of him. Long vertical strips of something . . . warmish, not metal, a texture that he associated with the Maze. He concentrated. Vellum. In the Maze they'd have been quest scrolls. But here, in the real world, they must be something else. Paper. No, the other one. Cardboard.

He was in a cupboard, with lots of . . . books?

The smell was funny, too. He breathed in, wondering how long he could stay in here before his nerve went.

Then he heard Daed's voice, and he leant forward, forgetting where he was.

11

Daed said, 'Hello. Can I come in?'

'Of course,' Perdita said. 'You don't have to ask.'

'Thanks,' Daed said, and then there was nothing.

Rick waited, wondering what was going on. Perdita said, 'Is there something . . . ?'

'Just checking on your progress,' Daed said. 'The iTank all on target, is it?'

'Time yes, budget no,' Perdita said, 'as always. Don't tell me you walked all the way down here to ask that?'

A pause. 'No,' Daed said. 'No.'

'Tea? I'll put the boiler on.'

'Kettle,' Daed said. 'A boiler was something else. No, thank you.' There was a rustle, as if he was getting something out of his pocket, and a little crackle, like foil. 'A glass of water would be nice, though.'

Water running, footsteps. Perdita said, 'Headache?'

'Not exactly.' Daed swallowed and coughed. A chair grated on the floor. 'May I?'

'Oh, shut up, Daed,' Perdita said. 'Why are you being so polite? We're friends, aren't we?'

Daed laughed, a little. He said, 'OK.'

'So,' Perdita said. 'You didn't want to vidcall whatever it is, so . . .'

'You've disabled your bugs, presumably?'

'I'm a Creative, Daed. I disable bugs as a hobby.' A moment of silence. Then she added, 'But —' and Rick knew she'd remembered, suddenly, that he was listening.

'But what?' Daed said.

'But . . . Maintenance were in here a few days ago, and I haven't swept since then.' She was lying, and she was rubbish.

'Never mind,' Daed said, and laughed. The laugh was breathy and voiceless, like his lungs weren't working properly. 'Who cares? I came to pick your brains, that's all.'

'About the iTank? The technology hasn't advanced much since my report. If you talk to —'

'I wasn't thinking of the technology, exactly.'

Silence. Rick heard water bubbling in the kettle, and footsteps. Then it clicked off, and he imagined Perdita at the workbench, mashing the teabag with a spoon, her back to Daed. She said, 'Since when did you need my brain for anything else?'

'Since Rick ran the Roots and screwed up my masterplan,' Daed said.

Another pause. Rick imagined Perdita staying still, where she was; but when she spoke, her voice was clearer, like she'd turned round. '*Rick* ran the Roots?' she said.

Daed laughed again; as if he knew he was the only one to see the joke. He said, 'Oh, yes. A minor irony.'

'And Paz sent Customer Services out to pick up some poor

innocent gamerunner who never hurt anyone? Gods, Daed. You make me sick.'

'Yes, all right. I don't like it any more than you. But it's just a detail. What matters —'

'And — wait. You told me that, about Rick, when I've just told you I might be bugged? Are you mad?' She said it calmly, like a med asking for symptoms.

'I didn't believe you,' Daed said. 'I thought you just didn't feel like talking to me.'

'Well,' Perdita said. 'OK. You were right. As it happens. But — Daed . . .'

For a horrible moment Rick was sure she was pointing at the cupboard and miming that he was there. But Perdita was decent; she wouldn't betray him like that.

Daed said, 'What?'

'If it's not urgent,' Perdita said. 'I've got a deadline for tomorrow —'

'It is urgent. It won't take long.'

'Daed —'

'Please,' he said. Daed never said *please*.

'I don't have time —'

'I need your help, Perdy. Please help me.'

Rick stared blindly into the dark. He was gripping the corner of one of the cardboard squares; he didn't remember taking hold of it, but now it was hurting his hand.

Perdita cleared her throat; but it seemed like an eternity before she said anything. Even then, when she spoke, it was only, 'Daed . . .'

'Do you want me to beg?'

'No, of course not!' Rick heard her turn on her heel and stride across to the window. She took a deep breath. 'Daed, you don't need my help. You've never needed anyone's help.'

'I do now.'

'Just because they've changed the terms of your contract —'

'Not quite,' he said. 'Not *just* because.'

Silence.

'All right,' she said. 'What do you want?'

More silence. Rick squeezed the cardboard between his fingers until it was damp and soft. Daed, saying *please* . . . He never said please, even to Paz.

Daed said, 'I want you to give me Asterion.'

There was a little noise, as if Perdita had opened her mouth and shut it again; and then silence. Rick wondered why this silence was different from the ones before it. There was no logic to it. But it *was* different.

He wondered who Asterion was; and why he mattered so much.

Perdita said, 'Yes, well, I want Paz's bank account details and a ticket to Deception Island. But I'm not going to get them.'

'Perdita —'

She laughed, but she didn't sound like herself. 'No.'

'Just let me expl—'

'Asterion wouldn't even *work*, Daed. It was just an idea I had when we were drunk. I didn't think it through. It was years ago, when we still thought everything was possible . . . I can't believe you're serious.' Her voice changed key, going up a tone. 'I don't even have the plans in soft copy. They're in a file somewhere in *ink*, on *paper*, and I haven't seen them for years. You must be desperate.'

'Yes,' Daed said. 'I am desperate.'

A pause. Perdita breathed, and breathed again. Then she said, 'Well. I'm sorry. But Asterion won't help you.'

'It *would* help me,' Daed said, and a cough surfaced and bubbled and barked before he swallowed it again. 'Come on! It was a perfect idea. You may have been drunk when you had the idea, but you worked on it for days. Remember? It was —'

'No.'

'I'll pay you for it, naturally.'

'*No.*'

'If it wouldn't work, you can give me the plans, can't you?'

'I haven't got them any more. I probably threw away all that stuff when I got promoted, all the silly mad ideas you and I had together. I don't have time for any of it now.'

Daed coughed again, softly. He didn't believe her. Neither did Rick, come to that, and he didn't know what they were talking about. But it was her voice: she was panicking.

Daed said, 'Then tell me what you can remember. I think I can work out most of it — but there's a lot of code that I can't reconstruct —'

'You've already been trying to reconstruct it?'

'Just playing around,' Daed said. 'Just doodling. But if I could invent a workable version —'

'Get out of my workshop,' Perdita said. Rick had never

heard her voice sound like that. It was a voice you could have sharpened a knife on.

'Perdita, please — I won't steal it, I'll credit you, I just need —'

'*Credit* me? Dear gods, you think I'm worried about *that*? Do you have any idea what you're asking? Asterion is . . . Daed, it's *evil*. It's an idea I came up with because I was interested in how it could work, that's all. It was just a game. I never, *never* thought about giving it to Crater, or —'

'*Evil?* I think you're overstating the case.'

'Out,' she said. 'I'm not negotiating. Get out.'

'Please, Perdy — I was there, when you thought of it, the idea's partly mine —'

'You will use Asterion over my dead body. *Over — my — dead — body*,' she said again. Rick saw her in his mind's eye: her dead body, ready to be stepped over.

'So it *could* be used?'

'I'm calling Security.'

'I've got full entry privileges to be in here.'

There was a creak, as if she was sitting down, and a little metallic tapping that Rick couldn't place. It went on, until he wondered if something awful had happened so quietly he hadn't noticed.

Finally she said, 'Please, Daed. I'm too tired to argue about this. My answer's no, that's all. It will be no, whatever you say. And if, somehow, you get hold of the roughs — and I don't know, I honestly don't know where they are — I will do everything in my power to sabotage the iTank and your expansion. I won't be responsible for Asterion, and if I can help it neither will you.'

It was probably the longest speech Rick had ever heard Perdita make. By the end of it she sounded as if she'd forgotten how to breathe.

Daed said, 'I'm dying.'

The tapping stopped.

'Ironic, isn't it? For an ordinary, human little disease to take me out? Too many cigarettes. How histro.' He paused. 'I don't know how long I have left, Perdita. Time to finish the expansion, probably; but after that I don't know. What do you think Paz will do with Rick, when I'm dead?'

It was a rhetorical question. The answer was silence.

'I can't leave Rick with nothing,' Daed said. 'He needs me. He needs protecting.'

'Asterion won't —'

'For as long as I'm here — for as long as I'm designing the Maze — my contract runs and Rick is safe. If I die, leaving nothing but a flimsy expansion that won't last a year, he's only got as long as it takes for someone to reach the end. If I hadn't been here when he ran the Roots, he'd have been out on the streets that night. Without a hood, knowing Paz. He's only a kid, Perdita. How long do you think he'd last out there? I *can't die*, do you understand? I need to be immortal.'

'Asterion won't —'

'As good as.'

'No, Daed, it won't! For gods' sake — what is it you *really* care about leaving? Rick — or the Maze?'

'Rick and the Maze need each other. I want them both to survive. Do you understand that? And for that I need Asterion.'

'Well, you can't have it.'

Daed coughed, and this time the cough went on for longer. Rick heard something wet hit the floor.

Perdita said, 'Do you want me to call a med?'

But when Daed stopped coughing, all he said was, 'I can get your workshop searched.'

'If you had a better way to get the plans, Daed, you wouldn't have asked me for them,' Perdita said. 'You might have been able to ask Crater for the sun on a wire, before Rick ran the Roots. But now? No, I don't think so. You try anything out of order, and your contract will be terminated, and some clever young thing will be in your office quicker than broadband.' She wasn't threatening him, just stating the facts. She was almost being kind. It made Rick hate her more than he'd ever hated anyone.

Daed said, 'Look at me, Perdita! I'm an old man. I'm desperate. Please. We were friends —'

'*Were*, yes,' Perdita said. 'Until the moment you asked me to give you Asterion. Who the hell do you think you are? Gods, I thought Paz was bad —'

'I give you my word that I'll use it on myself, first —'

'First. Exactly.'

'For Rick's sake, then! Do you want to see him thrown out on the streets? Do you want him to die too?'

Silence. Rick stared at the blackness in front of his face.

'That's unfair,' Perdita said at last. 'You're being cruel.'

'Am I?'

Another pause. Then she said, 'You really want me to spell it out for you, do you? OK, then. Yes. I would rather both of you died. I'm sorry, Daed. I love you both. But Asterion is not what you're looking for.'

Rick waited for Daed to reply.

But he didn't.

He'd given up.

And Rick understood, then, that Daed *was* dying.

There were footsteps, the click of someone logging out of the comms panel, and the *scrape-buzz* of the door. Rick wished he was deaf. He wanted to put his hands over his ears but they didn't obey him. He was still clutching the thin book-thing with his right hand, and the cardboard was warm and prickling like pins and needles. He wanted everything to go away. He was glad it was dark.

There were more footsteps. From the scuff of rubber on the floor Rick could imagine Perdita's shoes, in detail, grimy laces and rubber soles. He could smell the old-canvas, old-feet odour.

A stool creaked. There was a crash — a big, multiple crash, and the faint patter of something else falling a second later. Then something heavy hit the workbench, and he heard Perdita swearing, her voice muffled. Then she started to cry.

He didn't feel sorry for her. He wished she was dying, too.

Then the sobbing stopped, suddenly, and her breathing was louder, as if she'd turned to look at the cupboard.

Yes, that's right, Rick thought. I'm here. Remember? I heard it all.

Not that she moved immediately. Rick counted under his breath: forty-one, forty-two, forty-three. He got to forty-nine before she opened the door.

She was hoping he hadn't heard. She said, 'Rick?'

The space and light hit him between the eyes, like a punch. He wanted to get up, but he couldn't. He looked down at his legs. He knew that they ought to move. The joints ought to do clever things to make him stand up. But there was something missing. He thought: I need to reinstall software. If I could only reconstruct the code . . .

Perdita said, 'You heard.'

Every word, Rick said, but it stayed inside his head.

She understood anyway. He could tell from the look on her face.

He concentrated on getting up. He tried to lever himself up with his arms. The only thing that happened was that the book-thing fell off the shelf. He'd never seen anything like it. It lay face down with its covers spread, like a dead bird. He looked for a better place to put his hand.

Perdita said, 'Please, Rick, I'm so sorry you had to hear that . . .' She was searching his face as if he was a puzzle she had to solve. Her eyes had an extra layer of water. She blinked and a drop slid over her cheek.

Rick felt cold horizontal metal under his fingers, and pulled himself up. His legs felt like they were different lengths. There was too much air, too suddenly.

'Are you OK?' she said. 'Are you ill? Talk to me. Do you need a med?'

That was what she'd said to Daed. Rick shook his head.

'Say something,' she said. 'You're scaring me. Anything. Shout at me. Tell me you hate me.'

I do hate you. I *do*. But if I could say it, Rick thought, I wouldn't mean it. Don't you understand anything?

'I can't explain, Rick, but please, believe me, I wasn't — if I could help Daed I would, I promise, it's just that —' Her eyes overflowed again. It was disgusting, like she was incontinent.

He was still on his feet. His head was spinning. He was breathing too fast, too deep. But the door was only a few ems away. He thought about where he was and where he was trying to go. In the Maze there'd be a trap, somewhere. He'd probably die before he got to the comms panel.

He stepped forward. He thought: Oh. It *is* easy. I can just —

The floor blurred, rippled, and came up to meet him.

12

He didn't know where he was. He was lying on his stomach, like he'd been washed up from a shipwreck. His temple was pressed against something flat and hard. He remembered that something bad had happened before he remembered what it was.

Perdita's voice said, 'Rick? *Rick.* Oh, no. *Rick.* I'm calling a med. Are you OK? I'm going to call a —'

He wasn't supposed to be here. He didn't have clearance to be here. He said, 'Don't, *don't* call a med,' and then struggled to a sitting position. 'I'm OK, just, too much air, after the cupboard. I'll call a med when I get back to my room.' He didn't want to talk to her, but he had to make sure she didn't let anyone know he was here.

'Thank gods,' she said. 'I thought you were dy—'
Silence.

Dying. Oh really? Rick wanted to say. And did you care?

'Do you want anything?' she said. 'Tea? Water?'

Asterion, Rick thought. Whatever it is.

'Let me get you a glass of water,' she said. She got to her feet and looked around for a glass. The workbench was clear and everything was on the floor. Most of it was broken. Rick saw the glinting shards of a glass, and the two halves of his tea-bowl. Perdita stared helplessly at the mess, and then round at her shelves. But there was nothing to drink out of. She said, 'I'll be back in a sec.' She went over to the comms panel and logged out. The door opened and closed behind her.

Rick wrapped his arms round his chest and wished he could cry again. It had been like being sick: it got something out of his system. But he didn't know how to do it.

He didn't want Perdita's glass of water. He wanted to leave now, so that she came back to an empty workshop and nothing but mess on the floor.

He needed to stand up. He got on to all fours and hung his head, trying to summon enough strength. His foot caught on something and he looked round. He was still half in, half out of Perdita's cupboard. His foot was wedged between the cardboard spines of the book-things. He tugged it out, and they flopped forward. White rectangles spread out on the floor like wings. He thought: How histro. Paper. Ink. Handwriting.

He shuffled backwards, so that he'd be able to grab the shelves to get up.

The nearest bit of paper caught his eye. The writing was distorted and hard to read, like a page-long captcha. He focused, like a camera, and after a while words arrived in his head: *Thoughts for Daed re: Centre of the Maze. Ultimate solo — not instance? (Better name, perhaps? Heart of the Maze? Roots?).*

He imagined Perdita and Daed, getting drunk together, leaning towards each other. He thought Daed always worked alone.

The page underneath was full of sketches. He stared down at them, spreading his fingers on the paper. He knew they were Perdita's because of the clarity of the lines; Daed's drawings never looked like anything but ideas.

He thought: Traps.

Every trap he'd run, in the Roots of the Maze — every trap he'd ever seen — was there. He flipped over the next page, and the next, and after a while he felt like his spine was melting, slowly.

Daed's ideas, in Perdita's writing.

But Rick thought Daed had built the Maze alone. He'd thought Daed was —

It was stupid to care. Everyone worked together, didn't they? That was the point of Crater. There was a whole team of Creatives. Why did it matter so much, that they were Perdita's ideas?

But it did.

He remembered Herkules404: *Daedalus is a myth*. Rick wanted to block the voice out, but he couldn't. *You think one person could create this? It takes* hundreds *of designers, years of work, player feedback, and a hell of a lot of AI code to create this. Daedalus is just a convenient idea. Not a person.*

I'm so stupid, Rick thought.

Daed's probably not even my father.

He flipped page after page, and familiar things looked back at him. He got to the end of that book-thing, and pulled the next one off the shelf. He opened it, but he couldn't bring himself to read the handwriting. He ripped the pages across, and then into quarters. He dropped the bits, in hand-fuls. The cover was too stiff to tear, so he shook out the last scraps of paper and chucked it on the floor. None of that made him feel better, but he reached for another book-thing anyway. He covered the floor around him with white, like he was sitting on an island. He went through book-thing after book-thing until there was a pile of them beside his feet and only one left on the shelf.

The last book-thing — the *file*, Rick thought, that's it, I think it's called a file, like on a computer — was thicker than the others. It was a different colour, and dustier, and it had been wedged sideways in the corner of the cupboard. It had been hidden, before he'd taken out the other files. He wouldn't have known it was there.

He picked it up. It was heavy, and the cover felt softer, like skin.

It's older, he thought, without knowing how he knew.

He opened it.

He turned the pages. There was nothing here he recognised. There were drawings of things he'd never seen. Diagrams he didn't understand. There were whole pages of code — program code or maybe just a cipher, he couldn't tell — but nothing here was familiar. It wasn't the Maze; but it wasn't the real world, either.

Just — ideas. Ideas Perdita had never used.

But there were names, and the occasional phrase that made sense. *PROCRUSTES. APOCALYPSE — NB: some amendments necessary.*

He rolled a corner of a page between his fingers. The

paper was thicker, better quality. He wasn't going to tear it up. Not this file. Not this one. Because . . .

He already knew — didn't he? — what he was going to find.

He turned the pages slowly, his heart beating double-time.

He was sure, he was almost sure —

What had Perdita said?

If, somehow, you get hold of the roughs — and I don't know, I honestly don't know where they are . . . He'd believed her, when she'd said it. She *hadn't* known where they were.

But . . .

He turned the pages, and he was thinking: It has to be. The gods are on my side. They've given me this, for Daed. It *has* to be —

ASTERION.

It was coded, and there were pages and pages of it. After the word *ASTERION* there wasn't anything Rick could read: only numbers, letters and symbols that could have been Chinese or just invented. It took up nearly a third of the file, in dense unparagraphed text. There weren't any diagrams. Nothing broke up the pages, except lines of black where Perdita had made a correction.

But he didn't care, because Daed would be able to crack it.

He shut the file, and held it to his chest.

He looked down at the mess of white papers around him. It looked like an iceberg; and if it was an iceberg, it was melting. He had to get out. If Perdita came back —

But now he could move. He was the gamerunner he had

been, before he ran the Roots: slick, fluid, fast. He was himself again.

He flipped to his feet.

He logged out and got through the door. He knew he was untouchable. He knew he was going to get back to his room without anything going wrong. The door buzzed and closed behind him, obedient.

He crossed the atrium — the Nucleus — silently, holding the file over his chest, running lightly. Everything was going to be OK. The relief was like a drug: he couldn't remember how he'd felt an hour ago, couldn't even imagine it.

The comms panels let him through, like clockwork. He went up the stairs, up and up and up, and he wasn't even tired when he got to the top. He was laughing under his breath.

So this is the endgame, he thought. I love it.

He skimmed down his corridor, his feet hardly touching the floor. If he hadn't been carrying the file, he'd have front-flipped and tumbled, just for the hell of it.

He smacked his hand on to the comms panel outside his room and jumped from foot to foot while the door slid open. He bounced through the gap, through the antechamber and into his bedroom. He danced towards the window and spun, his arms spread out wide. His room whirled around him, high-spirited.

A door opened and closed, somewhere.

He stumbled, stopped spinning. The window blurred and suddenly he was dizzy. A shadow crossed his peripheral vision. There was the sound of rain on the chemiglass; and the rustle of clothing and feet on carpet.

He turned round. Everything slid to the left, uncontrollably, and then reset itself, over and over again. He cursed himself, thought: You're so stupid, Rick, making yourself dizzy, like a little kid, when you blacked out a few minutes ago, in Perdita's office . . . The floor rocked like a ship. Even his bed was spinning. He wanted to throw up. He was going to throw up.

And there were men in his room. Three men. In black uniforms.

They came towards him.

He opened his mouth to call for Security and had just enough time to realise there was no point. They *were* Security.

Then they'd got hold of him. One of them yanked his arms behind his back. He felt the soft merciless cuffs snap over his wrists. He tried to fight. But in a second he was on his knees, his head forced down, a half-em from the carpet. He shouted, 'Hey — what the hell — let me *go*, I haven't —'

Someone jabbed something hard into his kidneys, and a white wave of pain rolled up his spine. A voice said, 'Save your breath.'

He went on struggling, trying to get to his feet. He knew it wasn't any good; there were three of them, and he was in no shape to take them on. He said, 'I'll tell Daed about this —'

One of them laughed. There was a hand on his neck, and it tightened until he could hardly breathe. Someone said, 'It's Daed's orders, mate.'

'But we didn't need much telling,' the first voice added. 'Because we're loyal to our friends. And we don't like it when little losers like you send them to ICU. You better pray he doesn't cop it.'

Rick twisted his head, trying to see their faces — anyone's face. 'I didn't mean to hurt hi—'

A hand smacked across his face, from behind. It was deafening. For a fraction of a second it didn't hurt. Then it did; more than he could bear. He felt the water spill out of his eyes. Slowly he brought his face back to the front and tried not to sob aloud.

'Right,' one of the men said. 'Let's go.'

They lifted him half off his feet and half carried, half dragged him towards the door. Rick went limp. There was no point fighting. If he didn't fight, maybe they wouldn't hit him again.

But they went on hitting him anyway.

13

He's looking at himself.

At first he thinks it's a dream. Or is he in the Maze, a part of the Maze he's never seen before? It's strange, dead silent and still. He's in a chair, but it's made of glass or something transparent, so it looks as if he's sitting in mid-air. Behind him an infinite gleaming tunnel stretches away, the perspective finally squashing it to nothing. He can't move. Even his fingers are spread out flat, rigid. He can feel them, but they won't respond to his brain. After a while he thinks there's something holding him down: a layer of something invisible and unyielding. He's vacuum-packed, like a ready-meal. All he can do is blink.

He's looking at himself.

His hair is longer than it should be. His face is damaged but healing. His expression is blank. He looks —

Dear gods, I'm *dead*, he thinks. I'm looking at myself *dead*. What if this is —

Water rises in his eyes, as he feels a wave of panic; and then relief. He's not dead, after all. The face in front of him is wet-eyed, but the tears are here, too, blurring his vision. He's *here*; the boy in front of him is only a reflection, a mirror —

A mirror. He's disorientated, that's all. He squeezes his eyes shut, trying to get rid of the disembodied feeling. Then he opens them again, trying to understand where he is.

He's looking at a corridor of infinite rooms. There must be infinite Ricks, too, behind the one he can see; but the angle is so exact that they're hidden.

His head won't turn, but he looks as far sideways as he can. More mirrors on both sides. A cell of mirrors.

One-way mirrors, presumably. He opens his mouth — surprising himself — and says, 'Daed? Daed, what's going on?'

His voice is the first thing that really frightens him. It's not his own. He can't get enough air to make the right noise.

The sound dies, swallowed by the walls.

No one answers.

He tries to move. He can't.

He says, 'Daed? I know you're there. Please talk to me. Please . . .'

After a while he says, 'Anyone . . . ?'

Time blurs. He thinks he can see his hair growing. He's thirsty.

He says, 'Please . . . I need to go to the toilet. Please.'

He says, 'I don't know what you're doing. Daed, please, if you're punishing me . . . I'm sorry, I'm really sorry, I didn't mean to hurt that Security guard, I only wanted to get out of the complex, I'm so sorry. Please let me out. Please. Please say something. Anyone. Whoever's there. Please, just a word. Please.'

He says, 'Anyone. Please. Anything. I'm sorry.'

He cries.

He says, 'Daed, please tell me you're there, please, please, please.' He says *please* so many times he can't remember if it's a word or just the only sound he can make. He swears at his reflection, shouting. Then he cries again. He apologises. He begs for someone to let him out, for five minutes, for three minutes, thirty seconds, just to go to the toilet.

He promises to do anything, if only someone will let him out.

He promises to do anything if only they'll speak to him.

He watches his reflection wet himself. After a while the warm wetness on his skin starts to prickle and itch and go cold.

He cries. He watches himself cry. He stops crying and just stares.

The next time he needs the loo he doesn't bother to ask.

He thinks he might have died, after all.

He counts in his head. He lists prime numbers. He fights the voice in his brain that says: No one's going to let you out, ever.

They've forgotten you.

No one's even *there*.

No one's going to let you out, *ev—*

He thinks: Shut up. It's a punishment. Daed's orders, the Security men said. It can't go on for ever. They'll let me out soon.

But what if —

They're there. They are. They're just behind the mirrors.

A blank grey cushion of panic presses into his nose and mouth, making it hard for him to breathe. And he can't move. He's terrified. If he panics . . . If he can't move, the only thing that can give way is his brain.

I won't panic. I won't. Two hundred and forty-one. Two hundred and fifty-one. Two hundred and fifty-seven.

I can't move. I can't move. I can't *move* —

Two hundred and sixty-three. No, that divides by three. No, it *is* prime. Two hundred and — I can't move, *I can't move* — two hundred and sixty-nine. Oh gods, I can't move, *I can't move, I can't, I can't* —

Two hundred and —

Two hundred and —

If no one's even *there* —

You can't do this to me, Daed, please, you can't. I thought you loved me —

His reflection opens its mouth.

Rick thinks: This is it. I'm going to scream.

But he doesn't.

He says, 'Daed. Daed, if you're there . . . I heard you. What you said to Perdita. The thing you needed . . . I've got it. I found it. Let me out.'

Silence.

He says, 'Get a message to Daed. Tell him I've got it. Tell him I was there, and I've got it. Tell him . . .'

He looks into his own eyes. If this doesn't work . . .

His voice is rising. He has to fight to breathe. He says,

'Immortality. He said he wanted immortality. Well, tell him I can give it to — tell him — I found it, I can — please, Daed —'

He waits for an answer.

Nothing.

He shuts his eyes and feels the tears rolling down his face, the air rasping and changing gears in his throat. He thought it might work, he really thought . . . but now . . . he sobs aloud.

Then he starts to scream, until his throat burns.

Until —

There's a noise, like a door.

Daed's voice says, 'OK, Rick.'

And then there's a kind of coldness on his skin, and the smell of surgical spirit, and there are hands helping him up, gentle hands, and when he opens his eyes Daed is in front of him, and Rick can't stop crying, but now it's only relief, and anger. And Daed touches his face gently, and says something, and Rick wants to hit him but he's too weak, he can hardly stand up on his own, and then Daed puts his arms round him, and he's never done that before, and Rick lets himself lean into Daed's chest. He smells smoke and something rotten, something old; but he's happy. He leans against Daed's warm shirt and hugs him back. And even after everything, he thinks: It's all right. It's going to be all right, it's going to be all right.

PART 3

IMMORTALITY

14

He let Daed take him out of the door, through the grey-dark antechamber, and along corridor after corridor of silver-white. His eyes hurt. Daed put his arm around his shoulder and helped him to walk. It was like he'd been ill: everything was a little bit unreal, a little bit painful. He didn't want to think about the cell, and the chair, and the stuff on his skin that paralysed him; but that was OK, because he couldn't think straight anyway.

Daed said, 'Come on, then. Walk, that's right. Good boy.'

Rick opened his mouth and said, I'm not a kid. He said, Thank you, you rescued me, I couldn't bear it. He said, Wait, but they said, the Security guys, they said it was you, your orders . . . But none of it came out. Just his breath, smelling foul.

The corridors went on for so long he started to be afraid that it was just another part of his punishment; or that it was a nightmare, and he hadn't woken up. He looked at the doors as they went past and thought: If every room has someone in it . . .

Daed said, 'OK, nearly there.' There was a thick metal gate, a comms panel that took longer than normal to read

Daed's hand, and then they were through. Rick looked round and saw soft lighting and marble tiles and plants in pots and a twisting column of water that ran from ceiling to floor. He would have been sure he was dreaming, if he wasn't freezing. But no, it was all real. His clothes had bloody patches on them where the Security men had hit him. His bare feet stuck to the floor and made a sucking noise every time he lifted them. He could smell his own urine.

They took the lift. Rick wanted to stand on his own, but his ankles seemed to be made of some squashy material, like the handcuffs, and he couldn't keep upright. He held on to the wall. Daed gave him a quick look and rested a hand on his shoulder, lightly, ready to support him if he needed it.

The lift went up and up, making him feel sick. Then they were on the twentieth floor, and Daed was helping him out of the lift, like he was an old man. He wanted to cry again, because Daed had never been like this. Kind, like this. He could have told Security to take Rick back to his room; but he didn't. He was here, himself, making sure Rick was OK. They shuffled awkwardly towards Rick's door, out of step, and Rick felt an unlikely, ludicrous wave of gratitude. He held his hand up to the comms panel and waited to be let in.

The door opened; but Daed's hand tightened on his shoulder, and they didn't go in. Daed said, 'You said you could get me Asterion.'

Rick almost said, Yes. But something made him wait, just for a second. He looked down. He saw Daed's hand, still on his shoulder. He saw the tendons tighten, very slightly, as Daed waited for him to answer.

His stomach churned again, like it had in the lift. The happiness clicked out of existence like a light. It left a dark blot where it had been.

And he knew, clearly, without any doubt, that Daed had rescued him for that. And nothing else. For Asterion. For Perdita's densely-written code, for immortality.

Not because I cried, he thought. Not because I couldn't bear it. Not because I begged and wet myself. Just because . . .

He looked into Daed's eyes, and somehow there was a part of him still screaming in that cell, twenty-five storeys below. He hadn't escaped, after all.

He said, 'Yes. I stole the file from Perdita's workshop.' His voice grated and trembled like the power supply was on the blink. But the words were recognisable, just.

'You're sure? Where is it? Are you *absolutely sure*?'

Rick watched the skinny, clever-fingered hand on his shoulder. It tightened again, until it hurt. The nails were shiny. They dug into Rick's skin.

He looked through his open door. The door beyond had been left open. There was a stain on the carpet, and a long scuff-mark along the wall that he didn't remember making; but apart from that it was familiar, it was as he'd left it. And the file was on his bed, where he'd frisbee'd it, when he'd come in, that afternoon, whenever it was . . . No one had touched it. And why should they? Only Daed knew what it was. Daed, and Perdita.

Rick said, 'It's there, Daed. On the bed.'

Daed's hand released his shoulder. Rick took a step forward, but he couldn't keep his balance, and Daed pushed past without helping him. He reeled and leant against the wall of the entry hall, feeling desperately sick. Daed ignored him. He was already standing by Rick's bed; he flipped the file open and started to read, instantly absorbed. His face had a look like someone discovering they could fly. The moment when they took off.

He's not dying any more, Rick thought. That's the difference.

He thought: But — *immortality*?

Not even Daed, surely . . . ? Not even Perdita . . .

Daed glanced up, finally. He said, 'Rick . . . you should have a shower and go to bed. And get some food sent up, OK? You look terrible.' Then he carried on reading.

As if I had a late night, Rick thought. Or as if I've been a bit under the weather.

He wanted to grab the file and skim it through the archway into the swimming pool. He imagined the ink dissolving and swirling up to the surface, the pages drifting down to the bottom, blank. He said, 'Daed — the Security guys who took me down, they said it was on your ord—'

Daed shut the file and strode past him, towards the door. 'Get some rest, all right?'

'It was you, they said it was —'

'Yes,' Daed said. 'My orders. Although if I hadn't, Paz would've done. It wasn't just a punishment. I wanted you to be scared.'

'I was.' Rick wanted to laugh at the understatement.

Daed looked over his shoulder. His eyes rested on Rick's face. He didn't say anything.

'The man I — the Security man that I knocked down . . . Is he —?'

'He'll live,' Daed said. 'Probably.'

'I didn't mean to —'

'So you were scared,' Daed said. 'Good. Remember how it felt.'

He left. Rick watched the door close after him.

Then there was nothing but his empty room, and the rain against the windows, and through the archway, just visible, the shadow of the shark, biding its time at the bottom of the swimming pool.

15

He slept for two days. Not straight through — he had to get up to go to the toilet, to eat, to wash — but every time he was in danger of thinking, he went back to sleep. Dreams opened up like doors and let him in. He followed long dark passages, ran endless traps, called out a name that he couldn't remember when he woke up. The dreams slid slowly into nightmares, and finally he broke the surface, gasping, and then he went to the bathroom again to rinse away the sweat. He looked at himself in the mirror, and thought: Daed was *dying* . . . Just for a moment, for a second, he tried to imagine what it would be like, a world without Daed. But it was unthinkable. Everyone died, of course, eventually, but . . . He squeezed his eyes shut. Imagine it.

It was like trying to imagine infinity. It would be terrifying, if you could do it.

And he's *not* dying, Rick thought. Not any more. Not now I found Asterion and gave it to him, and he took it and went away.

And he didn't even say thanks.

He opened his eyes again. The nightmare was still ringing in his ears, calling to him from behind a closed door.

He turned away from his reflection and went back to bed. Because that was the thing about nightmares: they *were* nightmares. You could wake up. Which was more than could be said for the real world.

What brought him back to life, in the end, was Perdita.

She could have come straight in, if she'd wanted to; but she didn't. She waited outside Rick's door, waiting for him to give her permission.

Rick looked at the ceiling, and hoped that she'd go away. Just the sound of her voice made his stomach shrink. After ten minutes he rolled over and closed his eyes. But the comms panel buzzed again and her voice said, 'Rick? I know you're in there. Look . . . I brought you breakfast.'

He glanced at the window. *1702*. And he'd been back on full food privileges since Daed started work on the expansion, anyway. He could order whatever he wanted.

'Rick?'

Why was she bothering? He wanted her to go away. Daed hadn't come to see him; why should Perdita care? The last time he'd seen her he'd ripped up her files and stolen Asterion. And now she'd come to check he was OK. It was unbearable.

Finally, because he was too tired to do anything else, he said, 'OK, come in.' He'd been cold in the night, so at least he was wearing a T-shirt and underpants.

He knew immediately, from the way she looked at him, that she didn't know about Asterion. She'd got an armful of food and a thermocup balanced precariously between the topmost packet and her chin. She said, 'Rick . . . I just came to see how you were. I heard about the — about your getting punished . . . I can't believe they did that. You're only a kid, for gods' sake. Those cells are — grown men have gone insane, from being down there too long —' She stopped.

Rick took a deep breath. 'I'm fine, thanks.'

'Good.' She bit her lip and looked round for somewhere to put the packages of food. Her movements weren't quite right; she looked like an actor who hadn't rehearsed the scene enough.

'Perdy —'

'Listen —' she said, at exactly the same time, and they looked at each other and smiled.

'You go first,' Rick said. He watched her put the food down on the floor and even though he knew he had to tell her about Asterion he could feel the numbness in his stomach starting to thaw, a little.

'OK,' she said. She passed the thermocup to him. 'Green tea with lemon, supposed to be calming, worth a try, I thought, even if it's nonsense.'

'Is that what you came to say?' He almost laughed.

'No.' She waited until he had a firm grip on the cup. 'OK. I wanted to say . . . I'm sorry about what happened in my workshop. I know you were — you *are* upset, and you have every right to be. Of course. But I promise, no matter what happens, I'll do my best to protect you. When — if something happens to Daed, you won't be alone. I couldn't give him what he wanted, and I don't expect you to understand that. But please don't think I don't care about you, because I do.'

She sped up at the end and then stopped, like her battery had gone.

Rick looked down at the cap of the thermocup and swallowed. He said, 'Perdy . . . the files, in the cupboard . . .'

'It's OK,' she said. 'They were just ideas, old ideas. I've used most of them, anyway. There wasn't anything irreplaceable. Don't worry.' Her mouth twitched. 'Anyway . . . the thing about paper, Rick, is that you can tape it back together.'

'Right,' he said. He put the cup to his mouth, but he didn't drink.

'OK?' She crouched and came up with a green-grey box, glinting with old-fashioned lettering.

'The files in the cupboard,' he said again. If he said it often enough, she might understand, without him having to tell her.

'Macaroon?'

He didn't know what that meant. It sounded like a place, somewhere a long way away. He thought: I'd like to live there. He said, 'Perdy, there's something I have to —'

'Have a macaroon. It's going to be OK,' she said. 'You're not on your own. Don't worry.'

He sucked a mouthful of burning liquid through the thermocup and felt the water well up in his eyes, automatically.

He said, 'No, you don't understand, when I was ripping up the files in your —'

'Forget it,' she said. 'Honestly. Hello? No, I'm just — yes, all right —'

For a second he thought she was still talking to him. Then

139

he realised her earpiece was flashing, and she was grimacing at him, apologising.

She said, 'No, just for a moment, I'll be right back —'

A pause.

She said, '*What?*'

Rick filled his mouth with tea, and swallowed. It hurt. He felt the heat run all the way down his oesophagus.

'On whose authority? But I — there's no one else who is even in the same — no, you listen to me! Who the hell —'

Silence.

'Is this a joke?' she said. 'Because if it is, I think it's in decidedly bad taste.'

A murmur from the earpiece, as if it was starting to lose patience.

'I don't believe you. Why would he — no, this has to be Paz, this is *mad*, you're —'

And then nothing; just silence. The earpiece flickered and the light died. Perdita looked down at the box she was holding and made a strange noise. It was like a laugh; but it wasn't a laugh.

Rick was afraid of the silence, but he was more afraid of saying something.

Perdita didn't move. She looked like a screenshot: ugly face, with a trace of green and silver light reflected off the box in her hands. She didn't even blink.

Rick heard himself say, 'Perdita? Are you . . . all right?'

'I've been sacked,' she said. It sounded as if she wasn't quite sure what it meant.

'But . . .'

'By Daed. Daed has — sacked me. For no reason. I've got twelve hours' notice. I have to leave. I —' She stopped.

'Twelve hours?'

'Generous.' It must have been sarcasm, but it didn't sound like it. 'It could have been one.'

'But —'

'He's mad. He *needs* me.' She wasn't really talking to Rick. 'Even if he's angry . . . it's stupid, it's *mad*, Daed's a lot of things, but not *stupid* . . .'

Rick looked at her hands squashing the silvery pattern on the box, and tried not to think. She was right. Daed did need her; he needed all the help he could get. Or — he *had* needed her, before . . .

'He's lost his mind,' she said. 'He's not dying, he's self-destructing.'

I can't say anything, Rick thought. I can't tell her *now* . . .

'I understand,' she said, 'I do understand, if he wants to punish me for not giving him Asterion, if he hates me for that . . . I understand . . . but . . .' She swallowed. 'Surely he can see — if he sacks me, he's on his own. There's no *advantage*. What does he think he's going to achieve?'

She said it as if she really wanted to know. Rick pressed his lips together; and then bit down, to make extra sure.

This was his fault. If he hadn't stolen Asterion . . .

But why *sack* her? He thought it so loudly he was afraid she'd hear. It didn't make sense, even if . . .

She said, 'He doesn't trust me any more, I suppose.'

'Perdita . . .' In the Maze, sometimes, if you said exactly the right thing, you could change a hostile NPC to a friendly one, or open a locked door, or disable an enemy. Change the world. Rick wished he could do that now.

She seemed to see him, suddenly. Her eyes narrowed, and she looked round, taking in the room. Her gaze went down to the box in her hands. She said, 'Can I keep these?'

'What?'

'The macaroons. They're worth a bit. I might be able to get a refund from Housekeeping. Worth a try. You don't mind, do you? I'm sorry, I wanted to —' She stopped. She put the box on the bed. Then she grimaced, and bent over at the waist, very slowly, like the air going out of something.

And then she started to cry.

Rick knew, just from the way she was sobbing, that she wasn't going to survive, outside. And she knew it. They both knew.

Daed must have known, too.

He said, 'Perdy . . . do you want me to talk to Daed? He might change his mind . . . he's pleased with me at the moment, I could try —'

She didn't even bother to answer. Rick didn't blame her. Tears ran down her face and into her mouth. There was moisture dripping off her chin. A long plumb-line of spit swung and stretched towards the carpet.

'Perdy,' he said again. 'Please don't cry. Look . . .'

He knew how she felt, now, when he was in her workshop, when he wouldn't even answer her. He wished he didn't. He thought: My fault.

He said, 'Look — it'll be OK, I promise.' He was lying. He couldn't promise. But he needed to say *something*, because it was Perdita, and even if she'd refused to help Daed, she was still Perdita, she'd still brought him breakfast and waited for permission before she came into his room. He said, 'Listen, I reckon it's only a misunderstanding. All I have to do is tell Daed that you gave me Asterion, and you don't mind him using it, and then —'

'I won't give you Asterion!' The words were thick with saliva. She shook her head, and flecks of water speckled Rick's sheets. 'If he's trying to blackmail me into giving it to him, then tough, because I'd rather die. He can put me in one of his cells and leave me there and he won't get it. He knows he won't get it, he —' She put her hands over her face, pressing as though the flesh would come away from her skull if she didn't. 'Gods, I don't even know where it *is* . . .'

She was still crying, but silently. Her body was shaking as if someone had put an electric current through her spine.

Rick said, 'No, I mean . . .' He was such a coward. She was getting chucked out of the complex, and he was scared of owning up. 'Perdy . . . he's already got Asterion. The file was in the cupboard. I found it. And —'

She looked up. Her hands slipped down to cover her mouth. Her bottom lip bulged in the gaps between the fingers.

'He was dying, Perdy, and I don't know what Asterion does but it can't be wrong, can it, not that bad, and now he's going to be OK, he can keep working on the Maze. If he's immortal then, it's just that, I'm sorry but, don't you —' But all the sentences were dead ends.

She went on looking at him.

'Please don't be angry, I know it was wrong to steal it, but you wouldn't give it to him, and he needed it, and now if I just say to him that you let me take it, then he'll let you stay, you can help with the new expansion —'

'Rick,' she said. It was like a bolt snicking into place.

'I'm sorry,' he said, and almost wished he meant it. 'Sorry.'

She'd stopped crying. She straightened up and stared at him. She had a look on her face like she was listening. She said, 'You stole the file on Asterion and gave it to Daed. Is that what you're telling me?'

'Yes.'

She blinked. Her eyes were an odd colour; against the red of her eyelids the pupils looked lustrous, like oil. 'Do you know what Asterion is?'

'No, I —' He remembered her saying: *evil*. 'It's something to do with . . . Daed said it would stop him dying. That it would make him immortal. Perdy, that's not wrong, how can that be wrong —?'

She laughed. He wished she wouldn't; it was worse than when she was crying. She said, 'You think it's some kind of medicine, do you? A cure for cancer? Sure, I may design computer games for a living, but I'm into biochemistry as a hobby . . . And it's sheer bloody-mindedness that stopped me giving it to Daed of my own free will, is it?'

He tried to shrug. 'I don't know why you didn't give it to him.' *Evil* . . .

'Immortality,' she said, and the laugh was like something leaking. 'Oh, Rick, gods help us. You really have no idea what you've done.'

'Then tell me.' But he didn't want to know. He wanted to go on thinking she was overreacting, or just crazy.

She opened her mouth. Her face was gleaming wet, as if she'd been out in the rain: it looked painful.

Rick wished he could look away. He wanted to log out, once and for all.

She said, 'Where is he?'

It took him a second to understand. 'Who?'

'Daed. Where is he?'

'In his office, probably.' The answer came automatically, before Rick's brain caught up with his mouth. Then he thought: But Asterion? She was going to tell me about Asterion . . .

'OK.' She turned on her heel and walked towards the door.

'Wait —' Rick stumbled after her, through a grey fog of fear. He didn't know what he was scared of, but he was shaking. 'Perdita — tell me, at least *tell* me —'

'Daed can tell you,' she said, and then took a deep breath and turned round to face him. 'Rick. I'm not going to let Daed use Asterion. So it doesn't matter, does it? There's no need for me to explain, because it's entirely irrelevant.' Her eyes slid away.

'But —'

'Goodbye, Rick.' She swallowed, and met his eyes again. 'Good luck.'

He thought: I'm never going to see her again. 'Perdita —'

She hesitated for a moment and then walked towards him, until there were only a few centi-ems between them. She put her hands on his shoulders. They were too heavy; it felt like she was trying to force him to his knees. Then she kissed him lightly on both cheeks. He wanted to put his arms round her but he couldn't.

'Rick,' she said, 'one word of advice. *Stop doing stupid things.*'

They looked at each other.

Then she slapped him, hard, across the face. She was gone before he'd blinked the tears away. There was nothing but the *buzz-hiss* of the door, closing behind her.

16

He didn't know what to do. He stood in the middle of his room like a lemon. His cheek was burning, and his eyes were watering from the pain. Perdita might not have been state-of-the-art designed, but she had a lot of strength in her arm. Rick felt faintly surprised.

He sat down on his bed. The mattress subsided underneath him and the box of macaroons slid down into the dent. He opened it — he'd never seen a box made of cardboard before, and it took him a while to work out what to do — and looked at the macaroons. They were round, with a diameter the length of his thumb, and all different colours, like they belonged in the false sunlight of the Maze, not here. They didn't look edible. Maybe they weren't; maybe they were some kind of drug. Maybe you smoked them, or snorted them. Or injected them. He picked one up — it was turquoise — and considered it. He concentrated on it, trying not to think about Perdita.

He thought: Why would you eat something *turquoise*? What are these things, anyway?

He thought: The People's Republic of Macaroon . . .

And then he shut his eyes, and thought: What is she going to *do*?

He imagined her in Daed's office, demanding Asterion back. But she didn't have a hope; Daed would just laugh. Then he saw her in the glass entrance hall next to the Nucleus, putting her hood on, tightening her out-clothes, taking her time, because she knew that as soon as she stepped out into the rain . . .

He opened his eyes. His fingers had tightened on the macaroon, squashing the middle. He put it into his mouth, chewed, and shoved another one in before he had time to swallow. His teeth bit down on sweet crumbly dust. He bolted another one, almost choking, and another: violent pink, pale green, yellow. He wondered why they were expensive. When he tried to force another one down he sprayed wet crumbs of rainbow-coloured spit over his sheets. He wasn't going to think about Perdita. He focused on the taste of sugar, and the odd hint of other things, mint, bergamot, something flowery. Revolting.

The rain, he thought, in spite of himself. Outside even the rain can kill you. How could Daed —

Another macaroon. He felt sick. He *wanted* to feel sick.

But it's not my fault that she's been sacked, he thought. It's because she refused to give up Asterion — it was her choice, if she'd only agreed —

He was going to vomit. He threw himself towards the bathroom, smacking his elbow on the door frame, and got to the loo just in time. A saccharine, technicolor soup swirled and sank in the toilet bowl. He felt more tears seeping out of the corners of his eyes. Gods, what a mess, what a mess.

If I went and talked to Daed, he thought. If I pleaded . . .

Stop doing stupid things.

He leant his head against the sweaty mirror, and giggled weakly. But if I stop doing stupid things, what *am* I meant to do?

He wished he could see inside Daed's office, right now. He made his way shakily back into his bedroom and stared out of the window, even though Daed's office was in the other direction. The grey knot of Undone was spread out below him, smoking slightly. But the rain had stopped; that was something.

Maybe it *was* possible to live out there. Well — it *was* possible, obviously, there were millions of people who lived outside the complex, he knew that. But maybe it would be possible for Perdita; or for him . . .

He felt a surge of something he didn't understand. For a moment he thought he was going to be sick again. But it wasn't nausea; it was envy.

Suppose —

I could —

Suppose, when she left, I went with —

He rocked back from the chemiglass, feeling a new flush of cold sweat on his skin. He was afraid: but not just afraid.

He couldn't leave Daed. It would be mad. Daed was his father, probably. Daed protected him from everything he needed protecting from. Daed . . .

If I went with Perdita, he thought, I'd never be able to come back. It's not like before, when I just wanted to have a look, to know I *could* leave if I wanted to. If I go now, that's it.

For no reason, he thought of Athene. He'd never know what she looked like, in real life.

And he saw his own face, in the mirror-walls of the cell.

His trousers were crumpled on the floor beside the bed, and pulled them on, then his socks, then his shoes. Then he went to the cupboard where his hood was kept, in case of emergencies; he didn't expect it to be there, but it was. Someone must have put it back. Part of him wished they hadn't. He picked it up, turned it over in his hands. Was *this* enough to keep the rain off?

But right now it wasn't raining.

His heart was swollen and racing. But it's OK, Perdita, he thought. I'm not going to do anything stupid.

Well. Not *that* stupid.

He looked around. He could see the shark's shadow at the bottom of the swimming pool, moving restlessly back and forth. The sickness had changed to something else: a kind of oozing, uncomfortable heat. The blood was fizzing in his temples.

He thought: If this is the last time I see these rooms . . .

He looked at the bed — four ems wide, enough for three people — the space, the open door to the bathroom, the wall of chemiglass, the flicker of reflected water-light on the ceiling from the pool. Luxury, even for the complex.

But there was nothing here he could take away with him.

So he stared until it was all printed on his retina. He turned to the cameras, one by one, and gave each a deliberate V-sign.

And then he took his hood and went.

•   •   •

The comms panel at the bottom of the stairs let him through; there were more highlighted options than last time, but **outside access** was still unavailable. Not that it mattered; he chose **creative department**, and felt smug. He walked through the Nucleus, past the fountain, and even though it was huge, and silent, and made him think of Daed, he didn't feel much more than a tightening in his throat. If Perdita could leave, then so could he. Even if she had to be thrown out.

There was no comms panel outside the Creative Department door, but he half saw, half felt a glint of silver slide over his retina, and then the door swung silently open. He'd never been here without Perdita, but now he was allowed, apparently. As if Asterion was a password, and more powerful than he'd realised. He went down the corridor towards Perdita's door, and pressed his hand against the comms panel. But his luck had run out. The panel rippled silkily blue-green, but it didn't let him in. **I'm sorry,** it said, **Perdita isn't in at the moment. Would you like to leave a message?**

Not that he was surprised. After all, he was only Daed's kid; he wasn't Daed himself. Full-access privileges would have been too much to ask.

But he couldn't just wait in the corridor.

Gods, why hadn't he thought of this, five minutes ago?

Someone went past him — one of the Creatives, Rick was almost certain he'd seen him before — and gave him a funny look. Rick looked down at his manky slept-in T-shirt, the hood flapping in his left hand, and thought: Oops. I'm not exactly prepossessing.

He couldn't stay here.

He turned and followed the Creative, not too fast. Rick could tell that he knew he was there: his shoulder blades were tense, like he was afraid Rick was going to hit him from behind. When they got to the door at the end of the corridor he paused, his hand on the comms panel, and looked round. Rick remembered his name, suddenly: Jake.

'Hi,' Rick said. 'How's it going?' He couldn't remember the last time he'd tried to talk to someone he didn't know, and it showed. In the Maze there was no such thing as small talk; only negotiation.

Jake looked at him, and then away. He said, 'Oh, yeah, good, you?' His voice was flat, like he was counting. The door in front of him slid open and he glanced at the room beyond, then back at Rick. 'Er . . . listen, I'm just taking a break, I've been working for thirteen hours, really hard, I mean, I just need a coffee, you know —'

It took Rick a second to get it. Then he said, 'It's OK, Daed hasn't sent me to check up on you.'

'Oh.' He added, too late, 'Look, I didn't think he had —'

'Can I wait in there?'

'Er . . . yeah, sure.' He frowned and then smiled, too quickly. ''Course, no problem. Have a coffee.'

'Thanks,' Rick said, and followed him. It was the Ideas Space, and it had changed since he'd last seen it. It had been chaotic, full of gadgets and bright colours, cushions and inflatable chairs. Now it was white and minimalist, with doodle screens on every available surface. Apparently blankness was the new inspiration. Rick took the cup of coffee that Jake handed him and wanted to throw it at the wall. He thought regretfully of his technicolor vomit.

Jake said, 'So . . . we're all really excited about the iTank.'

'Great,' Rick said. He realised, with a weird sadness, that he didn't even know what the iTank was going to be like. A year, a month ago, he'd have been mad with anticipation, thirsty for every detail, begging to try out the prototypes. 'What's new? Better graphics?'

'You could say that.'

'Fewer bugs?'

Jake frowned, then laughed. 'You're joking, right?'

Rick shrugged. The coffee tasted burnt.

Jake said, 'You don't *know*? This is the biggest step forward since . . . well, since the game tank was invented. This is like the transition from flatgames to realgames. Seriously. Gods, where've you *been*?'

Something in his tone flicked Rick on the raw. I've been in the Maze, Rick wanted to say. In the Maze, and then in the endgame. But he didn't. 'So what's so great about it?'

Jake held his gaze, then blinked twice. His expression had changed. Now there was a gleam of pride in his eyes. He said, 'But Daed hasn't told you . . . ?'

Rick refused to answer. He was only here to wait for Perdita; this wasn't his world any more. He stared at the whiteness everywhere and wondered if he could give himself a nosebleed through sheer force of will.

Jake said, 'The iTank is . . . it's the pinnacle, it's the zenith, it's — we've been working on it for years, years and

153

years. I can't *believe* you don't . . .' He stared at Rick. He had very pale green eyes, and over-designed eyelashes. He reached out for the nearest doodle screen. He said, 'The iTank can *read your mind.*'

The words sent a trickle of excitement down Rick's back, even if he wasn't sure he knew exactly what they meant. 'You mean there's a direct link between the iTank and the player's brain?'

Jake rolled his eyes. 'There's already a *link*. How do you think we render smells? Or taste? There's already sense input from a game tank direct to your brain, that's how we adjust the details, that's why the Maze is as good as it is. That's what the cap's for . . . But now there's feedback *in the other direction.*'

'So what?'

'So —' Jake rubbed his finger over the screen, as if he really wished he was rubbing the skin off Rick's face. 'Imagine the power of the human brain, collaborating with what's already programmed into the iTank. Imagine the wealth of details that your subconscious would come up with, without your even *knowing* it . . . more than we could program in years. Or imagine there's a problem with the synchro, or a bug — as soon as the player realises there's something not quite right, the game knows and rectifies the error. Imagine a game that's created by your own brain *as you play it —* responding to your thoughts, tailoring itself to you so quickly you don't even notice. But it's still a multi-player game — it's still created by us, regulated by us . . . We give the stimulus — and it'll still be the complex, sophisticated programming that we already have in the Maze — but the player's own brain adds depth and believability. You won't even know you're playing a game . . . Imagine —'

'You sound like someone from Marketing.'

Jake's eyes unglazed, a little. 'No, but seriously. Seriously! You'll see, when you play in the iTank — my gods, you'll know the difference.'

'Right.' Rick stretched out his hand. Against the white of the sofa it looked dark, almost black. *Imagine*. He was trying not to be impressed. But if it was true, what Jake was saying . . .

'The two-way feedback was what we've been after for *years*. Sense input is easy, you just isolate the right synapses and stimulate them — but reading someone's mind . . . you have no idea how complicated that is.' Jake's voice was dreamy, now, and his finger drew a graceful, hair-thin arc on the screen. 'It's like . . . if you had a computer and a calculator, say, and the calculator could only count up to one . . . The calculator could say zero or one to the computer, no problem, but if the computer tried to say three or seven or nine back, the calculator wouldn't be able to read the figures . . . The simpler system can input into the more complicated one, but it can't receive. For real *communication*, you need a computer that's as sophisticated as a human brain — or nearly.'

Rick thought: He's right. It's amazing.

And suddenly he missed his old life so hard it hurt. He'd *lived* in the Maze, desperate to win, to get gilt and reputation, to be the best. He'd never thought about anything else. Life was simple. Nothing was impossible.

I could go back to my room, he thought, and forget about Perdita. I was happy before. I could be happy again. I could run the new improved Maze all day and eat what I want and it'd be fine, it'd go on for ever because now Daed's immortal —

(Jake was talking again, but none of the words got through.)

— now he's got Asterion and everyone's happy again . . . I don't have to escape. It'd be so much easier to stay here . . .

Rick shut his eyes, because the walls were too blank, like they were waiting for someone to write on them. He could see Athene. It was stupid; she wasn't even *real*. He didn't know why she was haunting him like this.

Or why he heard Paz's voice, from a long way away: *the thing about people is that they're . . . dispensable.*

Jake said, 'Let me know if I'm boring you, won't you?'

'Sorry. I was just . . .'

He wanted to stay — no, he wanted to *want* to stay; but he couldn't. He had to get out. This wasn't his world any more.

'I'd let you have a go, only the prototypes are being used — you know how it is, there's only twenty-one days left before the launch.'

Part of him lit up at the word *prototype*. Part of him would have given anything to try it — would have begged and threatened and bribed Jake until he gave in. But that part wasn't very strong, any more. The rest of Rick said: You're wasting time. If Perdita comes back to her office while you're in here, and you miss her . . .

'No worries,' he said. 'Listen . . . thanks for the coffee and everything, but actually Daed sent me to get something

156

from Perdita's workshop, only the system doesn't seem to have updated my entry privileges, so . . . I was wondering if you could get me in.'

'Er . . .' Jake looked round helplessly, as if there was an autocue hidden somewhere and he'd forgotten where. 'Well, look, maybe you should ask someone from Security, no one here has entry privileges for Perdita's workshop, it's only Daed and Marketing and all that lot. I mean, no other Creatives are . . . she's more senior than everyone else, so . . .'

'Daed wanted me to go through her stuff before the room was reallocated,' Rick said. 'Check for sensitive material. There must have been a glitch in the system . . . but surely there's someone who can let me in.'

'Reallocated?'

'Now that she's leaving.'

'Perdita's —?'

'Yep,' Rick said, almost enjoying the look on Jake's face. It said: Gods, if Perdita's going, who's next? It could be *me*.

'I didn't know she was —'

'The decision was only made this morning,' Rick said. He wiped his mind as blank as the wall opposite him and imagined he was talking about the weather. 'Unavoidable. We regretted having to ask her to leave, of course, but she was being a little bit obstructive, and teamwork is so important here.' His tone was greasy, sticky, like an oil-spill. 'There's so much pressure on all our departments, especially at a time like this, and even the smallest lack of cooperation can be crucial.'

Jake stared at him.

Rick shrugged, wishing his shoulders weren't so tight. He said again, 'Even the smallest lack of cooperation . . .'

Jake went on looking at him for a long moment, then took a big gulp of coffee. His throat bulged as if he was having difficulty swallowing. He seemed to be waiting for Rick to finish his sentence. Rick let him wait.

And it worked.

'But there's — we're not allowed to fiddle the comms panels,' Jake said, at last, 'they're an essential part of Crater's inter-departmental security —'

Good, Rick thought. He's going to do it.

'I mean, listen, I'd love to help out, but I need — it would be great if — maybe you could get Daed to confirm that he wanted . . . ?'

'Sure,' Rick said. 'Why don't you call his office and ask him?'

A silence. The air in the Ideas Space smelt stale. The coffee machine spat, suddenly, like someone who'd been winded.

Jake said, 'Well . . . he's notoriously . . . I know he doesn't like being disturbed . . . so maybe, could *you* . . . ? No, I guess not. Well. OK. Right. But — look, I can probably fiddle the door for you, but it's absolutely forbidden, so maybe if you didn't mention that it was me? If we just . . . you know, if we both forgot about it?' The question marks hung in the air like hooks.

Rick said, 'That would probably be OK.'

'Great.' Jake breathed out, and put his coffee on the

nearest doodle screen. The plastic bent, almost impercepti-
bly, and started to warp in the heat.

Jake stood up, and Rick followed him. Jake's office was
tiny, glass-walled, cramped even for a desk and flatscreen. As
soon as the door was shut Jake flipped the glass to mirror-
mode, and Rick stared into his own noncommittal eyes while
Jake hunched at the computer and hissed through his teeth.
It only took thirteen minutes, but by the end of it Jake's forehead was covered with tiny beads of sweat. He said, 'Look
— if someone finds out that I've hacked into the entry privi-
lege system, I'll be chucked out, you understand?' He said
chucked out like it meant *killed*. Then again, it probably did.

'Don't worry,' Rick said. 'My lips are sealed. So it's all set
up, then? I just press my hand against the panel, like normal?'

'Yes. It's all set up.'

'Great. Thanks. I really appreciate it. Hope the iTank goes
well . . .'

Jake's eyes narrowed, and he twisted round in his chair,
looking up at Rick. His mouth opened, but he didn't say
anything. There was a funny look on his face.

Rick thought: Oh, gods.

He wasn't sure what it was — saying thank you, maybe,
just being too friendly — but he'd given himself away. Jake
knew that he'd been lying. And he was shocked, and furious.
And absolutely terrified.

Rick wanted to tell him it was OK — don't worry, you won't
be found out, I'm not going to do anything stupid — but he
wasn't sure Jake would believe him. He said, 'Look, thanks,
sorry for taking up your time . . .'

'You'd better go.'

'Yeah,' Rick said. 'OK. Thanks.'

And he left. All the way down the corridor he could feel Jake's look — horrified, afraid, accusatory, the way Athene would have looked at him, if she'd known — and he rolled his shoulders, trying to shake it off. He'd never had so many enemies. He'd never *deserved* so many enemies.

But the comms panel let him into Perdita's workshop; and, after all, he told himself, that was what counted.

17

Perdita had cleared up the mess. Everything looked a little bit emptier than it had before; as though she'd had to throw a lot of things away. But there were broken bits and pieces lined up neatly on the workbench, ready for her to mend. Rick looked at them and wished he could fix them all, now, so that they wouldn't be left waiting like that for ever.

He sat down. He would have made himself a drink, except that he didn't know how to work the kettle. There were diagrams pinned up on the wall opposite him, but not of anything he understood. The cupboard where he'd hidden was open and bare.

He waited. Outside it was still not raining. A glint of platinum sunlight caught a tangle of wires on a shelf, making them shine for a few seconds, and Rick watched it, trying not to breathe. Then it was gone.

He stood up and peered at the little crippled bits of techno. He touched a few with his fingertips, very gently. Then he turned to the other shelves, ran his hands over the backs of books, fiddled with the old prototypes, bounced a ball against the ceiling. He wondered whether it would hurt Perdita, having to leave this stuff behind. He thought of his own room, and couldn't think of anything worth regretting.

He waited. He thought: Thanks, Jake. If it hadn't been for you, I'd have been sitting outside in the corridor.

He waited and waited. She didn't come. She was making the most of her twelve hours. He sat down again, stood up again. He opened drawers and filing cabinets, the ones that weren't locked. There wasn't anything very interesting. He went through to her tiny bathroom and wondered how she managed. He went to the loo. He went back into the work-shop and noticed her hood hanging on the back of the door. He got it down and put it on the workbench, to save time later. He checked that the breathing panel looked OK.

What was she *doing*?

For an odd, vertiginous moment he wondered if she could possibly have persuaded Daed not to use Asterion, after all. But —

He picked up the ball again and thumped it at the wall, trying to get as close as possible to the comms panel without actually hitting it. He imagined her in Daed's office. Suppose she won the argument, or Daed did; suppose they made up. He could see them laughing, drinking, trying out ideas for the new expansion. He threw the ball too hard and had to flinch as it bounced back, straight at his eyes.

Come on, Perdy. Come on. Let's go.

He'd have been less impatient if he wasn't scared, too. He wanted to get it over. He wanted to walk out through the Nucleus and the glass airlock, for it to be done and irrevoc-able. He hated this waiting.

He sat down. This time he sat against the wall, next to the

door. He leant his head back and shut his eyes. He breathed deeply, trying not to think about anything except his lungs and the air in them.

After a long time he heard the rain start again. The sound was so familiar it was soothing, like the pulse in his ears. He went to sleep.

When he woke up, nothing had changed.

It took him a second to work out what was wrong; at first it was just a feeling, like something was missing. Spot the deliberate mistake.

Slowly, painfully, he got to his feet. His back ached, and when he tried to turn his neck to the left the muscles twinged sharply.

He said, 'Time, please,' and the clock flashed up on the glassed-out rain-clouds. *0742.*

0742. But Perdita had only had twelve hours; she should have been out by 0530.

She must have come and gone. No. He would've woken up; he was right next to the door. She must've just gone, without even bothering to come back to her workshop first. Oh, *damn.*

He imagined her, alone, in the rain, walking the streets of Undone, looking for somewhere to stay. He imagined a small, anonymous figure in black out-clothes and hood, too ordinary for the cameras to follow. He thought he ought to pity her; but all he could feel was a cold, half-relieved stab of envy. She was outside the complex. She'd escaped.

Unless . . .

He thought: Daed wouldn't have changed his mind about getting rid of her. Surely . . . No. He wouldn't. He never makes any decision unless he's certain; so he never changes his mind.

Unless *she'd* changed *hers*. If she'd agreed to help with Asterion. Then, maybe . . .

He rubbed his eyes. He'd just woken up, but he felt so tired, so *tired*. What was wrong with him?

He took a last look around at Perdita's stuff — the rows of damaged components, lined up like a hospital ward, the books, the hood on the table like a black bag, the tangle of wire that shone like a crown yesterday — and then logged out of the workshop. He didn't meet anyone in the corridor, and he was glad.

He went up, up and up and up, to the twentieth storey, heading to Daed's office.

When he got out of the lift — he couldn't be bothered with the stairs — there was a strange odour in the corridor. It was something he'd smelt before, somewhere, but he couldn't put his finger on it. It was acrid and sharp, like a cleaning agent. It niggled at him, as though it was trying to tell him something important. He thought: Yeah, right, like that someone has *finally* been allowed to clean Daed's office . . .

Daed's door was locked. The comms panel was dark, as if it wasn't working. Either he really wasn't in, or he didn't want anyone to know he was in. The acidic smell was stronger, now. It hit the back of Rick's throat and made him cough. He put his hand on the panel and said,

'Daed?', but there was no answer, and he knew he wasn't going to get one. Maybe Daed and Perdita were in there together; or maybe not. He wished he knew where Daed's other rooms were.

He could have sat down outside the door and waited. But he was sick of waiting. All he ever seemed to do was wait.

He leant towards the comms panel and gave it another handprint, but it didn't even ripple. It was completely kaput. But then, Daed might have designed a kaput mode, just for situations like this one. It didn't mean anything.

So stuff it. Daed wasn't going to answer, even if he was in there; and either Perdita had gone already, or she wasn't going.

Rick coughed again — gods, that *smell*, like it had stripped a layer off his throat — and turned away. He went back to his rooms. There wasn't anywhere else to go.

He got in through the door and looked round at his room. He felt faintly sick. Outside the rain had started again. The shark in his pool was closer to the surface than normal; its outline was almost clear. The water rippled, blue and enticing.

Perdita must have left the complex; otherwise she'd have told him. Wouldn't she?

He stayed where he was, in the vestibule, and said to the comms panel, 'Housekeeping, please.'

Hello, Rick. How can I help you?

'Er . . . listen, I wanted to order a meal. For someone else, but from my account.'

Certainly. Please choose your food options.

He struggled to think. 'Just . . . um. Chips. Just chips. With salt and vinegar, and —' There wasn't any point getting carried away; it's not like he was going to get to eat it. 'That's all. Thanks.'

One portion of chips, with salt and vinegar. Where would you like that delivered?

'To Perdita, in the Creative Department,' he said. 'Please.'

I'm afraid I don't recognise the name. Do you have an alternative?

'To Workshop One, in the Creative Department,' Rick said. His hand was still pressed against the comms panel, and it was slippery and cold.

I'm afraid there's no one registered at that address. Do you have an alternative?

'Er . . . look, Perdita Sands, she used to be a Creative, I mean, until this aftern— until yesterday afternoon. Can you look up your records?'

I'm afraid I don't understand your request. Would you repeat it, please?

He took a deep breath. 'Request personal response, please.'

A pause. **One moment, please.**

Two seconds later, the comms panel said, **Yes? How can I help you, Rick?**

He wished they wouldn't be so polite; he never quite believed that they were real people, even though they said they were. He said, 'Look, I'm trying to send some food to a

friend of mine, and the system's saying she's not registered.
Can you tell me what's going on?'

What is her name, please?

He went through it all again, slowly, with his heart skitter-
ing in his ears.

I'm afraid Perdita Sands isn't registered with us.

'I know, that's what the computer said, but — she was
here yesterday . . . Maybe she got fired or something —'

That's possible.

OK, Rick thought, it *is* a real person, because the computer never interrupts.

**I'm not sure exactly what's happened, but I *can* tell
you for certain that she is no longer in the building.
Technically the information is sensitive . . . But as it's
you — the voice softened, like something going sticky in the
heat — I think I can say that if she had been fired, this
is exactly how it would show up on the system. *Exactly*
like this. Does that help?**

Rick's disappointment gagged him for a second; he had to
bite down on it before he could make the words come out.
Then he said, 'Yeah. Thanks.'

**My pleasure. Would you like the food order sent to
a different location?**

'Yes,' he said automatically, 'send it to me here, please.'

No problem. Can I help you with anything else, Rick?

'No.'

Well, please don't hesitate to contact me again if —

He walked away from the comms panel and let the voice
talk to itself. That was it, then. Perdita had left, without

going back to her workshop. He'd waited for her, and all the time she was already outside, probably. He stood at the window and watched the rain. The grey towers and streets of Undone were spread out in front of him like a 3D map. It wasn't anything like the Maze; but the shine in the chemiglass made it look beautiful, almost. Dangerous — but beautiful.

He heard the click of Housekeeping signing in, and the noise of the delivery box opening and closing. He didn't move, even though he could smell the vinegar-and-hot-fat perfume of the chips. He'd thought he was hungry. But he wasn't. The smell only made him feel queasy.

I used to be hungry, he thought. I used to sleep well. The only things that hurt were injuries I got in the Maze. What's happened to me?

He stood up, dragged the duvet off his bed, and sat down in the corner of the room, next to the window. He wrapped it round himself, half cloak, half nest. Then he leant his head against the chemiglass, watching the huge blurred raindrops on the other side of the window, too close to focus on. It was hard to believe they were poisonous. From here they just looked like water.

He stayed where he was. He drifted into a kind of trance, watching the rain. It wasn't quite sleep, because his eyes were open; but time passed quicker than it should have done. Until it was dark, and he was watching the lightning, long thick fingers of white light, like the roots of stars.

And there was something in his head; something with sharp corners, so that when he thought it dug into him, not letting him get comfortable. Something he'd seen, or something he'd heard, or touched, or smelt . . . Something that was germinating now, pushing a little tendril out into his brain. What . . . ?

He got up, leaving the duvet where it was, hollowed into the shape of his body. He stood for a moment in front of the darkened window, watching the lightning snatch at the clouds like it was looking for something. The rain slackened for a moment, and stopped. There was silence. The sudden quiet pressed against his brain.

And then he was logging out of his room, running along the corridors to Daed's office, and when he got round the corner there was the stench of ammonia, thick as a brick wall, and Daed's door was open and there was light spilling out.

He said, 'Daed? Daed, I need to talk to you —'

And then, in spite of the smell, he went in.

He had just enough time to see the world breaking in through the window, the shards of chemiglass on the floor like frozen petrol and the chair with its legs in the air like an insect. Then he took a breath — he couldn't help it — and he was blind and choking and his lungs were full of molten metal.

Someone grabbed him and pushed him backwards, gripping his shoulders as if they wanted to tear handfuls out of him. They were shouting but Rick couldn't focus on the words; whatever was in the air was eating into him, turning his skin inside out. He let himself fold down on the floor, choking so hard it felt like someone else was doing it. His eyes were streaming and everything hurt.

Something liquid poured over him, through his hair and down his face. It was cool, slightly sticky, and the pain washed away with it. His throat still burnt, but his skin was shivery and relieved, as if it was covered in frost. He gasped and coughed, and his mouth filled with the taste of bleach. He tried to spit it out. Something thick slid down his chin, leaving a trail of stinging slime. He wiped it away with his hand, and blinked the last drops of water out of his eyes.

There was a woman in front of him, her hood hanging down her back, her out-clothes undone at the collar. She said, 'Gods, are you trying to kill yourself? What on earth are you playing at?'

Rick said, from a corroded voicebox, 'What happened?'

He meant, what happened in the office; but the woman either didn't understand, or didn't want to tell him. She said, 'You took a lungful of outside air. I rinsed you off, but you should see a med to check for internal damage. If it was raining, you'd have been killed.' Her voice was flat, but she was shaking. Of course: he was important, he was Daed's son. If he'd got killed, it would have been her fault.

'I only wanted to see if Daed was in there,' Rick said.

A man's voice said, 'Did you leave the door open? What were you —'

She didn't look round. She said, still looking at Rick, 'The mechanism's broken. I couldn't close it. Get on with the job.'

The man snorted. It made an odd, muffled sound, because he was still wearing his hood. Then Rick heard him go back inside Daed's office.

The woman searched Rick's face with her eyes. 'How're you feeling?'

'OK. What happened in the office? I mean — the window —'

'A minor incident,' she said.

Which is why you're fixing it now, at night, when no one'll see, Rick thought. But he didn't say anything. He closed his eyes and saw the missing window, the last splinters of chemiglass clinging to the frame like teeth. The taste of Undone's air filled his mouth and he wanted to spit again.

'The chair,' he said. 'Someone wrecked the office.'

'No,' she said, 'just a minor incident. Daed's fine. He's been checked over, and he's fine. Nothing for you to worry about.'

'He was *in* there? When the window broke?'

'He's fine,' she said again. 'It wasn't raining, and he was only in there for a few seconds. He knew to get out as soon as possible, and the air didn't corrode the comms panel right away, so there was no problem opening the door . . .' She paused, as if she'd realised she was talking too quickly. 'Really, it was a minor incident.'

'So he was in there,' Rick said. He coughed. He was never going to get the taste of ammonia out of his mouth. 'What happened? Why did the window break?'

'An accident. Let's get you to a med.'

'Because the glass was too old?'

'No,' she said, a sudden defensive note in her voice. 'The Maintenance records are completely up to date. We can't be held responsible.'

'It didn't just implode?'

'No, it certainly —' She narrowed her eyes, then her face smoothed itself out. She was trying not to give anything away. But it was too late. She stood up, and hovered for a second, looking down at him. 'Go back to your rooms and ask for a med, urgently. OK? You can do that? Do you need someone to come with you?'

He wished she wouldn't tell him what to do; but the irritation was a long way away, behind a veil of grey. He didn't want to think about Daed, or his office. The broken window was like a mouth, trying to tell him something. Daed had been in there; Daed had broken the window, even though he must have known how dangerous it was. And he'd left the office in a mess, with the chair overturned, as if there'd been a fight . . .

He said, 'No.'

She thought he was answering her question. She pulled her hood up. 'Great. Can you ask the med to contact Maintenance after he's seen you? Just for the paperwork. Thanks.' Her gloved fingers ran over the seams in the outsuit, checking the fastening. 'Right, better get back to work. Go and get yourself checked out.'

She went back into the office, giving him one final look over her shoulder. The corridor light reflected off her hood, blanking out her eyes.

Rick stood up. His skin still felt cool, tingling like the top layer had been lifted off. He looked at his hands and half expected to see the bare muscles, tightening and drying out in the air-con.

Daed had been in there. And when he'd left, the chair was

overturned and the window had a hole big enough to throw a person through.

Rick thought of what it would be like, to stand at a broken window twenty storeys up, with nothing between you and the poisonous air. What it would be like to fall.

He squeezed his eyes shut. He thought: Maybe no one fell. Maybe Daed threw something at the window — the other chair, the desk, an old flatscreen . . . Maybe whoever was in there with him walked out through the door. Maybe there *wasn't* anyone in there with him.

And Perdita —

He wished he hadn't thought of her name.

He could almost believe that she was OK. He could almost, almost make himself believe that after she went to see Daed she walked out of his office and went down to the ground floor and left through the airlock, the way she was supposed to. He *would* believe it, if . . .

He breathed in and the smell of chemicals rose, filling his nose and mouth.

Against the dark of his eyelids he could see Perdita's work-shop, the way he'd left it: the wounded techno lined up to be mended, the empty spaces, the bare workbench.

Bare, except for Perdita's hood.

That was what had been niggling at him, the thing he couldn't get hold of. That, and the smell of rain.

The hood. The one thing no one would leave the complex without. Unless . . .

Unless they had to. Unless they fought with someone in an office twenty storeys up; unless somehow — in a blur, in a mess of words and movement that Rick can't imagine clearly — somehow — they smashed their way through the window, fell, disappeared, probably asphyxiated before they even hit the ground. Or . . . unless they were pushed.

Unless they were killed.

For example.

18

Rick tried and tried to get back into Perdy's workshop. He pressed his hand against the comms panel and closed his eyes, willing the door to slide open. The workshop would be just as he remembered it, except without the hood on the workbench. Because he was tired, wasn't he, and imagining things. Or it must have been his own hood that he'd left there. An easy mistake to make, especially when you weren't thinking straight.

He tried and tried; but the door stayed closed. Either Jake had only arranged a one-off entry for him, or the system had been swept.

After a while the comms panel said, **This office is temporarily unassigned. Can I help you with anything else?**

He shook his head, as if the comms panel was human, and genuinely offering to help. He put his back to the door and pushed, which was stupid, because it opened sideways. The metal was cool and unforgiving against his ribcage. It hurt; but then everything did. His skin was still painful. He didn't think anyone would be able to touch him, ever again. It hurt to move, or get out of bed, or put his clothes on. Even warm water was unbearable. The med had said he was fine, and given him painkillers, 'just in case', but they didn't work.

Then again, he knew it wasn't the airburn. It was the thought of the broken window, and Perdita. If he could only be sure she was OK, the pain would go away.

But the door stayed closed. And he remembered getting her hood down, and putting it on the workbench; he remembered it too clearly, like something behind glass. He'd never been so sure in his life.

He spun awkwardly away from the door, and stumbled down the corridor to the Ideas Space. He wanted . . . he didn't know what he wanted, but he couldn't stay here. The panel let him in, without pausing, and he stood in the doorway looking at all the whiteness. He wanted to be like that: blank. He wanted to run a bleach-covered cloth round the inside of his skull, and start again from scratch.

A group of Creatives looked up at him, and stopped talking.

He opened his mouth: nothing.

A tall woman with sparkling hair said, 'Hi, Rick.'

He thought he was going to ask where Perdita was; but he heard himself say, 'Where's Jake?'

'Jake?'

'He's a Creative. His office is down there.' Rick pointed. 'He's got light hair. He's tall.'

'No Jakes,' she said, and you could have cut diamonds with her eyes. 'If you mean Jason, he got asked to leave. For hacking the system. One-hour notice and no reference. Wonder how long he lasted, in Undone.'

'He was . . . thrown out?'

'Yeah,' she said. The other Creatives watched her, and

stayed very still. 'Funny, he said he thought he was doing it on Daed's orders. What a rubbish excuse. He should have known better. Right, Rick?'

It was like being punched on a frostbitten limb; the pain was vague, only just breaking through the numbness. Rick said, 'Oh.'

'Coffee?' she said.

He shook his head. He thought: They hate me. Of course they do.

He said, 'Could someone get me . . . I want to check something, in Perdita's old office . . .'

There was a silence. It fitted the room perfectly, wall to white wall, like it had been ordered especially.

And then they laughed.

He'd never heard people laugh like that. They laughed like the joke was death, and terror, and all the worst things they could imagine. And they were laughing at *him*. He stood there, and if he could have died right there, right then, he would have done.

Finally someone else — a man, with a shiny, sculpted face, too GM'd — said, 'No, don't think so, mate. Sorry.'

There was contempt in his voice, as well as hatred. The same old trick, it said. How stupid do you think we are?

They'd stopped laughing. Now they were just staring at him. The hostility made his skin tingle, like the airburn had.

He turned away. He knew Perdy was dead. He'd known it ever since he'd seen the broken window in Daed's office — but now it was just *there*, an unassailable fact, like gravity.

As he left someone said, just loudly enough, 'And he couldn't even get Jason's *name* right.'

Time passed. There was nothing Rick could do, so he did nothing. No one came to see him; but that was OK, because the thought of seeing anyone made him feel queasy and afraid. Once he thought he heard Daed's footsteps outside the door, and his stomach swirled and plummeted. But no one came in. And he was glad. Fiercely, defiantly glad.

He swam and practised the slowfight form on his own in his room, so at least he'd be hungry. Then he ate and slept. Strangely enough, he slept well, without dreaming.

Time passed. Hours, days, a week.

He was asleep when the door opened, and he dreamt that someone had come into the room and was sitting at the end of the bed. He rolled over, wishing they'd go away, but they didn't, and finally he had to admit he'd woken up and they were still sitting on his feet. He opened his eyes and looked at the faint reflection in the window. A ghost of Daed was sitting on a transparent bed, in twenty storeys' worth of mid-air. Rick wondered vaguely what was keeping him there.

'Awake?'

'No,' Rick said, 'I'm still asleep.'

'Security said you might be ill. You've slept fourteen hours out of the last twenty-four.'

'I don't have anything else to do.'

'Find something.'

'I don't want to.'

'What's up, Rick?' Daed's voice was soft, unexpectedly concerned. It made Rick sit up — slowly, because his head was spinning — and peer at him. Daed smiled, and Rick's unease faded. 'Good. I *thought* you were awake.'

'Go away, Daed.' He lay back down.

Daed stood up. For a second Rick thought he'd won, and felt a stupid surge of disappointment that Daed hadn't tried harder. He heard Daed go back to the door. Daed said, 'Lights, please.'

'Hey — Daed —' Rick squeaked in outrage and dived under a pillow, sheltering from the light as if it was a bomb-blast. Everything was muffled but his eyes still ached. He hadn't had the lights on for *days*.

'Yep — through there, please, there's a studio, the door — no, that's the bathroom — gods, be careful, do you have any idea how much that's worth? Yes, there, that's right, ignore the corpse in the bed, it's just a teenager.'

Rick raised his head. There were two workpeople shuffling round his bed with a box — a kind of white cylinder — the size of a coffin. They glanced at him as they went past. One of them smiled, but Rick was too confused to smile back.

Daed said, 'Yep, through there, normal power supply, normal networking, software already installed. Can I trust you two to set it up?'

The smaller workperson said, 'Er . . . well, actually —'

'Set it up,' Daed said, dismissing him.

'But —' The workpeople exchanged looks. The little one cleared his throat. 'Erm, we're not actually — our training isn't — not for new hardware — the insurance —'

'Oh, for gods' sake,' Daed said. 'It's not hard. Just do it. I'll check it later, OK?'

They exchanged another look, and then the woman shrugged. She said, 'OK, Daed, no problem,' and they started moving again. They paused at the door to Rick's studio, and the comms panel let them straight through, without a qualm. The door shut behind them. Rick turned his head slowly and stared at Daed.

'The iTank,' Daed said. He'd got a faint grin, like a skull. 'A little present for you. Not connected to the Maze yet, obviously, but there's a demo on there.'

'Thanks, but I don't want it.'

'Tough,' Daed said. 'You've got it.'

They looked at each other. Then Rick buried his face in his pillow again.

After a while the studio door opened again and the same unfamiliar voice said, 'All set up. Anything else, Daed?'

'No. Thanks.'

The silence swirled round the workpeople as they left, and then washed back into the room. It was cold.

'You should try it,' Daed said.

'Try what?' Rick said. 'Blackmail? Murder? Oh, right. I get it. You mean the iTank.'

Another silence. Then Daed said quietly, 'Ah.'

Rick rolled over, until he could see Daed's face, the way the electric light shone off his skin, how everything looked too thin. He said, 'Ah? Is that all you've got to say? *Ah?*'

'I'm sorry about Perdy's — I'm sorry about Perdy.'

'You killed her,' Rick said, spitting the words like they

were made of something. He wanted to see them hit Daed's shirt and leave a mark.

'Yes.'

'You *murdered* her — you pushed her out of the wi—' Rick stopped. His heart stuttered, like it was trying to catch up. 'What?'

'I said, yes. I pushed her out of my window. I did kill her.'

Rick blinked. He almost wanted to laugh. He waited for Daed to explain, change his mind.

Daed looked back at him, expressionless.

Rick put his face back into the soft breath-smelling pillow, and started to cry.

Daed let him cry for a long time. Then, finally, Rick felt the mattress sag and tremble as Daed sat down. He didn't touch Rick, but the air got warmer.

Quietly — so quietly Rick had to stop crying, just to hear the words — Daed said, 'Everything I do is because of you.'

Rick sat bolt upright, and if he'd been close enough to Daed to hit him he would have done. 'Don't you dare say that! Daed, you killed her, you *killed* —'

'Yes. And everything I do is to make sure you're safe, that you'll always be safe. I'm sorry about Perdy. But you're more important.'

Rick stared at him. Part of him said: Come on, it's *Daed*, of course he knows how to say exactly the right thing. Gods, you don't *believe* him?

The other part of him stayed resolutely silent, because all it could think of was: Really? You think I'm important? Really?

'OK?' Daed reached out a thin, nicotine-stained hand: the

hand a skeleton would have, if it chain-smoked. He brushed Rick's hair off his forehead. 'I'm sorry. I know it upset you.'

'How did — why did you have to —?'

'She was going to sabotage Asterion. I tried to get her out by gentler means, but . . . We had a fight. I realised then that it was . . . inevitable.'

The way he said it reminded Rick of Paz: *the thing about people, Daed, is that they're . . . dispensable.*

But Rick didn't say anything. And he let the silence go on, until finally it swung shut, like an old-fashioned door, and the subject was closed.

Daed said, 'Anyway. The iTank's fantastic. I think you'll like it. Hardware isn't my area, of course, but when you see the demo . . . I'm proud of it.'

'Good,' Rick said, without feeling anything.

'Try it. The atmosphere downstairs is . . . I've never felt anything like it. Even Marketing are happy.' Daed laughed. There was pleasure in his voice, but something else, too. Rick would have thought it was bitterness, if that had made sense; but it didn't. 'The launch party is going to be big. You're invited, of course. I think you might enjoy it.'

'I don't want to go.'

'Let me rephrase that,' Daed said. 'I think you *will* enjoy it.'

'I don't want to go.'

'Tough,' Daed said, shrugging. 'You're going. And you won't insult anyone or GBH any Security guards, either.'

Rick opened his mouth to make the 'I' sound. But it disobeyed him. 'All right.'

'Good.' Daed coughed, and covered his mouth with his hand. The fit went on for thirty seconds, easily, and when he stopped he wiped his hand on his trousers. It left a dark stain in the shape of two fingers, giving Rick a dispassionate V-sign.

Daed was sick. He was *still* sick.

But —

Rick thought: Wait, I thought —

'Daed — you're OK,' he said, in a rush. 'You're OK, aren't you? You're going to be OK?'

Daed looked at him, and his eyes were like a curtain, ready to be drawn aside. For a moment Rick was afraid, because he was going to see what was behind Daed's face, what Daed really looked like.

Then Daed raised one eyebrow. 'Yes, Rick. I'm OK, you're OK, we're both OK, everything's going to be OK. OK?'

'OK,' Rick said, before he could stop himself.

'Try the iTank demo. You'll like it. I'm a genius.' He stood up. 'Must be fun, being related to a genius.' He winked.

Rick smiled back. He stored the word away, to be re-examined later. *Related.* It was something.

Daed raised a hand — like he was a god, calling down blessings on the household — and turned to leave. It would have been a smooth exit, except that he started to cough, and had to steady himself in the doorway. Rick watched him, and then looked away, uncomfortable. It was like watching something private, like he shouldn't be there. He let his gaze rest on the shark under the swimming pool.

Daed gasped for breath, the air rattling in his throat.

Something blackish and clotted hit the carpet at his feet and soaked in.

Immortality, Rick thought. Not all it's cracked up to be, apparently.

Something inside him gave way. He couldn't help it. Something broke, something split cleanly down the middle. He'd had enough. He couldn't go on.

'Why did you do it?' he said, hearing his voice rise suddenly, out of control. 'I know this is all my fault — if I hadn't won against the Roots . . . but *you* designed it, you put the end there, if you hadn't—'

'What? Made it possible?' Daed was smiling; how could he be smiling? 'I had to, Rick. Nothing is impossible, remember? If word got out that I was designing dead-end quests . . .' His cough mastered him again.

There was a silence, and Rick hated him: for being right, for always being right. For letting things get to this. For Letting *Rick*—

He said, in spite of himself, 'Daed, I want to go. Please can we go?'

Daed straightened up, struggled, and finally drew a whole, ragged breath. 'Go where?'

'Anywhere. I can't stay here. I can't do it any more. Please.'

'Leave the complex?'

'Yes. Please, Daed, please.' He was like a kid, pleading for sweets. He remembered Perdita's macaroons and felt queasy.

'No.'

'Please —'

'*No.*' The cough came back, only this time it was a laugh. Rick felt his throat tightening. What was so funny? Blood speckled the corners of Daed's mouth, and when he wiped it away he left a long mark on his chin, like a pennant. He said, 'Oh, Rick. Gods. You're priceless.'

Rick opened his mouth to say something — to argue, to insult, to plead, he didn't know what — but Daed got there first. And something in his voice told Rick to shut up, because maybe, just this once, Daed might be telling him the truth.

'Rick,' he said, 'I've spent my whole life trying to keep us here. Everything I've done . . . And I've done it too well. We couldn't leave if we wanted to. And now, with Asterion . . .' He stopped short, as if he'd caught himself on the edge of saying something he shouldn't.

'But —'

'Shut up and listen.' Daed leant against the door frame, crossing one ankle over the other, so he looked like a screen-shot from the Maze, a vagabond loitering outside a tavern. You wouldn't have seen the tension in his shoulders and ribs, unless you'd been looking for it. 'Rick . . . we needed Crater. We needed shelter, and food, and money. So I came here, with you, and offered to work for them. You were too small to remember. And I worked so well that they promoted me, and kept on promoting me, until now I'm indispensable. I *am* the Maze . . .' For a second he paused, looking past Rick at the rain spattering the window. 'Now they won't let me go. I'm too important. If I went to Crater's competitors . . . well,

Crater wouldn't like it. And you — they'd be scared of letting you go, for the same reasons. We know too much. Do you understand what I'm telling you?'

Rick thought he did. But he shrugged. 'Just say it, Daed. With nice short words.'

'I can't leave. Neither can you. Ever.'

Rick nodded. Not because he agreed, but because there was nothing else to do. He said, 'The complex . . . it's a prison, isn't it?'

'For you and me, yes.'

'And you . . . not even you can think of a way to get out?'

Daed laughed, briefly. 'I can think of hundreds of ways to get out,' he said. 'It's just that we wouldn't survive the next twenty-four hours.'

'Because of — Undone, and the gangs, and the rain —?'

'We could survive those, probably. No, because of Crater. And Customer Services. They'd track us.'

They looked at each other.

'There's nothing we can do,' Rick said. 'Really, nothing?'

'Nothing,' Daed said, but his voice was hollow, with something hidden inside it, like a box. 'Just stay here. Make the most of it. Enjoy the party.'

Enjoy the party. It had an odd ring, like an insult. Rick couldn't help himself. He said, 'We'll be here for ever.'

'Until we die,' Daed said, and he closed his eyes, as if he was too tired to go on. 'There's always that, to look forward to.'

It sounded like a joke. It had to be a joke. But . . . no, it *didn't* sound like a joke. Not quite. A kind of empty grey horror rose through Rick, and he clenched his hands on the duvet to keep himself still. It was like one of those dreams, where you couldn't run or move out of the way. If he'd looked up, he'd have seen the ceiling collapsing, falling towards him in deadly slow-motion.

'Rick . . .'

He looked up, surprised.

Daed had opened his eyes. They shone, weird and beautiful in his old man's face. He looked . . . worried. He said, 'You're not really *unhappy*, are you?'

Rick blinked. Then *he* wanted to laugh, or to cry. But he was frozen, speechless. Someone's hacked Daed's account, he thought, blankly. Same face, same avatar, but the person behind it is someone I don't know . . .

The silence went on. And finally, like a trickle of moisture pushing its way gently through a dam, Rick thought: Maybe he *is* my father. Maybe he really *is*.

He thought of Athene, who was dead now, and Perdita, and Jake — no, Jason — and the Security man, who might be dead or alive, Rick didn't even *know*. The panic rose and swirled like a flood. He took a deep breath.

'No, Daed,' he said. 'Relax. I'm just a bit under the weather. You're right. I'll enjoy the party.'

'Good.' Daed's gaze slid away. 'You should be glad to be here. Food, shelter, unlimited access to the Maze . . . luxury . . .' He gestured vaguely at the swimming pool. The shark flipped its tail and changed direction.

'That's right,' Rick said.

A pause. Daed nodded. 'See you later, then. At the launch,

if not before.' He sounded hundreds of years old. Perhaps he was.

'Yes,' Rick said. He'd never felt so lonely in his life.

He watched Daed go. The rain splashed and clattered against the window, relentless. He thought about throwing a chair through the glass. But it would have been painful, to die like that. And he didn't want to die.

In the end he got up and went to look at the iTank. He stood outside it, running his hand down the smooth white contours, admiring the design. It wasn't quite cylindrical; the curves were subtle, like something organic. He wanted to go inside. He wanted to like it.

If I try it, he thought, that's it. I've lost. I'm giving up. I've stopped fighting, and I'll live here for ever. I'm letting Crater and Paz and Customer Services win. That's the choice.

There's nothing else I can do.

The tank responded to the touch of his hand, rippling faintly silver. The door slid open, inviting him in.

He stood there for a long time.

And then — inevitably, without even feeling much, except tired — he went in, and the door shut behind him.

The ruins of somewhere beautiful are spread out around him. Above the last ribs of the roof there's a clear sky, just beginning to glow red with the sunset. In the emptiness between the pillars there are leaves drifting down, slowly, glinting gold and scarlet and crimson where they turn in the sunlight. Underfoot the paving-stones are overgrown with thin yellow grass and moss.

And space. There's so much space. The scale of it . . .

He feels the hair rising on the back of his neck.

He pivots on his heels, looking around. He swallows, and swallows again, caught off-guard by so much loveliness. The other side of the sky is a pale blue, throwing the outlines of the ruins into silhouette. He sees broken towers and a stair-case that leads nowhere, a little tree pushing out horizontally from a wall.

Oh, Daed . . .

He can smell . . . but he doesn't have words for it. Something fresh, something clean. No, not clean. Things growing. A garden smell. But not a synth smell, not how it would smell in the Maze. Oh, the *difference* . . . He blinks. Water runs down his cheeks. He laughs. He doesn't want to exhale; he wants to keep inhaling, for ever, always breathing this air, always smelling this smell. It's the smell of everything he never realised he wanted. It's the smell of quietness and seeds and peace and sunlight and and and —

His lungs are going to burst. He breathes out, in a rush.

Finally he takes a step forward. The stones are hard under his feet, except for the overgrown bits. He crouches and runs his hand over the moss and it feels like velvet. He pulls at it and it peels slowly away from the ground, the roots ripping softly like very polite Velcro. It comes away in his hand like a green rag. When he drops it, it stays where it is. So does the bare patch. He watches them for ages, waiting for them to melt back to how they were; but they don't. He stretches an arm out, picks up a fallen leaf and crunches it between his fingers. When he looks at his palm there are little fragments of brown leaf-dust clinging to the skin. He makes a noise that's half sob, half hiccup.

A sudden coolness slides over his face, and the quality of the light changes. For a moment he thinks something's gone wrong. Then, when he looks up, he realises that the sun has dipped a little further, that's all. Now it's hidden behind the ragged wall opposite; but if he tilts his chin he can still see it, blinding, impossible and unfamiliar. The sun in the Maze is only a ball of light. Here it's . . . he can't describe it. He thinks: I've never needed these words before. None of the words I know are good enough.

The part of his brain that isn't reeling, dazzled, adds: Wow. An environment that exists in real time. I wonder if it changes with the season . . .

He shakes his head again. Daed, he thinks. You're right, this is amazing, this is . . . I don't believe it. It's not techno, it's *magic*.

And this is only the demo.

He gets to his feet. Now the sun is lower, the air is cool, brushing his face with its fingers, making him shiver. He says, 'Er . . . help. Please.'

How can I help you?

It ought to break the spell, but it doesn't. He says, 'I'm cold.'

Would you like to: a) change iTank settings?

b) learn how to affect the playing environment?

He chooses the second option.

Anything you can do in real life, you can do here, too, the iTank says to him. **But you also have a few magical powers. Would you like to try them out?**

In the Maze, Rick doesn't bother with magic, because it's lame and takes too long. Hardly anyone does — only the weekenders, and the kids, people who can't be bothered to take it seriously. And they stay in the lowest levels, quibbling with each other and learning spells off by heart when a bit of training would mean they could just fight for real. Magic isn't worth the trouble.

But here . . .

To set something on fire, point at it and imagine it bursting into flame.

Rick laughs. This is weird, and incredible, and isn't going to work. He points at the nearest clump of grass and imagines CGI fire exploding out of it. Nothing. It's too real; it's like pointing at his bed and expecting *that* to catch fire.

Sometimes speaking can help you to concentrate. Try saying, 'Burn, burn.' Don't worry if it takes a few goes. If you concentrate hard enough, it will happen.

He says, 'Burn, burn.'

He says, 'Catch fire. Go on. Catch fire.'

He says, 'Fire, fire, fire, fire, fire, I feel really stupid.'

He says, 'Burn, baby, burn.'

His arm is starting to ache at the shoulder. He thinks: Did they really think this was going to work? He shuts his eyes. He imagines what it would be like if it *did* work. He thinks of a tiny spark running round the edge of a dry blade of grass, smoking, catching light, the first little lick of flame, and then a tiny *whoomph* as the rest of the clump catches light —

And he smells smoke, and when he opens his eyes the clump *is* alight. The flames dance and give out heat. He stares and stares.

It read my mind, he thinks. It really did. It *read my mind*. Gods.

Well done. Now let's learn how to fly. This could take a little time, so don't worry if it doesn't work straight away! First, you need to take up a stable stance, with your feet hip-width apart. For safety reasons, you will not be able to lift off unless your body is balanced and relaxed. Breathe deeply. Now —

He thinks of flying in the Maze, which is boring, actually. You have to stay upright, and you feel like you're walking, except that everything moves faster, and you're three ems up. And you can only do it when you're a ghost. It's rubbish.

He takes a deep breath, makes sure he's balanced and

relaxed. He shuts his eyes and thinks of becoming weight-less. He imagines gravity letting go of him, slowly. He thinks about how he's in control, and free, and how he's safe here, and he can do anything he wants.

The air thickens around him, holding him. It's odd, almost unpleasant. He pushes down with his hands, spreading his fingers, and he feels the resistance like a current, pushing back. His stomach tightens. He can still breathe, but it's just —

He opens his eyes.

And he's in the air. He's flying.

Well, not exactly. To be honest, he's hovering, only a few ems off the ground — which is just as well, because as soon as he looks down, the disbelief surges and he drops back to earth. It knocks the breath out of him. Or would, if he wasn't already breathless with excitement. Oh, Daed, he thinks. Oh, Daed. This is so good. This is . . . how did you *do* this?

The sun, he thinks. The sky. The smell of things that are alive. *Leaves*.

He sits up, a little painfully — although not as painfully as if he'd really fallen two ems, obviously — and wraps his arms round his knees. The tuft of grass is still burning, smoking and giving out heat. He imagines it blazing higher and fiercer, and it does.

And once all this is linked to the Maze, with the other players . . . Wow.

The next step, he thinks, will be for it to stop being a game at all. Funny, how they try to make it more and more real until you're hardly playing any more.

He shuts his eyes, and listens to the little rustlings of leaves, the gentle whisper of wind through the grass and the ruins. He can still feel the warmth from the fire, dying now, and the last caress of sunlight on his face. On impulse, he runs his finger over the ground and puts it in his mouth. The skin is gritty and tastes of damp and mould. He opens his eyes again and takes in the red radiance of the sky, the glorious sunset that makes him think: rose, ruby, vermilion . . . words he didn't even know he knew.

He thinks: Suppose *this* is the real world, and the other one is just a . . .

The sky flashes black. Everything flashes black, a sickening negative of itself. The ruins and the trees and the sun go dark and slide sideways and elongate at the corners. Something is screaming at him. His mouth is full of pepper. It *hurts*. He struggles for breath. Oh gods, oh —

He gasps, 'Log out, log out, log out —'

His blood rushes to his head and away again, as if the tank is rolling over and over. He's falling. There's a smell of bitterness, burnt plastic, maybe. He has time to think: Not rain, at least, that's something.

Then he's flat on his stomach, and everything is pale and shining white, and his mouth is empty and sore. But he can smell something burning. He can still smell something burning.

'Open the tank door, please,' he says. The *please* surprises him.

It slides open, immediately. He kneels up and crawls out on his knees, falling forward on to the soft studio floor. He's shaking and clammy with sweat. Sickness rises and falls with every breath, and the worst thing is it's coming from his brain, not his stomach. The iTank is flashing red, a red-behind-white glow, like an opal. It says, **There has been a malfunction. Please tell Crater about this problem.**

Rick says, 'Ha.' It's half a word, half an exhalation.

He can see the malfunction. It's the connection wires, at the back. They're smoking. As he looks, a gaudy blue and green flame stretches up and rolls its shoulders, then slides forward and starts to lick at the carpet. He watches it for a few seconds before he realises that it's got anything to do with him.

He takes off his T-shirt and drops it neatly over the bad connection. After a while the smoke dies. When he lifts the T-shirt away again it's got a blackened hole in it; but the fire's gone. The smell of it is still stuck in the back of Rick's throat. He's got a headache the size of Ingland.

Ouch. At least the old tank couldn't make you *ill*.

His knees give way. He drops into a sitting position, lean-ing against the iTank wall. He wishes it didn't have that trendy curve in it.

Daed forgot to check the installation. That's all. The work-people weren't trained, and they didn't plug it in right. When the wires overheated the tank started to malfunction. Just an accident. It's OK. No harm done . . .

He wonders what it would have done to his brain, if he hadn't logged out.

He thought he was wondering it idly, in an academic sort of way. But he starts to shiver, and he can't stop.

He stays there until the nausea has passed, and then he stands up and sends a message to Daed about the malfunction, and to get the tank rewired.

There's no point worrying, he thinks. This is my life, now. This is the only thing I've got.

And later, in the end, he ordered food which he couldn't eat, and had a shower and went to bed. He told himself nothing terrible had happened. It was only a malfunction.

And in a way he believed it. Everything went wrong occasionally. It was a fact of life. And the workpeople had *said* they weren't trained . . .

But when he went to sleep, he woke up again and again, sweaty and paralysed, his heart pounding. He'd never been so terrified. He had nightmare after nightmare, relentless and repetitive, full of nothing but sunlight and falling leaves.

PART 4

ENJOY THE PARTY

20

Prototype malfunction duly noted. Thank you, Rick.
That was all Daed's message said. Rick waited for a day,
another day, a week, but no one came to take the iTank
away. No one came to rewire it, either. Or to sort out the
burnt patch in the carpet. No one came.

The only other message he got was the invitation to the
launch party. And that wasn't an invitation; it was an order.

It was an order; so he followed it. That was what he did,
these days. The night of the party advanced on him merci-
lessly, and he ignored it for as long as he could, until finally
he was getting ready to go, putting on the suit Housekeeping
sent him, struggling with the cufflinks . . . He cursed, furious, because it was safe to get angry about cufflinks.

He looked at himself in the mirror, and it was a shock. Not
just because of the histro clothes — which would shock
anyone, Rick thought, gods, I look like someone from before
the world was in colour — but because of the face and the
hair and the gaze. He looked years older than he used to. His
eyes were purple round the edges.

He leant forward, bracing himself against the washbasin.

The cold porcelain pushed back, like it didn't want him there. His wrists were shaking.

Behind him, his alarm went off. The nearest comms panel said, **Hello, Rick. It is 1830. Please get ready to leave. Don't forget your invitation!**

'Thanks,' he said, to shut it up. He looked back at himself, wincing. He felt sick. He didn't know what was wrong, but something was.

He shut his eyes. All this week he'd been on the edge of understanding; or that was how it felt. As if every time he spoke to Housekeeping, or heard blurred, excited voices going past his door, or glanced at the fire-eaten hole in his carpet . . . as if every little thing was pushing him towards a conclusion, as if any moment now he was going to under-stand. He squinted into the dark of his eyelids.

Nope. Nothing.

A tired, ironic voice said, over his shoulder, 'What are you doing, exactly?'

Rick opened his eyes and looked into the mirror. Somehow he felt faintly surprised that Daed was solid enough to have a reflection. He said, 'How long have you been in my rooms?'

'You look good,' Daed said. 'Just Paz's type.'

Rick turned round to look at him. He was dressed up, too, but his face was taut and grey. He looked weird; like a default avatar, before you'd bought a better model. Rick shrugged.

There was an odd, fractured kind of silence, as though someone had cut the sound. Then Daed said, 'Have you got a moment?'

His voice was polite. It made Rick blink and hesitate before he said, 'A moment . . . ? Er . . . yes.'

But Daed didn't seem to have heard. He stared past Rick, into the mirror, while the pause stretched. Rick wanted to say, Is that all you wanted? Ten seconds of silence? But he didn't dare, quite. He could smell nicotine and ash.

Finally Daed met his eyes. He still didn't speak; instead, he took Rick's elbow and piloted him through the bathroom door, through the archway and along the side of the pool. Rick felt the cold from the tiles seep through his socks.

'Daed, where are —?'

'Shut up,' Daed said, and opened the door of the hammam. The steam billowed out in a cloud and for a moment Rick could smell eucalyptus and lavender instead of cigarette smoke. Then Daed's hand was between his shoulders, pushing him forward.

Rick stumbled and sat. The thick warmth filled his lungs; his face and hair were already dripping. 'Daed, what — this suit is — what am I supposed — what are you —?' But he had too many questions to finish any of them.

'Oh, well, I just wanted to ruin your lovely new clothes,' Daed said, and suddenly his voice was the one Rick knew: mocking, unsympathetic. He looked at Rick and laughed, shortly. 'My apologies for the indignity, Rick, but this wasn't an exchange I particularly wanted to share with Security. No hidcams in a hammam,' he added, when Rick frowned. 'Far too much trouble to maintain.'

'An exchange?' For a second Rick thought, madly, that he

meant a real exchange, that Daed wanted to sell him something, or buy . . .

'There are a few things I need to tell you.'

'Now? Right now? Look, Daed, why don't —'

'Yes,' Daed said, and he took hold of Rick's wrist, like a handcuff made of finger bones. 'Right now. Sit still and listen.'

Rick blinked the water off his eyelashes. He turned his head aside and looked into the fog of steam. He wanted to laugh, because he was in a steam bath, fully dressed, and his party clothes were ruined and Daed had gone mad — or always had been mad, maybe — and if he laughed he could pretend it was only funny, when it was horrible.

Daed seemed to be waiting for an answer, so Rick swallowed a bulb of phlegm that tasted of eucalyptus and said, 'OK.'

A pause. Water ran down the walls.

'Tonight,' Daed said, 'is my great triumph. Tonight is the pinnacle of my life's work.' His voice was flat. When Rick heard the word *triumph* he thought of a wall in the Maze where someone had graffitied *RED* in huge blue letters: you saw the word, but it didn't mean what it normally did. There ought to have been something he could say, but there wasn't.

'I need you to promise me something,' Daed said, so quietly, suddenly, that Rick only heard the consonants. 'Will you?'

'What?'

'Promise first,' Daed said. And laughed, as if he'd made a private joke.

Rick opened his mouth to say *no*.

'*Promise me.*' Daed's hand tightened on Rick's wrist, grinding the bones together. 'This is important. Trust me.'

Rick's tongue pressed against his front teeth, getting ready for the *n*. The world blurred and dripped. He thought of everything Daed had let happen — Athene, the mirror cell, Perdy — and wanted to chew up the word *trust* and spit it back at him.

Daed said, 'You're my son, Rick, and I love you. Trust me. Please.'

Rick blinked. Water rolled down his cheeks and dripped off his chin. He felt it soaking into his collar. When he licked his lips he tasted salt, not eucalyptus. He said, '*What?*'

Daed gave him a look that could be a smile. Through the fog of steam his face looked half rubbed out. Another minute and he'd have disappeared entirely.

'Light of my life,' he said. 'Apple of my eye. Of course I love you, Rick. Otherwise I'd have strangled you long ago.'

Silence. Wet, hot, blind silence. Rick ran his hand over the slick warm tiles, pushing with his fingertips like he was trying to find a handhold. He breathed in, trying to imprint everything on his memory: the smell of the steam and his wet clothes, the feel of water soaking into his collar, Daed's hand on his wrist . . . *Apple of my eye*. Rick would've thought that was sarcasm, before.

And he said, 'Yes, I promise, Daed. Anything. Whatever you say. I promise.'

Daed breathed out, so long and so deeply it could have been his last breath. The steam danced. He said, 'The Maze expansion isn't safe. There's a malfunction. Promise me you won't run the Maze until I tell you it's OK.'

Rick didn't know what he'd been expecting, but it wasn't that. 'But — the malfunction —' He coughed and had to swallow. 'Wait. You haven't fixed the malfunction?'

'Not the same malfunction. Yours was just the iTank wiring.'

'So —'

'So promise.' Daed leant forward, so the contours of his face loomed through the steam. 'It's not the iTank, it's the Maze. I'll get someone to rewire your iTank, there won't be any problem with that. You can play the demos all you want, any of the solo player games. But not the Maze.'

'There's a malfunction in the Maze? You're launching the new expansion while there's still a malfunction?'

'Please, Rick, it's rather tiresome to have to repeat everything.'

'But —'

'We're in a steam room, Rick, let's not get hung up on the details. Promise me you won't go into the Maze. It's important.'

Rick almost agreed, right then. But he was still struggling to work it out. The Maze wasn't safe. They were launching it anyway. 'Does Paz know?'

'Yes,' Daed said. 'Well. More or less.' But he didn't sound worried; just impatient. 'Rick —'

'But you're going to fix it? The malfunction?'

'Rick.' Muscles flickered over Daed's jaw. Then he reached out and linked his fingers behind Rick's skull, pulling his head forward. 'Just promise me. *Now.*'

'All right, I promise,' Rick said. 'But how soon will it be fixed?'

Daed kept his hands where they were and looked into Rick's face. Rick stared back, wondering what Daed could see in his eyes. The veil of steam between them rippled and thinned.

'Thank you.'

'That's OK,' Rick said, and suddenly he was scared that he'd promised something bigger than he knew.

Silence. Then Daed got up. Rick heard the moisture dripping off his clothes as he moved. He wondered if Daed had ever said *thank you* to him before.

Daed reached out and pulled him up by the wrist. Rick could feel him trembling, right up into his shoulder. He was afraid to let him take his weight; but afraid not to, too.

He didn't let himself think. He said, 'You're OK, aren't you, Daed? With Asterion?'

Daed's hand tightened and loosened again, like a spasm. 'What about Asterion? What do *you* know about Asterion?'

'I —' Rick got to his feet. 'Nothing. I mean . . . only what you said about it. That it makes you —' *Immortal* sounded too dramatic, but he couldn't think of another word. 'It stops you dying. Daed . . .'

'Stop worrying.' Daed opened the door of the hammam and the cold air swirled over Rick's face and tingled on his lips. 'I'm OK.'

'You were sick,' Rick said. 'You kept coughing, and —' But he still coughed, didn't he? He still looked like he was being eaten from inside.

'I'm OK.'

'You were sick,' Rick said again, as if it was a game.

'Shut *up*!' Daed rounded on him. His hand was raised, at the height of Rick's face. 'Gods . . . you don't know anything about it. Asterion is —' He stopped, suddenly, and when he blinked the condensation rolled down his face like tears. 'Rick. Just do what I say, and everything will be fine. You keep that promise, OK?'

'OK.' Rick felt like he'd heard *OK* so many times it didn't mean anything any more.

Daed looked at him for a long time. He let his hand fall, slowly. A wisp of steam coiled round his wrist and faded. Then he walked away, without a word. As he went past the corner of the swimming pool he glanced down, and the shark rose a little and flicked its tail, as if in greeting.

Rick watched him go. At the last minute, he said, 'Daed?'

'What?' He didn't turn round; just halted, his hand poised over the comms panel. His shoulders were sagging.

'Is it a real shark?'

'What?' Now he did turn.

'In the — under the pool. It's not real, is it?'

Daed's eyes narrowed. He said, 'Have you ever seen it being fed?'

'No, but — but you can't see right to the bottom. You can't see the shark all the time, only when it surfaces.' Rick could feel the blood tingling in his cheeks, as warm as the wall of steam behind him. But you *can't* see all the way down, he thought. It *could* be a real shark . . .

A fractional pause; as if Daed was listening for something

Rick couldn't hear. Then he said, 'Of course it's not a real shark, Rick. Relax.'

'Oh.' He was disappointed, somehow: that the world wasn't scarier, nastier, beyond his cell of glass. Stupid.

'Honestly,' Daed said. 'A real shark. Would I?' He didn't seem to expect an answer. He leant his hand on the comms panel, until the bones shone white through his skin. The door slid open.

Then he turned round and smiled at Rick. It was a strange smile; on anyone else Rick would have thought it was affectionate. No, not just affectionate. *Loving*. It was a gift, a miracle of a smile. It made Rick take a deep breath.

Daed said, 'I've got to go.'

'See you later,' Rick said. 'Downstairs — in the party . . .' He took a step forward, and another, until the hammam door swung shut behind him and he was trembling in the cold. His wet clothes were sticking to him. 'Daed —'

'Goodbye, Rick.'

And then he went, and Rick was left standing on the brink of the swimming pool, shivering.

21

The Nucleus was full of people; more people than Rick had ever seen in one place. They were in black and white, most of them, but their faces and hair were so bright and varied Rick couldn't work out what was GM and what was make-up. They milled about, talking too loudly — at least someone had turned the sound-deadener off — and occasionally glancing over their shoulders at the giant staircase as if it gave them the creeps, even with all the lights and the decorations. Their champagne glasses were round-bottomed, with the same trendy curve as the iTank. There were already a few empty glasses on the floor, spinning and rolling as people caught them with their feet. Rick paused where he was, ignoring someone hissing impatiently behind him as she came through the ticket gates, and just *looked*. Gods.

And he saw that the decorations were a kind of sci-fi version of the iTank demo: skeleton trees, leaves of copper foil drifting down from the roof, 2D ruined walls, like lazy graphics. Either the ceiling glass had been tinted red, or outside there was an unusual glow in the sky. It made him think of the time he'd spent in the demo, the way a skull would make him think of a face. He hated it.

And if he closed his eyes, he thought of the black sickening flash-out when the tank malfunctioned. What the iTank could do to a brain.

He looked round. He needed something to drink; or just something to hold. The champagne glasses were hanging from the trees, like tall pale green fruit. He pushed his way through the jostling groups of people and grabbed for one. It was cool and slippery with condensation, but it didn't have a proper stem and he had to cup it in his hand. He heard someone say, 'Gods, whose bright idea was *this*? It won't stay cold longer than a minute.'

'Yeah, and if you put it down it doesn't stay upright. Not that there's anywhere *to* put it down . . .'

Rick glanced round, and then quickly away again, because it was the group of Creatives that had laughed at him, when he'd tried to get into Perdy's office the second time. But he could feel them staring. He hoped it was because of his clothes — the histro suit was ruined, so he was wearing a slim-cut black pyjama instead — but he thought he could sense hostility heating the back of his neck like sunburn. He really didn't want to be here. He took a long swallow of cold champagne and tried not to drop the glass.

There was a sweet, clear, chiming noise, like a bell. Slowly the noise subsided. Everyone looked up.

There were vidscreens set up, just too high to be comfortable to look at. Rick hadn't noticed them before, but now they flashed into life: first the Crater logo, then a CGI sequence from the Maze, then, finally, a man's face. He was badly designed, with a clumsy nose and weak eyes, and after the CGI it was a bit of an anticlimax.

He said, 'Welcome, my friends — guests, employees, gamerunners and gamepros. Welcome to the launch of the iTank, the biggest virtual reality product the world has ever known.' He pressed every word like it was a button. 'This is not merely an upgrade of the gametank; this is not merely an expansion of the Maze.' He paused, and his amplified breath hissed into his lungs. 'Friends, guests, employees . . . The Maze —' the vidscreen flashed up an ® symbol — 'was already the biggest game ever played. Crater is the biggest employer in Ingland. We have already achieved worldwide — and *breathtaking* — success. The Maze —' another ® — 'is not only a world so vast, so complex, and so *adored* that it has its own economy, not to mention a higher GDP than Ingland itself; it is also a work of art. You already share in that success; you are the heroes, the creators, the owners, and the gods of our virtual world. And please — don't make the mistake of thinking that a virtual world is somehow less real than the real one.' There was a little titter of laughter: not amused, Rick thought, but smug.

'But that is all in the past,' the man went on. He lowered his voice — for dramatic effect, obviously — and went on talking. Rick tuned out and let his gaze wander from the vidscreen. With a strange jolt, he realised that the man was actually there, live, on a platform at the foot of the giant staircase. When he looked back at the screen he saw that there was a time-delay on the camera, so the man wasn't in sync with his real self. It made Rick feel seasick.

'Let us,' the man was saying, 'focus on the *now*. Crater has never been content to rest on its laurels. To be human is to create, to improve, to evolve. There is no rest for humanity. Time enough to rest when we're dead.' There was another laugh, although Rick wasn't sure it was a joke. 'It goes without saying that Crater's products far outstrip our competitors'. But they can never be good enough — not for us, not for you, not for our consumers. And so the gametank as you know it, my friends, is finished — despite its success, despite the amazement and excitement that it still inspires. The gametank, and the Maze — the old hardware, and the Maze itself — were, *are*, a magnificent achievement. But we just weren't satisfied. We wanted something better.'

There was a pause. Rick heard the crack of someone stepping on a fallen champagne glass, and the stifled syllables as they swore under their breath.

'Imagine,' the man said, and leant forward, his face expanding on the screen. 'Imagine the days of flatgames. Imagine the consoles, how impressive they must have been, at first. PlayStation,' he said, savouring the word. 'Xbox. Dreamcast. And yet —' he gulped with mirth — 'imagine the difference, for those first realgame players, when they stepped into a tank. It was the end of an era; the end of a world. And now, my friends . . .' He paused, and this time no one broke the silence. 'My friends, what you are here to witness is as dramatic, as wonderful as that moment must have been. We, too, are poised, ready to witness the beginning, ready to discover a new universe. The iTank is beyond everything you have ever experienced; the Maze expansion exploits every new possibility the iTank provides. Together they are — literally — *incredible*. I hope you enjoy yourselves tonight, my friends, and I welcome you on Crater's behalf. I hope you all have a fantastic evening. But, please, believe me when I say that this is not simply a launch party. This, tonight, is *history*.'

Rick felt his back teeth grinding together; but applause erupted around him, loud enough to drown out the sound. He was glad he'd got his drink, because it stopped him having to clap. He didn't know why he was so annoyed; after all, the man was right. He looked round, wondering whether the smiles and wide-eyed nods were real or put on. Unexpectedly, he saw Daed, alone, leaning against a fake tree, a few ems away from the PR man's platform. He seemed to sense Rick's gaze; he looked up, met Rick's eyes, and made a tiny humorous gesture as if he wanted to be sick. Rick grinned, feeling a tiny release of tension in his jaw.

And then Paz stepped on to the lowest stair of the giant staircase, and there was silence like a flash of lightning. Rick held his breath, waiting.

She didn't need the screens; they'd gone blank. She stood still, and the sheen of water on the step below her reflected every detail of her body. She was holding a glass of champagne, and she held it to one side without looking and let go. Someone scuffled and crouched to get to it before it hit the ground, but too late, and it smashed. Paz smiled.

'Thank you,' she said. 'As my esteemed colleague says, welcome.' She paused, and the silence wrapped round the words, glittering, so it hardly mattered what she said. She looked about her; Rick could have sworn she was looking directly at him. 'Everything he said was true — but let's not beat about the bush. We're not here because we want to make history. We're not here to amaze our consumers. We're not here because we want to create works of art. We're here to make money. And the iTank will make us more money than you can imagine. Combined with the new Maze expansion, it will make us money beyond our wildest dreams.'

More silence. And slowly, one by one, people started to smile again. A new light was coming into their eyes.

'Most of you aren't my friends,' Paz said, with an ironic glint in her eye that — Rick thought — made everyone think they were one of the exceptions. 'But you are all my guests. You all share my values. So . . . Guests. Mazerunners, Mazepros, colleagues. The toast I propose isn't to our Creatives; it's not to Daedalus.' For a moment her eyes rested on Daed, and Rick was impressed despite himself, by the way she was almost thanking him, but not quite. 'It's not even to Marketing or PR. I'm not going to be polite. Why should I?' She paused, and no one moved or made a noise or breathed. She held out her hand to the side, and this time someone was ready, and when she lifted it again it had a new, full glass of champagne in it. She said, 'This is my toast. Let's raise our glasses to the money we're going to make. And the world we're going to rule.'

There was a pause, and then a murmur, as people echoed the toast.

And then there was a ray of light falling on her, blazing copper and gold, striking sparks of rose and orange off her dress and the curtain of water behind her. She looked up, into the beam, and smiled.

Rick followed her eyes, expecting to see a lighting rig. But it wasn't an effect; it was coming from the sky. There was a break in the clouds, and the gash of light was gaping like a wound, scarlet-edged, glaring platinum, more beautiful than anything Rick had ever seen. It hurt to look, but he couldn't help it.

'The heavens are smiling on us,' Paz said. And Rick knew everyone else was staring, too, that there was no one in the Nucleus looking anywhere but at the sun.

The *sun*.

Rick couldn't remember the last time he'd actually seen the sun.

He felt water rising in his eyes and he blinked it away, not wanting to miss a second of this light — *sun*light — this wonderful unbearable hole in the sky, dazzling, unlike anything he'd ever seen. I want to go outside, he thought. I want to see it properly.

The world seemed to stop where it was, for a second, for ten seconds. Then the clouds closed up, their edges knitting together like broken bones. The light went grey and faded; the strange electric stillness went out of the air.

'Thank you for your attention,' Paz said, and it was like she'd been in charge, all the time, like even the sky belonged to her. 'And now the last speech of the evening. I promise.' And she gestured to Daed.

Daed looked up, almost as if he was surprised. Then he smiled, and went to the little low platform where the PR man had been, a few minutes ago. The crowd shifted restlessly; Rick could feel their impatience. Another speech . . .

Daed cleared his throat. 'The iTank was mostly the invention of one Creative,' he said, 'and I don't mean me. Perdita Sands was one of the most talented technicians I've ever known. She was killed in a tragic accident a few weeks ago. I know she would be very proud of the iTank.' He paused, and his shoulders spasmed as if he was trying not to cough.

'On the other hand,' he said, his voice tight, 'the Maze *is* almost entirely my own work. My life's work. And the new expansion even more so. The Maze is the creation — the work of art — without which the iTank technology would mean nothing. And I think you'll be impressed.' A silence. Rick thought: He isn't even *trying*.

'Enjoy the Maze,' Daed said. 'But be careful. It has some surprises in store.'

Silence. No one clapped. No one seemed to realise he'd finished. They watched as he stepped painfully off the platform and retrieved his drink from someone's hand.

Then people stopped listening and turned away. A couple of Creatives started to applaud and then stopped, looking foolish. The murmur rose, like a sea washing footprints off sand.

And it was as if Rick was the only one who'd actually heard what Daed had said. Rick was the only one who stayed still, the back of his neck tingling, wondering what was going on. Everyone else took a swig of their drinks, smiled, or snorted with mirth at a wisecrack. They were going to enjoy the party.

Only Daed caught Rick's eye. He held his stare for a second; and then glanced quickly — too quickly — aside.

•   •   •

The party went on. Rick couldn't work out whether time was going too fast or too slowly. He leant against one of the champagne-trees, watching the nearest glass swing gently in and out of focus. He felt sick; he'd drunk too much, and there wasn't any food. The noise of five hundred people talking at once battered at his ears, drowning him. How long had he been here? How soon was he allowed to leave? It wasn't like anyone cared that he was there . . .

There was a hand on his shoulder. For an odd, dislocated moment, he thought it was going to be Perdy: Don't worry, Rick, I was never really dead, it was all a big practical joke . . . But when he turned, it was Daed.

'Having fun?'

What do you think? But it came out as, 'Whasshink?'

'Evidently,' Daed said, without smiling. 'Sorry about the speeches. Should've warned you. Oh, and don't drink too many cocktails — they're champagne and absinthe. Lethal.'

Rick didn't know what absinthe was, but he'd already worked out the *lethal* bit. He said, 'Great, thangforelling me.'

Daed looked at him, his head tilted to one side. He looked grey. There was a tightness around his eyes and lips. Through the alcoholic haze Rick thought: Sick, he's sick, sick and scared . . . Then he dug his nails into his palms, trying to concentrate, because Daed was fine, really, when he was sober he knew that. Didn't he?

'Gooparty,' Rick said. He smiled, hoping the muscles in his face would obey him. 'Nishe.'

'Glad you're enjoying it,' Daed said. 'Another three-quarters of an hour and you can leave. Or you can stay all night if you want. It's up to you. But don't leave for another forty-five minutes, or Paz might notice and be angry. OK?'

'OK,' Rick said. He wasn't exactly enjoying himself, but he could bear another forty-five minutes, just about.

'Good,' Daed said. 'See you later.' He paused, and then turned to leave.

'Daed,' Rick said. 'Congradguladguns. Forlife's wor. I meanid.'

Daed turned back and looked at him; and then, like something breaking, he started to laugh. He laughed until blood flecked the corners of his mouth, and then he hunched his shoulders and coughed into his hand. Finally the attack died away.

Then he pulled Rick into an awkward embrace. It seemed to last for a long time. He said, 'Thank you, Rick. I love you.'

Rick stayed as still as he could, swaying slightly.

In the end Daed detached himself. He pushed Rick away gently and disappeared into the crowd. Rick saw him emerge on the other side, near the PR platform. Paz turned to look at him and reached out, brushing his shoulder with her fingers. It made Rick's stomach twist; they looked like friends. Or lovers. Gods . . .

Daed leant forward and kissed Paz on the mouth.

Rick tasted acid and champagne in the back of his mouth and gulped it back, trying not to vomit. He couldn't take his eyes off the kiss. It looked . . . painful.

And then — without waiting for Paz to react — Daed pulled away. He glanced around, and somehow Rick knew Daed was looking for him, to see if he'd seen. He ducked his head, forcing his gaze to the floor. When he lifted his eyes again Daed was making his way to the ticket gates. He was leaving.

Not fair, he thought. *I* have to stay for another forty-five minutes. Daed said I had to stay . . .

He looked back at Paz. She was watching Daed, too; and the expression on her face was so strange that it took Rick a moment to work out what it was.

Surprise, he thought. She's *surprised*.

It was stupid; it wasn't a big deal. There was no reason why Paz shouldn't be surprised, occasionally. There was no reason why it should have sent a current of cold running down Rick's back, or made him fumble and almost drop his glass. But it did. As if the dread that had been building inside him for weeks was suddenly alive, hatched, fully formed, digging its claws into his nervous system. Paz, *surprised* . . .

He thought: If *Paz* doesn't know what's going on . . .

He held on to the tree, pulling himself upright, narrowing his eyes. Daed was through the gates, now, making his way down the corridor towards the stairs. He was walking with his shoulders hunched, as if he was trying to be invisible — and quickly, as if he had something to do . . .

Don't leave for another forty-five minutes.

And like something catching fire, the grey ache of dread leapt into fear. Rick heard his heart thunder in his ears, tapping the roof of his mouth like a finger. Oh, gods. What was going on? He felt cold sweat in his armpits and the small of his back. It smelt bitter.

And he couldn't help himself. Not even though he heard

Perdy's voice, clear as black and white: *Stop doing stupid things.* He let go of the tree and staggered towards the gates, weaving through the people, apologising, pushing when he had to. He had to get out; he had to follow Daed. It seemed like an eternity before he got to the gates, but they let him past without a problem. And then he was in the corridor, walking as quietly as he could, trying not to stumble or wander from side to side, tracking Daed like a monster in the Maze.

22

By the time Rick got to the last door, Daed was already gone; but Rick could hear his footsteps in the stairwell, climbing round and round above him. Rick clung to the banister, out of breath, wishing things didn't split into two whenever he took his eyes off them. Already the fear had lost its edge; he was just being stupid, it was only a drunken panic. There was nothing to be scared of. But all the same, he started to climb the stairs.

Up and up and up, until Rick stopped being careful to tread lightly. He stopped listening for Daed's footsteps. All he could think about was the dizziness as the stairs unwound in front of him, and the nausea as he lurched forward. Where was Daed *going*? Maybe Rick would finally find out where his rooms were. Up and up, and *gods* he was sick of —

The door he'd just passed had been open.

He staggered backwards, and then leant on the wall, staring. It was closed now, of course; there was no way of knowing whether it really had been open or whether he'd imagined it, that centi-em-wide gap . . . He looked at the comms panel, wondering if the trace of moisture on it was condensation from the air or the mark of a hand. If he'd been sober, he'd have trusted his instincts. Now, though . . .

But there was nothing else to do, was there? Except keep going up the stairs, and right now he'd almost rather be wrong.

He pressed his hand on the panel and nearly fell through the door when it opened. Why hadn't someone *told* him there was absinthe in the champagne — whatever absinthe was?

And in front of him there was nothing but an empty corridor. It looked familiar, but then all the corridors looked the same.

He wondered how many of the forty-five minutes had elapsed; he said, 'Time, please,' but the numbers on the wall didn't mean anything. He ought to have looked at the time when Daed said it. Slowly he made his way down the corridor, trying not to make too much noise, in case Daed was only just ahead, beyond the next fire-door. He eased it open with his shoulder, and peered through the gap. Nothing, no one. But there was a faint smell — was there? — of cigarette smoke and unhealthy sweat.

He looked to one side, then to the other, and chose at random. He trod softly, trailing his hand along the wall beside him, breathing deeply. But that elusive smell of smoke and sickness wafted past him and disappeared, until he wasn't sure whether he'd imagined it or not. He wasn't scared, any more. This was all stupid. He wanted to sit down on the floor and go to sleep.

He got to the end of the corridor, the last corner, and realised where he was.

The twentieth floor. Where the tanks were. Only now they'd been replaced, and there was a line of iTanks, glinting clinical white, stylish and unexpected against the petrol-grey light from the window. He thought: That was quick. And then: But I can't go into the Maze yet. Not until Daed said it's OK. I promised.

But he took a step forward, drawn towards the tanks in spite of himself. One of them — the furthest away, where his favourite tank had been — was shimmering, ripples of green and blue and purple running under the white like paint in milk. It meant someone was inside, playing already. It was beautiful. Rick could happily have stayed and watched, hypnotised. But he tore his eyes away and turned on his heel. Daed must have gone in the other direction; and now Rick had lost him. Damn.

He ran back the way he'd come, sacrificing stealth for speed. When he'd run the Maze every day he could sprint silently, but he'd lost his condition now. There was no need to be quiet, anyway; even if Daed heard him, there was nowhere for him to hide.

Rick got to the end of the corridor. No one. He stared at the blank walls, the window, and thought: He's disappeared. Into thin air. Where —?

The forty-five minutes must be nearly over. If something's going to happen . . .

Daed must have gone to his office, Rick thought. I must have imagined the door closing, the handprint on the comms panel. Because —

The toilets.

He'd been past them so many times he hadn't even remembered they were there.

He shook his head, half laughing at himself. Daed was on his way up to his office, because the party had got too much, and then urgently needed the toilet . . . OK.

He retraced his steps, pushed open the door — no comms panel, which was either democratic or just sensible, depending on how you looked at it — and walked in. The row of closed cubicles looked back at him, deadpan. He said, 'Daed?' and then felt himself blush because, well, honestly . . . But no one said anything. Not even: Gods, Rick, what is the *matter* with you? Did you follow me to the *loo*?

He said it again, a little louder, but still no answer. There was a tap trickling water, and the noise filled the silence as if it was trying to tell him something. Automatically, he moved to the sink and turned it off. The porcelain was dirty, smeared with foamy soap and hair and something that could have been blood. He looked down at it, wrinkling his nose, cleared his throat ready to call Housekeeping. And then stopped. Wondering . . .

Someone had shaved their head. Someone who had had longish hair, to start with; some of the strands clinging to the sink were the length of Rick's thumb. And the blood . . . Either they'd been in a hurry, or they hadn't had much practice. Not a regular gamerunner. Someone trying the iTank for the first time.

Rick looked down at the mess. There was a safety razor on the side of the sink, the triple blade shining redly. The same kind he used.

He said again, '*Daed?*'

And then he started to run again: past the cubicles, past the showers, and through the other set of doors, out into the other branch of the corridor. Daed could have come this way, without Rick seeing him. He hurried round the corner. He saw a glimmer of his reflection in the nearest iTank, like a ghost behind a white fog. The two nearest iTanks were still dormant, like white marble. The only colour he could see was from the furthest iTank; but it wasn't swirling blue-green any more. It was winking red.

There has been a malfunction. Please tell Crater about this problem.

He threw himself against the door of the iTank, but nothing happened. He said, 'Manual, manual, open the door, activate emergency procedures,' and the door clicked and buzzed slowly open. As soon as there was a big enough gap he caught it with his hand and pulled, trying to accelerate the movement.

The door finally slid aside. Rick stood in the doorway and looked. There was someone inside.

He was sitting against the wall, knees up, feet splayed, head and arms hanging forward. He had a bare, whitish skull, with tufts of badly shaved stubble and a caked dribble of blood where his spine started. The skin had a pale, obscene look, like something naked. You couldn't see his face.

Now that the door was open, the iTank stopped flashing. The white shell went opaque again; only the places where Rick was touching it stayed silver, glimmering under his fingertips like water.

He knelt down in the tank, in front of the sagging body. Suddenly, strongly, he could smell faeces. He gagged, tried to get up, stumbled. He found himself on the floor, retching. He put his hands over his mouth and breathed shallowly until he was sure he wasn't going to be sick.

Then he reached out, past those dangling hands, and lifted the head to see the face.

It was so heavy he could hardly manage it. The skull was slick and prickly under his palms. He felt a shiver of revulsion go down his back. He squeezed his eyes shut, gritted his teeth, and made himself do it. He'd looted bodies in the Maze; why should this be so different?

Then Rick opened his eyes, and it was Daed.

And Daed was dead.

23

It was the eyes that told him. The eyes stared. They looked straight through Rick, already cloudy, like stagnant water, already with specks of dust clinging to the membrane over the eyeball. They didn't look weird any more, or too old; they just looked dead. They fitted the rest of his face. For the first time, Daed looked like a normal person — just, a normal person who happened to be dead.

Daed, thought Rick, is dead. Is dead, is Daed, is dead.

He can't be.

This is a game. This is the endgame. Log out, log out.

But . . .

What happened? He thought: It's important, I have to know what happened. It's really important. If I know what's happened, I can undo it. Think. What *happened*?

(He can't really be dead. This can't be happening. I must have got something wrong. He can't be . . .)

Rick rocked a little on his heels, feeling the blood fizz and settle again in his thighs. I'm imagining it. He's not really dead.

Only . . . he is.

What *happened*?

Rick thought: He wanted me safely downstairs for forty-five minutes. He didn't want me to find him before it was too late. He *knew*. But —

Something cracked neatly in Rick's brain, like a fortune cookie, and said: Suicide.

He did it on purpose. He even said goodbye.

But *Daed* . . . Rick couldn't believe it. Yes, he thought, he's dead. He knew it was going to happen. He didn't want me to stop him . . . but *suicide*? *Daed*? It doesn't make sense. Daed, who wanted immortality, who would *never* —

And what about Asterion?

Rick put his hands over his eyes and pressed. There was too much light, even behind his eyelids, splurging and whirling in splodges of purple and orange. He couldn't think straight. He kept his hands there until he realised he could smell sweat and the tang of nicotine, from where he'd touched Daed's skull. He took them away from his face and wiped them on his trousers. He was shaking; he hadn't noticed.

Asterion was meant to make Daed immortal. Wasn't it?

So what went wrong?

Rick thought: He'll never fix the malfunction, now. He'll never tell me the Maze is safe. I'll never run the Maze again . . .

He heard himself gulp, as if someone had hit him in the stomach. The world wavered wetly, and then overflowed. Is that how much I loved him, then? he thought. So much that it's *that* that makes me cry?

He looked at Daed's body. He took in the details, as if he was going to draw it. The stubble on his scalp, the slick of saliva on his chin, the pale, receding gums above his perfect teeth. Daed was already decaying, as if he couldn't wait to be gone. Rick understood how he felt. He knew a moment of the purest, most absolute despair he'd ever felt. Nothing, he thought, will ever be any good again. Nothing is worth the effort. I wish I could die, too.

There was a malfunction in the Maze. That was what had killed Daed. So he *could* die, too, if he really wanted to. If he meant it. Easily.

He lifted his head and stared into the middle distance, meeting his own imagined gaze. *Do* I mean it? Do I really want to die?

The answer came as instinctively as his next breath: No. Of course not. But . . .

Can I imagine life without Daed?

He waited.

Well? Can I?

And I can't leave the complex; they won't let me go, not even now. Daed said that, and I believe him. Twenty-four hours, and Customer Services would find me. Like Paz said: people are dispensable.

Oh, gods.

He was drowning in greyness. He couldn't bear to think; couldn't bear to keep his eyes open. If only he could just — stop . . .

And if he went into the Maze now — well, at least he'd be doing *something*.

There used to be a welcome screen, while the tank booted up; now he's in a quiet, old-fashioned room, with a wooden floor and high windows. He stands still, waiting for the door to appear in the opposite wall. It takes a long time to load. After a while he walks forward, but the wall recedes in front of him, and when he looks behind he's still in the centre of the room. Of course, he can't interact with anything. There's nothing to do but wait.

The tank says to him, **Hello, Rick. Welcome to the new iTank, and a new, expanded version of the Maze — but don't worry, you don't have to start again from scratch! I'm just transferring your details now. Please wait for a moment while I upgrade your account.** A pause.

And then there's the door — a neat, white-painted door, simple and unthreatening — and suddenly he can move towards it.

Would you like to return to your last location?

He frowns. His last location? The garden at the end of the Roots? No, that was Athene . . . His last location was . . . gods, the gate outside the solo he was running, all those weeks ago. He remembers his corpse, slumped on the steps, and feels sick, because that isn't what a real corpse looks like. He knows that, now. He says, hastily, 'No.'

Please choose another available location.

He says, 'Alpha Omega Guildhall,' and somewhere in the back of his head he's shocked at how unfamiliar the words feel on his tongue, when he used to *live* there, practically. 'Please.'

Thank you. Please wait for a moment —

And then the door opens, and someone comes into the room.

Rick recoils, stepping back instinctively. No one comes *into* the loading space. Nothing happens here; that's what it's designed for. He doesn't understand.

The figure stays where it is, a few ems away, watching him.

And —

Oh gods, oh gods, no —

It's Daed.

Or . . . *almost* Daed. There's something wrong with him; he's hard to look at, as if Rick's eyes don't match up with what he's seeing. The image is there, steady and solid, but there's still something flickery about him, something blurry. As if Rick's idea of Daed and the computer's aren't the same.

Rick lets his breath out, concentrates to stay upright. He wants to say something — but what? Daed, I thought you were dead. Daed, you *are* dead. What are you doing in a place like this? This isn't the afterlife, is it?

The waiting-room silence goes on, until Rick thinks the tank's crashed.

Daed laughs. Something about the tone of it — soft, faintly lost — makes Rick think, stupidly: Oh. So this *is* the afterlife . . .

Then Daed says, 'You promised, Rick. You shouldn't be here.'

'Sorry.'

'You promised,' Daed says again. 'Honestly. You're useless.'

'I know,' Rick says. 'I'm sorry. I wanted —' but he doesn't know what he wanted. He's scared to step forward, in case Daed retreats; but he reaches out with his hand, lets it hover a micro-em from Daed's sleeve. He says, 'Daed . . . what happened? Why are you here? Please . . .'

Daed smiles, a little. He steps forward and puts his arms round Rick, and there's warmth and solidness and for the first time a smell that isn't nicotine and something rotting but a smell like — like clean clothes, or bread, or green tea, something healthy . . . Rick swallows and holds on, and *this* is real, he thinks, the other was only a nightmare. Oh thank you, thank gods, thank you.

Daed says, 'Rick, you are a stupid, pig-headed little oath-breaker, and I'm thoroughly disgusted with you. OK?'

Rick laughs and nods into Daed's shoulder. 'Yes,' he says. 'Fair enough. OK.'

'You're lucky,' Daed says, 'that I'm such a genius. Happily for you, I can lock you out of the system without having to rely on your honesty. The iTank, you see. We identify people by their brainprints, so we can bar them for life. Clever, isn't it?'

'Yes,' Rick says. He doesn't care what Daed says, he'll agree to anything.

'Yes,' Daed says, mocking him. 'Yes, I thought so.'

'Why are you here?' Rick says. 'I mean . . .' A cold idea begins to grow in his stomach, like the beginnings of nausea, but he ignores it. 'You were — I found you in the tank, you were —'

'Dead?'

'I —' It seems tactless, to say it aloud.

'I'm sorry,' Daed says. 'You weren't meant to find me. Wait —' He narrows his eyes. 'I told you to stay in the party . . . Oh, for gods' *sake*, Rick, can't you do *anything* I tell you?'

The cold idea is icy now. It won't be ignored. Rick thinks: He's not real. He's just a — not a ghost, but something pre-programmed, he's just a, a non-player character . . . It's like an insult, a sick joke. Daed, an NPC.

Rick pulls out of Daed's embrace, because it's too much to bear. He wants the real Daed, the one who's slumped in the tank with that obscene bare skull.

He says, 'You programmed yourself . . . what are you, a guide? What do you do in the Maze all day? Give out quests? Or are you a kind of automated GM?'

The corner of Daed's mouth quirks up; as if it's *funny* that Rick doesn't think he's real. He says, 'What is this, Rick? The Turing test?'

'What?'

'Never mind.' Daed shrugs, as if it really doesn't matter.

Rick thinks: That's the one thing NPCs don't do. They always think you're important.

Rick says, 'What's going on, Daed? I thought . . . you're not really here, are you? I mean . . .'

What a stupid question. But Daed doesn't seem to despise him for asking. He says, 'Yes, Rick, I am. I am *really* here. This is me. Truly.'

Silence.

'It was Asterion, Rick. It's a brainscan program. I'm here, I'm thinking. I'm immortal. In a manner of speaking.'

'That's it?' Rick says. He thinks, for no reason, of an empty box, of shadows, of nothing, nothing but dust in the corners. He can't believe it. '*That's* Asterion? You wanted to be an NPC?'

'Not —' Daed stops. He takes a little breath, turning his eyes to the side wall. There's light coming in from the windows. Then he says, 'Yes, that's right. More of less.'

'I don't understand. What's the point? And why did Perdita say it was —' He's going to say: *evil*. But Daed interrupts him.

'Never mind, Rick. Just trust me, OK? And now —'

'Now —?'

'Now let's get you out of here.'

'But —' No. No, he can't. If this is where Daed is . . . and *why*, Rick still doesn't understand, there's something wrong, something missing, Daed's lying —

'Sorry,' Daed says. 'But you can't come back. It's for your own good.'

'But why — no, Daed, please, let me at least come back to see you — please, don't bar me, *please* . . .' He's desperate. He runs towards Daed, trying to grab him. He'd drop to his knees and plead like a little kid, hanging on to Daed's legs, if he could; but Daed cheats, and the world slides away and no matter how fast Rick runs he's always in the same place. 'Please, Daed, don't do this — at least *explain* —'

'It's better if you don't know —' Daed hesitates. 'If you don't know the details.' For a strange moment his voice takes on a kind of pleading tone; as if Rick's the one in control. 'I've set it all up for you, Rick. You can stay in the complex for ever. You'll be safe, and well fed, and looked after; you'll be *important*. They'll even give you a job if you want one. Please, Rick, trust me. The Maze is your inheritance, even if you can't run it. And I've sacrificed myself for it — for you. Don't worry about Asterion. Now I'm here, it's just . . . it's not important. Please.'

Rick thinks: How odd. Both of us saying *please*.

And: I wonder what it is, what he's not telling me. I wonder if I want to know.

And: Daed, please don't lock me out, if this is where you are, it's not fair to lock me out, please don't, in the real world you're *dead*.

He says, 'Daed, please don't lock me ou—'

'Goodbye, Rick. Trust me.'

He reaches out, desperate for another touch, desperate to stay. He wants to ask question after question: who are you? When you said you loved me, you meant it, right? And my mother — please tell me, who was my mother? If he doesn't ask now, he'll never know. It's his last chance. He says, 'Daed, please — tell me —'

But the room disappears. Everything, the windows, the light, Daed's new-young face — is gone. There's only a gun-metal grey mist, wrapped round him like a curtain. A padded cell for the brain.

And the iTank says to him, **Sorry, there seems to be a problem with your account. Please contact Crater Customer Services.**

234

24

When Rick found himself again, he was staring into his own ghost-eyes, his reflection hanging in the air twenty storeys above the streets of Undone. It was still not raining; there was still a lurid tinge in the sky. Fine weather. You could survive ten minutes, out in that without a hood — or half an hour, a whole hour, maybe.

He leant his forehead against the chemiglass, spread his hands out, pressed. Break, break . . .

Behind him Daed's body was hunched against the wall of the furthest iTank. Rick should call a med, or Housekeeping, or whoever dealt with corpses on the night shift. No doubt there was someone who was used to it. Customer Services, at a pinch.

Daed was dead.

Or, if not exactly dead, he was gone. Irrevocably and absolutely gone. Rick would never see him again. Other people will, he thought. Gamerunners. Random consumers who don't even care, don't even know who Daed *is*; but not me. Daed's locked me out. I'm the only person in the world Daed doesn't want to see again. And he's made sure he won't.

You can stay in the complex for ever. You'll be safe, and well fed, and looked after . . .

Oh, gods. Please, no. I can't do it. The rest of my life, here?

The sky outside flickered, but it wasn't lightning. The clouds were thinning; for a second Rick thought he saw a blazing red circle, behind the grey haze. Then it was gone. It said to him: Freedom.

But I can't leave. Daed's sacrificed everything for me, to make sure I'm all right. Whatever he's hiding, whatever he was lying about . . . I trust him that far. I think. Don't I? He *is* protecting me. He always has.

And I can't leave anyway, even if I want to.

So this is my life.

He looked through the chemiglass. Outside there were kids running wild, abandoned or orphaned so young they couldn't speak Inglish; there were gangs who'd mug you for your hood, leaving you bare-headed in the rain; there were people starving. There were people who'd sell themselves for an hour in a tank, to collect gilt, to sell it on the black. He tried to feel sorry for them. But all he could feel was envy.

Slowly, like an old man, he turned away from the window. He made his way along the corridor, back the way he'd come, and up the stairs.

He logged into his room, took off his clothes, dived into the pool. He wanted the cold water to come as a shock, but it felt tepid, undemanding. The shark saw him from the opposite corner, but stayed where it was, bored. He floated naked, face down, trying not to think. Lucky Daed, to be dead. It was one way to escape the complex.

He felt something welling up in him, like he was going to be sick, like he was drowning. He opened his mouth and gulped in air and water together. He floundered, struggling to find his feet. He waded to the end of the pool and put his hands on the bars of the steps, ready to haul himself out. Daed is gone, he thought. The only person I had. My father; or whatever he was. For ever, gone. He put his arms round me. He said he loved me.

And then all Rick could do was cling on tight.

Time had never gone so slowly. When he called for the clock digits it was only just past midnight, and the same evening as before. Downstairs the party must still have been going on. Nobody would have found Daed's body yet.

He was lying on his bed, looking at the ceiling. He was going to do a lot of that, in the rest of his life. While he was safe, and well fed, and looked after . . .

What had Daed been hiding?

Evil, Perdita's voice said, in his head. He tried not to believe it. But . . .

Even if it was something bad. Even if Asterion was something worse . . . if it wasn't just Daed's way of programming himself into the Maze . . . if it was something more, something . . . yes, something evil . . . Even if . . .

What would you do, Perdita? But he knew, already: she'd stay here, in the complex. Wouldn't she? She'd choose to be well fed, and safe, and . . . well, who wouldn't? Especially if the alternative was to be dead.

Who wants to be dead? Rick said to himself, and then wished he hadn't. Because — yes, he thought, me. *I* do. If this is my life, safe and well fed and looked after. I don't want that. On my own, in the complex, with nothing to do but eat and sleep. I'd rather be out in the streets of Undone, fighting for my life. Or dead.

This isn't really how I feel. I don't mean it.

Yes, I do. I don't want to die. But —

Wait —

Oh my gods, he thought. Oh —

The ceiling was white and blank and full of nothing and suddenly —

Suddenly —

He sat up, breathless, his heart pounding.

If I —

I can't leave, because they'll follow me. Customer Services will track me down. But if I were dead —

If I were *dead* . . .

It won't work. It can't work, he thought. It can't. Can it? But if it *did* . . .

He heard himself laughing, softly, delightedly, like someone who'd just thought of the best joke ever. He could *feel* every door in the complex swinging open, silently, invisible to everyone but him. He could feel the air and space, beyond the confines of his rooms. He could feel the sun, sliding high behind the clouds, the most precious secret in the world. For the first time in his life, he felt like Daed's son. He knew what it would be like, to create something you were proud of.

He got up, changed his clothes, shaking, the pit of his stomach crawling with nerves, because what if he was wrong, what if there was something he hadn't thought of? He tried not to look at his plan head-on; but when he caught sight of it, it still seemed like it would work. He was trembling so much he could hardly dress himself. And he was still laughing.

I'm going to do it, he thought. I'm going to escape.

The actual *leaving* bit would be easy. Tonight, with all the guests leaving the complex, there'd be a way to get out through the airlocks. He trusted himself to cross that bridge when he came to it, and he was pretty sure he wasn't being over-optimistic. It was like Daed had said: there were hundreds of ways to get out.

He tried not to think about what would happen if someone caught him. That cell, with the one-way mirrors . . . but what was the worst that could happen? He'd go mad anyway if he stayed here, one way or another.

What mattered was not being caught by Customer Services, after he'd got out of the complex.

And they wouldn't follow him if he was dead already.

And accidents happened, didn't they? Terrible, shattering, tragic accidents. They happened just by chance: because of a malfunction, because someone had left something in the wrong place, because something had been wired in wrong . . . The kind of accident that could destroy the hidcams, or wipe out a whole floor, so dramatic there wouldn't be anything left except debris and ash.

Not even a body.

He should stop laughing, or the hidcams might pick it up. He couldn't look happy. Soon he had to get angry — well, that should be easy — but he couldn't look excited. Right now he should look despairing — and then convincingly furious. He had to have an adolescent tantrum. But he didn't want anyone to notice — or care — what he was doing, before it was done. Once it was over, it wouldn't matter.

He'd put his favourite clothes on. He looked at his reflection in the window, and gave himself a curt nod. Then he went to the comms panel, opened his door, stood there for a second or two, and then stepped back into the room, as if he'd changed his mind. But as the door slid closed he slipped a wodge of toilet paper into the gap; the old trick, but it worked. The door almost closed, but not quite. Now it was on manual; he could drag it open with his hands, if he had to. *When* he had to.

He turned his back to the nearest hidcam, and got his hood out of the wardrobe. He hovered for a moment, wondering what to do with it, and then shoved it up his top. It made him move awkwardly; but he could cope with that, and he'd need it, later.

He would have liked to take more with him, but he didn't

want anyone to see him packing. He couldn't look like he was planning anything. Or, at least, not what he really *was* planning.

He just had to hope it would work.

25

He trashed his room, carefully.

It was harder than he'd thought it would be. Some of it was fine — the bathroom, the far side of the bedroom — but when he dragged his sheets off the bed he almost stopped to wonder where to put them, and caught himself on the brink of a pause. He threw them down, and then kicked them into the right position, punching the air with his fists. He swore loudly. The sound might not get through to the surves, but no doubt they could lip-read. Luckily he'd sobered up a bit, but not too much: they'd be ready to believe he was drunk. When he'd finished cursing, the sheets were in a long loose curve between the doorway to the studio and the arch that led to the swimming pool. He remembered suddenly that there were cold, oily chips still sitting in the delivery box. He ran to get them out and sprinkled them along the twisted length of bedclothes. All that grease. That should help, a bit. They were packed in polystyrene and a bit of histro newspaper, transparent with fat. He crumpled that and kept it in his hand, trying to look as if he'd forgotten he was holding it.

He spread piles of clothes on the carpet, found a stash of

used tissues in the bin and scattered them artlessly among the most flammable-looking garments. In the bathroom he discovered a bottle of bath oil that he'd forgotten about. That was oil, right? So it should burn . . . He wanted to cheer. He splashed it everywhere, scowling.

Almost everything in his studio was plastic; he looked round, despairing, and almost forgot to sweep everything off the shelves on to the floor. It might burn, at a pinch, but he needed things that would catch fire easily. If only he had some books; but he'd never been much of a reader — he couldn't be bothered with all that ancient stuff. Now he regretted that. Books would have been perfect. He just didn't have enough *stuff* — nothing really existed. His music, films, games were all in the ether somewhere. He stared round, desperately. Oh, come on, there had to be something . . .

And then he thanked Daed silently, over and over again. The posters — vintage realgame ads, from years ago, birthday presents that Rick never really wanted, that he thought were naff and boring. Daed had been into that kind of thing, not him. He'd put them up, dutifully, but only in his studio — on the wall opposite his flatscreen, where he'd never actually see them. He looked at them now and grateful water welled up in his eyes. Even the slogans seemed to speak to him: **go for it**, **heaven is here**, **nothing is impossible**. He reached for the nearest one, tore it down and started to roll it into a tube before he remembered he was meant to be trashing his rooms, not building a fire. **welcome to the real world.**

He chucked it down, with the greasy chip-paper, so that they fell across the half-burnt-away wire leading to the iTank. The sight of it made him nervous again: what if the wire was melted? What if it wouldn't conduct electricity at all? What if it didn't behave the same way, the second time? He ignored the questions and kept ripping the posters off the walls. No use wondering about that now. He had to try, that was all.

And when he'd taken down the last poster and was dragging his arms across his desk to clear it — the flatscreen toppled, landed on its side on the floor, made a cracking noise — he was in luck: his elbow caught one of Daed's cigarette lighters, left there months ago. He flicked at the wheel and there was a flame. Not empty, then. He threw it to the floor with a casual, contemptuous gesture that left it next to the iTank wire and the corner of the poster, exactly where he wanted it. He paused for a moment, looking round. Not bad. A convincing mess. The kind of mess that was a fire hazard in itself . . .

And now, he thought, for the pièce de résistance.

He went back through to his bedroom, kicking at things viciously and grabbing a pillow off the bed as he went past. He threw it into the swimming pool and watched it sink. He opened the door to the little sauna but there was nothing there he could pick up or break. He opened the hammam door, too, and the smell of steam reminded him so strongly of Daed that his throat ached. Then he turned away. He was only pretending, anyway, just so what he was about to do next didn't look premeditated.

Because on the other side of the pool was the filter room, with the heater and the temperature regulator. And the chemicals.

It was hard to get the door open — so hard that he was afraid he looked too determined, wrenching at the old-fashioned handle. But it was stiff, not locked; he went in from time to time to change the thermostat. It was just the moisture that had got into the hinges; after all, that was why it wasn't electric, like the other doors. He swore and sweated, pulling until the muscles in his back burnt with effort. Finally the door burst open, and he staggered back, almost slipping on the slick tiles. There was the smell of chlorine and chemical salts. He thought, with a strange sort of detachment: Hmmm. This might be dangerous, actually . . .

He pulled at the nearest canister, and as he tried to get hold of it the metal slid under his hands and the labels came into view. Corrosive, poisonous, highly inflammable. Excellent. He picked it up, and heard the salts shifting about inside. This one had already been opened, so he took it into the studio and tipped the salts out on to the floor, making sure he scattered it around a bit. That should help the fire get going.

He piled the other canisters in his bedroom, a few ems from the studio doorway. He was afraid it looked a bit calculated, so he kicked them, afterwards, and found a few more bits and pieces to chuck into the pool. The shark had seen the pillow and was nosing at the glass, as high as it could go. When it saw Rick's shirt sinking to the bottom, the arms waving, it flicked its tail and moved towards it. It looked purposeful, hungry; Rick had to remind himself that it wasn't real. He crouched and wiped his face with some of the pool water, trying to get the sting of chemicals out of his nostrils. It was worse than the smell of rain. Tears ran down his face and dripped into the pool, and every time he blinked his eyes felt full of pepper. Gods, he'd better be careful, when he started the fire . . .

It was dark outside; he hadn't noticed, but suddenly there was a clear, white light shining in through the window. He looked up, and there was a disc of silver slipping sideways through a gap in the clouds. At first he thought it was some kind of ship. Then he thought: The moon.

Had he ever seen moonlight before? Real moonlight, not in the Maze? He didn't know. He'd never noticed, never cared. It wasn't like sunlight; it didn't make his spirits lift. But it made him feel cool, sure, fatalistic. Now, somehow, he wasn't afraid of anything.

It was like a code word. *Moonlight*.

Let's go.

He got up, letting his shoulders sag, like he was tired, finally defeated, like he was wondering how the hell he was going to explain *this* to Housekeeping tomorrow. He made sure he didn't glance at the hidcams.

He slouched past his bed, dragging his feet. He looked for a long time at the bare mattress; then rubbed his forehead, and made his way through the doorway to the studio. It all felt stupid, so exaggerated he could hardly believe they hadn't come to interrogate him already. But no one came

And there was the iTank; innocent, going silver under his touch, like a pet wanting to be stroked. And when he opened the door and went in, it said to him, **Hello, Rick**.

Thank gods it wasn't connected to the Maze; he wasn't barred. He could still use the demo.

He took a deep breath. Was everything ready, outside? He ran through it in his mind, trusting that there weren't any hidcams in here — or that if there were, no one would think it was odd for him to stop and close his eyes. The greasy paper and the poster, where the flame should start; and the cigarette lighter, ready to melt and catch fire, ready to explode and spit burning lighter fluid everywhere. The sheets, draped in a loose curve, to give the flames room to breathe . . . the scattered chemical salts, the scented bath oil. He thought: Well, at least it should smell nice.

And I need to be in the tank long enough for the wires to overheat. Until it malfunctions. The same as last time.

Just the *idea* of the malfunction made his skin crawl. But it wasn't the same malfunction that had killed Daed: it was only the wiring on this iTank, just the wiring. Nowhere near as bad . . . Anyway, he'd survived it before, and there was no reason why it should be any worse this time. Except that he'd be expecting it, of course — but that might make it easier. You never knew.

Oh, gods . . .

But it was too late to change his mind now. Just stay logged in, he thought. Just until it overheats. Then you leave the tank, you pretend not to notice the flames, you collapse on the bed like you're feeling ill — and you wait. Got it?

Of course I've got it, you prat, I *thought* of it. Stop talking to me like I'm thick.

He opened his eyes, half grinning, in spite of himself.

He said, 'Open demo, please.'

26

Night, in the ruins.

Rick stands where he is and looks round, wondering if he'll ever see it again. The moonlight glints off pen-and-ink trees, shines through the gaps in the walls. The thin flags of clouds in the west are blazing at the upper edges, silvery and soft below. The rest of the sky is deep uncompromising black, sprinkled with stars. The ruins are silhouettes.

Rick thinks: It's as though someone took death and made it beautiful, made it a place you could live in.

Daed understood death, then.

How could they think that the party decorations even came *close*?

But then, that's the point, isn't it? That's what they do. They take real life and make a shoddy version of it, an easier version, to suck you in.

Not that this *is* real life, of course.

He realises, suddenly, that he must still be a bit drunk. It's not the most reassuring thought he's ever had.

And the sky soars above him, the clouds low and long, the stars cold and fiery. It's freezing; Rick shivers.

Come on. Pull yourself together. Remember why you're here.

So the demo environment does change in real time, then. He tries to be interested in that, but it's not easy.

He waits.

He takes a few steps forward, a few steps back, trying to get rid of the cramping feeling that's started to come into his forehead. Any moment now . . . but the malfunction doesn't come.

He thinks: If it doesn't come, at all, ever . . . oh damn, I *will* have to explain the mess to Housekeeping tomorrow. He giggles, weakly.

But he needs the malfunction. He's dreading it; but if it *doesn't* come . . .

What did I do before? he thinks. Setting fire to things. Flying. He doesn't have the heart for that, now. He runs his hands over his scalp, feeling the prickle of growing hair. Moonlight and ruins, he thinks. The last leaves, clinging to the branches. Silver. Oh, for gods' sake, I don't *care*, just get on with it . . .

He sets his gaze on the tree that's growing out of the wall. He likes it. It's the nicest tree he's ever seen.

He thinks: Burn, burn, *burn*. He imagines gold and red bursting into this black-and-white world. Fire; the fire that will be his way out. Go on, please. Burn. Fire that will translate into real fire, somewhere.

He closes his eyes; but it isn't the tree he sees, it's the wire. He sees plastic — melting, bubbling a little — and a tiny cushion of flame inflating around the copper. He tries to think of the tree, but he can't. Just the wire. It has to catch fire, it *has* to. Please.

He smells smoke. When he opens his eyes the little hanging tree is blazing. He laughs, watching it. And then looks at the other trees, focuses on them, and sets them alight too. Magic. He's going to miss this.

And then —

The malfunction —

Black and shining, like a bullet in the head —

No — please no this is worse this shouldn't be as —

Gods —

This is no this *no* black not black dark like fire burning the inside a brain sucked out through — hole in the universe this is — how Daed died like this is it — please please log out log out log —

'Log out — log out — log *out* —'

And thank gods he's said it. Thank gods.

It's stopped. He's back. He takes a deep breath.

The iTank is white and flashing red. He can't stand straight.

There has been a malfunction. Please tell Crater about this problem.

And as he stumbles out he can smell smoke, and it's acrid plasticky smoke, not the clean woodsmoke of the demo. He looks down, and yes, there's a flame. He ought to care, and if he wasn't feeling so sick he *would* care. That's good, isn't it? A flame . . .

He staggers through the doorway and collapses on to his bed. That was the plan, anyway, wasn't it? Which is just as well, because he can't do anything else. He wants to be sick and go to sleep and die, all at once. He hears someone breathing in great gasping gouts, and he pities them, because they must feel even worse than he does, right now. Then they start to cough. It's the smoke, the fire that must be taking hold — so quickly, he never thought it would happen so *quickly*. Must be the chemicals, he thinks. All that *highly inflammable* . . .

I can't move, he thinks. I want to go to sleep.

I mustn't go to sleep.

I had a plan. What was the plan? I — had — a — *plan*.

He puts his hands over his face again, trying to concentrate. The smoke . . . too much of it. Why isn't the alarm going off? What's happened to the alarm? Oh no. Gods, what a fool I was, why didn't I *think* of the alarm?

Daed switched it off. Ages ago. Because he wanted to smoke a cigarette. As if — as if he knew . . . Rick laughs, choking on the taste of fire. Oh, Daed. Just for that. Because he wanted to smoke.

And the thought of Daed is something to cling on to: a cornerstone. Daed, he thinks, who sacrificed everything for me. So that I could stay here and be safe and well fed and looked after. Daed, my father.

He opens his eyes.

OK.

The fire . . . well, his plan's working. That's got to be good, right?

He stares at it, wondering how he could have thought this would work. It's dangerous . . . and even with the fire alarms turned off . . . The sheets haven't caught, yet, but the chemical salts are alight, and the poster is burning merrily. He wants to watch it; the flames flicker and dance.

They shimmer blue and green and sodium yellow, as the fire eats through different colours of ink. There's smoke, filling the room, black and grey and white. It hangs like a veil between Rick and the window. How can the surves not *notice*?

Either they're all at the party, or it's already too hot for the hidcams.

Now that he thinks of it, it *is* hot.

He was supposed to wait here until he was sure the hidcams weren't working any more. Until anyone watching saw the cameras crash. Until the last recorded moment was him sitting on the bed, surrounded by fire.

But he can't. He hasn't got the nerve.

He laces his hands together and looks down at them. He can feel the heat on his face. He stays still. It's a game, he thinks, and I want to win. There's light flickering on his skin: hot, orange light, shifting from dark to gold to . . . hypnotic. His brain is tired. Or . . . I could stay here, he thinks. Because once those canisters catch light, it'll be all over. I won't know anything about it. Quick.

Not exactly peaceful, though.

He stands up. He's not going to leave, not yet. But he can't stay still. He feels safer over the other side of the room; which is stupid, he knows. When those canisters —

How long can I leave it?

He blinks smoke-tears out of his eyes and looks at the canisters. They look fairly safe, still. They're sitting in a nest of flames, like a phoenix before it hatches, but they don't look . . . awake, yet. Mind you, there's a lot of fire, now. It's starting to feel urgent. Rick is starting to think he ought to leave.

Stop doing stupid things.

This probably qualifies as stupid, doesn't it? Sorry, Perdy.

But it might work; really, if he does it right, exactly right, it might work.

He leans against the door panel, watching his life go up in flames. Count, he thinks. Just count. One, two, three . . . when you go into triple figures, you can go. But no gabbling; that's cheating.

And it was a good idea. He has to believe that. They'll believe he's dead; they'll let him go . . .

When the canisters explode, they'll take out the whole floor. So he needs to be downstairs when they go; those cameras will go down, too. He'll have time to get downstairs unseen; and with his hood on, he'll be one more anonymous figure, wandering through the complex on launch-party night. Well. Until they start the evacuation. He wants to giggle; it's the first time it's occurred to him, that they might evacuate. That he might cause that kind of chaos.

He's lost count. He stares at the flames — roaring now, hungry, licking the chemiglass as if they're eager to get out, too. Sixty, he guesses. Sixty-one. Sixty-two. Sixty-three.

I should get out.

I should get out *now*.

He goes to the door and runs his fingertips down the gap. He can pull it sideways; but when he does, there'll be more air. He imagines the fire, billowing up in a great rush; and the smoke gushing into the corridor. Would Daed have turned off those alarms, too? Rick prays that he has.

Eighty. Ninety. Ninety-nine and a half.

OK.

Here goes.

Out through the door. The corridor. He's running like it's the Maze, as fast as he's ever run. It doesn't seem quite real, but that's OK. It's easy. He hardly even needs to breathe. Behind him the flames are taking over, calling him back, spitting and roaring. He can hear them. He keeps running.

He's done this before. He knows he can do it. No problem.

The game, he thinks. *This* is the game. I understand now. And gods, it's *fun* . . .

Down the stairs — the first few stairs —

Yes, he thinks, almost, yes, it's going to, *I'm* going to —

And —

Too late.

3

EPILOGUE

WINGS OF FLAME

The blast ripped through the twentieth storey of the complex, spitting flame at the sky of Undone. It exploded sideways, in a ball of gold, spotted with red and black, like the sun up close. People on the streets of Undone looked up, wondering. There was a cloud of steam — another explosion, like an afterthought — and a generous spray of shattered glass. Scraps of clothes, a sad little flag of torn bedsheet, a few bloody lumps of shark flesh. The debris spewed out over Undone like largesse. A charred, many-toothed jawbone fell into the gutter, twenty storeys below.

In a way, Rick had done well. He'd been right — for what it was worth. The hidcams *did* go down. All the cameras did, in fact. On the twentieth storey, the nineteenth, the eighteenth . . . No one would ever know what had happened, exactly. Not those last few seconds. The film cut out, just before the blast; although they'd be able to work it out from the rest of the footage, more or less. Give or take a few details. Like Rick leaving, for example.

But he didn't get far enough. He was only a few storeys below his room. He felt the blast, he didn't hear it. He knew it was too late. The floor moved under his feet, shifting up and down, like a ship. He looked down and somehow, stupidly, expected to see the sea.

And then the fire boiled down the stairwell towards him, sucking the oxygen out of the air.

He didn't realise he was screaming, but he was.

And the explosion kicked away his feet from under him. He'd put his hands over his face to shield his eyes, and he nearly dropped to his knees; but there was no time for that. A second wave of fire shoved him forward, roughly, like a friend, one hand on either shoulder blade. Get *out*.

And when he stumbled, it picked him up and threw him, straight through the window ahead of him. He burst into the open air in a knot of scarlet and broken glass and fire. To anyone looking up he was like one of the old gods: glorious, silhouetted against a dying sky. Then he fell.

No one can fall sixteen storeys without dying.

Not straight down, anyway. But Rick landed on the sagging power-cables over the streets of Undone, bounced and jerked like a fish on a line, and then dropped again. The fire in the Crater tower flapped upwards, sending smoke towards the clouds. Anyone unlucky enough to be out on the streets of Undone turned to look, momentarily distracted from whatever they were doing. It was as though someone had trapped a star in the tower, keeping it prisoner. Its fury reflected off the other skyscrapers, far too close for comfort.

And Rick fell, still. His clothes were burning. He hit the top of the Crater fence, where it was curved outwards to stop climbers. The wire hooked into him, ripping him to shreds, but it broke his fall, again. He hung for a moment, between worlds. And then, against all the odds, he struggled, convulsed, and flopped *over* the fence, falling the right way. He landed on the concrete like a dead thing; but he was on the right side. The Undone side, that is.

He should have been dead; but he wasn't. Not quite.

Not that he'd have been grateful for it, if he was conscious.

And when they found him, later, he was still alive. Just.

The rogue sun had burnt out, at last. The complex was surrounded with flashing lights, evacuation vehicles, the last bewildered party-goers struggling to get out of the Undone air, relieved it wasn't raining.

Someone stood in front of Rick's face and nudged at him with one foot; and briefly, before he dropped back into blackness, he opened his eyes. He had time to notice how it hurt to breathe — how everything hurt, in fact. How the darkness was flashing, and he could hear voices, and he didn't know where he was. How no one was helping him, or calling for a med, and that meant he must have escaped. How he was in agony. How the plan must have worked, and what a stupid plan it had been, after all.

How he was alive.

How he was free.

And how his back, especially . . . how, even through the

rest of the pain, he could feel the material of his top melted and clinging to the skin where the explosion had caught him, drawing on him, leaving two terrible burns: symmetrical, running the whole length of his back, like wings.

Read on for the first gripping chapter
of the mind-blowing

THE TRAITOR
GAME

by B.R. Collins

WINNER OF THE 2009 BRANFORD
BOASE AWARD

'A rites-of-passage novel of unusual power and skill'
Sunday Times

ONE

It made sense that it happened on that particular day. Michael could see there was a kind of sick logic to it. Like someone had developed a sense of humour. If it was going to happen, then, well, *obviously* it would be on that day. Not that there was anything special about the date – just, it was one of those mornings when you actually feel pleased to be alive and up and going somewhere. You know, one of those morning-has-broken mornings, a God's-in-his-heaven morning. Not that he believed any of that stuff, of course, but he could see what they were on about.

That morning as he walked to school in the October sunshine, leaves everywhere like yellow paper, he felt sort of better about everything – sort of *good*, actually. St Anselm's was always pretty – that's what you paid for, red-brick buildings and striped lawns – but that morning, with a blue sky overhead and no one around, it took his breath away. Michael was whistling as he went through the school gates. He looked at the drifts of leaves at the base of the wall and thought about kicking them up into the air, because it wasn't like there was anyone around to laugh at him, but in the end he didn't. You get hedgehogs hibernating in piles of leaves, and it wouldn't be fair to disturb one.

He turned left, the way he always did, past the music block, on to the playing fields, and down towards the belt of trees. For a moment, looking into the glare of sunlight, he thought Francis hadn't got there yet. Then he saw him, leaning against a tree in his shirtsleeves, his jacket hung on a branch. Francis was the only person he knew who took off his jacket when he smoked. Michael grinned and jogged across the field, the bag over his shoulder bouncing.

'Hey.'

'Good morning.' Francis reached automatically into his pocket and offered the cigarette packet. Michael took one. It was a rule. You had to have a cigarette before school, just like you had to bunk off early on Friday afternoons. He used to feel queasy smoking first thing in the morning but now it was luxurious, taking deep lungfuls of thin smoke and autumn air, standing in silence. He leant against a tree a little way off from Francis's and closed his eyes against the light.

'How was the wedding? On Saturday?'

Francis laughed. 'Really awful.' He took a last drag on his cigarette and stamped it into the mud. 'All those people. Having that many relations is just scary. And they all look the same.'

'Like you, you mean?'

'Exactly. It's horrible.'

Michael squinted at him sideways, smiling. 'I can see that.'

'Yeah, shut up. The whole experience is just purgatory. Seriously. Even getting there's like some kind of medieval torture. You wouldn't believe how long it takes just to get everyone in the car. And then when you get there it's all, haven't you grown and aren't your little brothers and sisters lovely and do *you* have a girlfriend, Francis?' He laughed again, but briefly. 'I mean, Jesus, they can *see* my little brothers and sisters and they're clearly *not* lovely. What's that about?'

'Compared to you, maybe.'

Casually Francis flicked two fingers up at him. 'And of course they all say, how nice that you still want to come to these family things, how nice that you don't have anything better to do. And I want to say, actually, Mum made me come, I *do* have better things to do. Frankly I'm seriously pissed off that I have to be here at all.' He shook the cigarette packet pensively, then got another cigarette out and lit it. 'But that should be it for a bit. I mean, Saturdays as normal from now on. Thank God.' He smiled and flicked ash at a pile of leaves.

Michael nodded and breathed out smoke. 'Good.'

'Which reminds me –' Francis crouched suddenly, his cigarette between his lips, and dug in his bag. After a few seconds he surfaced with an A4 envelope in his hand. 'Here.'

'What? Oh – thanks.' Michael held it for a moment, wanting to say, *No, not here, give it to me later . . .* But that was silly, paranoid. Francis would think he was crazy. It'd be fine. Just because they'd never given each other stuff at school before. What could happen? It wasn't like anyone was going to go through his bag. Anyway, Christ, it was just an envelope, just a plain brown envelope.

It was like Francis read his mind. 'It's not hardcore porn, you know. Unless my mother switched the envelopes.'

Michael forced himself to smile. 'Yeah, right.'

'I guess it could have waited till Saturday.'

'No, it's fine.' Michael started to kneel down and caught himself before he got mud all over his trousers. He crouched carefully and pushed the envelope into his bag, between two books to keep it flat. As he leant forward he felt the key round his neck swing coldly against his skin, like a talisman. 'What's in it?'

Francis winked. 'Wait and see.' He stamped on the butt of his cigarette and added, 'Nothing world-shattering. Don't get too excited.'

'No fear.' They grinned at each other.

They heard the sound of the five-minute warning bell carry across the playing field, clear and shrill. Francis sighed and picked up his bag. 'God, I hate Mondays.'

Michael shrugged, agreeing. They walked back towards the main building, away from the sun. There were more people around, now. Michael could hear shouts from somewhere, pre-pubescent shrieks that sounded like they were coming from the music-block roof, and the scuffle of a game of football from further away. Francis kicked genially at a pebble. It skittered forward and Michael chased it and kicked it back. When they turned the corner he wasn't even looking where he was going. He only knew something was wrong because Francis stopped dead and grabbed his arm. He turned round to look, stumbling. A little kid – a second-year, maybe, skinny and miserable –

stood unhappily on the grass, surrounded by a straggling circle of older boys.

Someone said, '*Bent dick?* Is that really your name?'

But the voice would have stopped Michael in his tracks, wherever he was. It was sly, malicious, *gentle*, so that you answered back, so you made things worse for yourself. He felt a sort of disbelief rise up in the back of his throat, outrage like nausea. *Not here, not now, it can't be.* He stared at the group in front of him, hardly noticing Francis's grip on his arm. The kid in the middle was small and thin and scruffy. You wouldn't have looked twice, except for the expression on his face. Michael stared and then wanted to turn and run. That expression. He felt the muscles on his own face tense, like he was trying to mimic it.

The voice said, 'Is that because your dick is bent? Or is it because you're a dick and you're bent? Was that why your parents called you *bent dick*?' He was leaning against the wall, smoking, like he wasn't paying much attention. Tall, dark, with hair that was just too long. Dominic Shitley. Shipley, really, but they called him Shitley because he was a shit.

Francis said quietly, 'Old Condom Shitley. He can talk.' Michael wanted to smile but he couldn't. He wanted to turn round and walk away but he couldn't. No one had seen them. They could just turn round and go the other way, round past the cricket pavilion. No one would know. But he didn't move.

Shitley said, 'So, Bent Dick, which do you think it is?'

The kid knew the drill. His eyes flickered to Shitley's face, then down. Answering would only make it worse. Michael knew he was thinking, *Just get it over with*. But he wished the kid would say something, anything, just to fill the pause.

Shitley stepped forward, peeling himself away from the wall like something reptilian. He moved in a semi-circle so the kid had to turn to face him. He flicked his cigarette ash casually towards the kid's face. 'Personally, I'd guess you're bent.' He gestured, like a teacher giving a lesson. 'You know. A poofter. A fag-got. A *pansy*, if you like . . .' And for a moment the imitation of Father Markham was so good Michael almost smiled, like it was all a big joke. They'd got it wrong, it was just a kind of game . . . But when the other fifth-formers laughed, the kid flinched. Shitley waited until they'd finished. He took a drag of his cigarette and leant towards the kid, blowing the smoke straight into his face. 'That's right, isn't it, bender-boy?'

Michael felt Francis step forward. He grabbed his arm, wrenching him back by the sleeve of his jacket. He felt the tension in the fabric as Francis tried to pull away, and then the material relaxed under his fingers. Francis turned to stare at him. 'For God's *sake*, Michael!'

'Leave it. Please. Just leave it.'

Francis frowned. '*Leave* it?'

Michael shrugged helplessly. He still had Francis's sleeve in his hand. He held on to it, like he was anchoring himself, like if he gripped hard enough this wouldn't be happening. He swallowed frantically. 'It won't help. Whatever you say. It won't help.' His voice sounded small and pathetic, and he hated himself.

Francis narrowed his eyes. Then he looked away, pointedly. He could do that, he could turn his head away so that you felt *dismissed*, shutting you out like you just weren't there any more. Michael had seen him do it to other people. It made him feel cold. He looked away himself, scared of what his face was doing.

Shitley said, 'Is that what you get off on? Working away at that little bent dick of yours?'

The kid raised his eyes and looked at Shitley. His face was rigid, blank. Michael felt the force of his hatred as though it was inside him: the hatred that ate you up, that froze your face into stone. It was dangerous, because it made you want to fight back. You had to brace yourself against it, like a wave.

Shitley shook his head slowly, smiling. 'Looks like I've touched a nerve.' He laughed. 'Oh, yeah, baby . . . Bet you're turned on now, just thinking about it.' He stood there, still, daring the kid to hit him, to retaliate, and Michael knew, with a spasm of shame that knotted his stomach, that the kid wouldn't do it. He wouldn't be able to. He couldn't even stare him out. Shitley said, 'Or would you like to . . . ?' His hand went to his flies. *No.* No. *Oh God, he can't.* Disgust hit the back of Michael's throat like a finger.

Francis hissed, 'Jesus *Christ*,' and stepped forward. He started to say something, loud and clear, 'Hey, Shitley,' but before he'd finished – maybe even before he'd started – Shitley had stepped towards the kid. Michael heard the kid's sob of revulsion, then saw him force himself to stay still, not to flinch, to keep his clenched fists at his sides. Shitley brought his cigarette up to his mouth and took a long drag. Then he brought the glowing end of it down on the back of the kid's hand, grinding it down into the pale space above the wrist. The kid cried out and stumbled backwards.

'Stop it! Piss off, Shitley, leave him alone –' Francis ran towards them. But underneath his shout you could hear the noise the kid was making, the dry hoarse sobbing that you can't control, like your body's trying to shake the pain out of you, like it's trying to break it down into manageable bits. Almost like laughter. Sometimes they thought you really were laughing, and that made it worse; or if you were crying, properly, with tears, that made it worse as well. But now all Michael could think was, *Thank God, thank God it's over, thank God that's all*. He felt relief push up warm from his gut and despised himself.

Shitley swung round towards Francis, leaving the kid to drop to the ground. His henchmen followed his gaze. 'Mind your own business, Harris.'

'You sadistic bastard, Shitley, what the hell d'you think you're doing?'

Shitley blinked, twice. 'What did you call me, Harris?'

'A sadistic bastard.' Francis held his look, cold, challenging. Michael looked round at Shitley's mates and wondered if they'd fight another fifth-former. Surely not. It wouldn't be worth it.

Shitley shook his head slowly. 'Before that.'

'What?' For a second Francis looked genuinely confused. Then he said, 'Oh. Shitley. It suits you better than Shipley, don't you think?'

Shitley looked at him consideringly. Then he flicked his cigarette butt away. 'You'd better watch yourself, Harris. Don't mess with me.'

'What, is that a *threat*?'

Shitley shrugged. Like, it wasn't that he didn't know what to say, only that he couldn't be bothered to say it. He glanced down towards the kid, who was hunched over, knotted into himself, cradling his hand, still gasping. Then he started to walk towards the main building. He looked Michael briefly up and down as he passed. Michael met his gaze. It wasn't like Shitley could see inside his head. After he'd gone past, Michael was pleased he hadn't flinched, hadn't given anything away.

The henchmen followed, giving Francis dirty looks. He stared them out. Michael wished he could do that: keep his cool, gaze back at them flatly until they looked away. But it wasn't courage. Not really. It was only not knowing how things could be.

The kid pushed himself up with one hand. He was still breathing heavily, with a kind of catch in his throat on every in-breath. Francis said, 'You OK?' When the kid didn't answer he said, 'You should go to the medical room. Get that looked at.'

'I'm all right.' He wasn't.

'Want one of us to come with you?'

'No. Thank you.' The words came out tight with misery. He'd hunched his shoulders like he could curl completely into himself. Michael knew he didn't want them there.

'Look – I'll skip Prayers, make sure you're OK –'

Michael said, 'No.'

Francis looked up at him sharply, like he was surprised he had the gall to speak at all. 'I wasn't talking to you.'

'He doesn't want your help.'

'Like he wanted Shitley to stub a fag out on him, you mean? Like he wanted us to leave him to be tortured by those creeps? Like he wanted us to *leave him*?' Francis didn't expect him to answer.

'We can't *do* anything to help,' Michael said, trying to sound as though he was talking about something academic, something that really had nothing to do with him. 'He wants us to go away and leave him alone.'

The kid walked past him without looking up, as though he wasn't there. He disappeared round the corner, holding his hand up to his chest, across where his heart was.

Francis followed him for a few more seconds, but he stopped when he got to the corner. Then he turned on Michael. 'What the hell is *with* you? You selfish, arrogant, *cowardly* bastard. What the hell would you know about what he wants?'

Michael wanted to hit him. He wanted to smash his head against the wall. He wanted to tell him, for God's sake, he *did* know, better than anyone, how the kid felt. He wanted to hit Francis over and over again, until he gave up trying to fight and just took it. He wanted to knee him so hard he made the same sound as the kid had. He wanted to make Francis understand – wanted him to know himself how it felt, the shame of it, the way you wanted never to talk to anyone again. And the humiliation of knowing someone had *seen* – how that, sometimes, was the worst thing of all. He swallowed, turned away, and said nothing.

'You're not scared of Shitley?' A pause. Michael felt Francis look at him. 'Are you?'

'No.' And in a way it was true. Not Shitley, not

personally. Not of being beaten up, or burnt, or whatever else they did to people. Not that.

'What, then?' Francis's voice had changed. He wasn't having a go any more. He really wanted to know. That was worse.

'Nothing.' Michael thought, *Please let it go. Please.* He couldn't talk about it, he couldn't bear it. He looked down, away, anywhere but at Francis. A pause that stretched out like string, so taut it might break. Then Francis swung his bag back on to his shoulder and started to walk down the path. Michael followed him. His throat ached.

Francis said over his shoulder, 'His name's Benedick. Benedick Townsend. He's in the third year – Luke's class.'

'Benedick. His parents really should have known better.'

'Yes. Although if it wasn't his name, it'd be something else.'

'Yeah, I guess.' For Michael it had been being clever. Not that he was, especially, except that at the comp anyone who could spell their own name was clever. Or even pronounce it properly. That was him. Clever Boy. Even when he started to fail tests, stopped reading, couldn't think at all any more. Even then, they'd made him 'explain' Pythagoras' Theorem before they started on him, mimicking his accent. He remembered thinking, that day, *At least they didn't kick me in the hypotenuse* . . . laughing weakly all the way home, because if he cried someone might notice.

They walked past the hall. Prayers had started. Everyone was on their knees. They went round the long way, so as not to walk past the windows, and up the stairs to the fifth-form corridor. Michael tried to think of something to say, to explain, so Francis wouldn't think he was cowardly or cruel. But his mind stayed blank. Francis was first to the top of the stairs; he stopped right in front of Michael, and said, 'You should be in Prayers.' It took Michael a second to realise he wasn't talking to him.

Luke was standing at the lockers, his uniform already dishevelled, even though it was only ten to nine. He stepped aside for Francis to get past. He said, 'I was late.'

Francis had his head in his locker. 'Well, if you get reported and Mum goes ballistic and blames me, you're going to regret it.' His voice was muffled.

Michael went to his own locker and started to get out his books. Luke was still standing there, rolling his tie up and down his finger. He wore it short, like a flag, the way they all did. Trying to fit in, trying to be cool. Luke said, 'Will you take me paintballing on Saturday?'

Francis straightened up and cracked his head on the ceiling of his locker. He pulled his head out and stared at Luke, rubbing a hand over his hair. 'No, I will not.' He shoved a couple of textbooks into his bag. 'Why are you asking now, anyway?'

'Mum won't let me go unless you come with me.'

'Tough. I wouldn't touch a paintball with a barge-pole.' Francis caught Michael's eye and gave him a quick ironic grimace.

'Why not?'

'It's puerile. Anyway, I have better stuff to do on Saturdays.'

Luke put his head on one side and stared past

Francis at Michael. There was real hostility in his eyes; Michael felt it register somewhere inside him, like something cold. 'Going round to Michael's, like you *always* do. Are you two gay or what?'

Francis said, 'Get stuffed, Luke.'

'I just –' Luke changed tactic. Michael could have told him he'd blown it, but you had to give him marks for trying. 'Please, Francis. You'd like it. And I'll do your chores for two weeks.'

Francis finished putting his stuff back into his locker. There was a silence, and he looked up at Luke, like he was surprised to see him. 'Are you still here?'

'Michael wouldn't mind. It's only one Saturday.'

Michael said, 'How do you know Michael wouldn't mind?'

Luke looked at him – that expression again, like Michael was the scum of the earth – and didn't answer. He turned ostentatiously towards Francis. 'Francis, please. Please please please. All my mates are going.'

'In that case, *definitely* not. I told you, *no*. My Saturdays are mine. Ask Dad to take you.'

'He won't. You know what he's like.'

'Then you'll have to find someone else.' Francis slammed his locker shut and turned the key in the door. 'Piss off, squirt.'

'I hate you.'

'It's entirely mutual. Go on. I said fuck off.'

'I'll tell Mum you said that.'

'I look forward to it.' Francis raised his eyebrows at Michael. 'See you at break?'

'Yeah.' Michael watched Francis stride off. When he turned back to his locker Luke was still glaring at

him. *Stop looking at me like that. It's not my fault.*
Although possibly it was, possibly Francis knew how
much the Saturdays meant to him, how desperate he
got if they had to miss one. It was pathetic, really,
how dependent you could get. But Luke didn't know
that – did he? Michael said, 'What?'

Luke watched him in silence for a moment. Then
he turned and went down the stairs, without saying
anything.

Michael left it thirty seconds, then shouldered his
bag and trudged to double French. He sat down in the
sunlight next to the window, the desk where he
always sat, far enough back to piss around but not
too far back, not where Father Peters always looked
for troublemakers. Not that he felt much like pissing
around today. He looked at the trees outside.
Benedick. Bent dick. He was in Luke's class, Francis
said. That made it worse, somehow, although why
should it? After all, Luke was an annoying little
git . . .

And Shitley. What would he do? *If anything*,
Michael thought sternly to himself. *He might not do
anything.* Anyway, he'd been OK here so far. It was
just a one-off. It wasn't like the comp. It *wasn't*. It
couldn't be. He pushed away the dread, the voice that
said: *Feeling safe, Michael . . . how stupid can you
get?* He was being paranoid. No need to worry. He
settled back and tried to concentrate on the lesson.

When the bell went for break he felt better. He
fought his way back upstairs – *Get textbooks, then
coffee* – and made his way to his locker, pushing first-
years out of the way on the stairs. There was music
coming from the common room. He stooped to push

books into his locker, cramming them in precariously, but there were too many, and the bottom ones started to slide towards him. He grabbed them and tried to steady the pile.

There was a folded bit of A4 paper wedged into the bottom of the locker, as though someone had pushed it under the door. It said, *MICHAEL THOMPSON*. It wasn't handwriting he knew. Michael slid it out, bracing the books against his chest, and flipped it open.

It said, *I KNOW WHERE ARCASTER IS.*

That was when the bottom dropped out of everything.